Theatre of Chance

ALSO BY GERALD VIZENOR

Blue Ravens: Historical Novel

Native Tributes: Historical Novel

Satie on the Seine: Letters to the Heirs of the Fur Trade

Waiting for Wovoka: Envoys of Good Cheer and Liberty

GERALD VIZENOR
THEATRE of CHANCE

*Native Celebrities of Nothing in
an Existential Colony*

WESLEYAN UNIVERSITY PRESS

MIDDLETOWN, CONNECTICUT

WESLEYAN UNIVERSITY PRESS

Middletown CT 06459

www.wesleyan.edu/wespress

© 2025 Gerald Vizenor

All rights reserved

Manufactured in the United States of America

Designed and typeset in Parkinson Electra

by Eric M. Brooks

LIBRARY OF CONGRESS CATALOGING-IN-PUBLICATION DATA

NAMES: Vizenor, Gerald Robert, 1934- author.

TITLE: Theatre of chance: native celebrities of nothing in an existential colony / Gerald Vizenor.

DESCRIPTION: Middletown, Connecticut: Wesleyan University Press, 2025. |

SUMMARY: "A group of native puppeteers from the White Earth Reservation in Minnesota hold creative puppet parleys in the context of the historical moment and the existential colony of an urban reservation of Minneapolis" — Provided by publisher.

IDENTIFIERS: LCCN 2024026878 (print) | LCCN 2024026879 (ebook) | ISBN 9780819501547 (cloth) | ISBN 9780819501554 (paper) | ISBN 9780819501561 (ebook)

SUBJECTS: LCSH: White Earth Band of Chippewa Indians—Fiction. | White Earth Indian Reservation (Minn.)—Fiction. | LCGFT: Novels.

CLASSIFICATION: LCC PS3572.I9 T54 2025 (print) | LCC PS3572.I9 (ebook) | DDC 813/.54—dc23/eng/20240617

LC record available at https://lccn.loc.gov/2024026878

LC ebook record available at https://lccn.loc.gov/2024026879

5 4 3 2 1

In memory of

DANE WHITE

There is but one truly serious philosophical problem, and that
is suicide. Judging whether life is or is not worth living amounts to
answering the fundamental question of philosophy.

ALBERT CAMUS
The Myth of Sisyphus

Bunker Boy Beaulieu was more at ease as an outrider or solitary
swing man in cowboy stories than as a student of social studies,
grammar, science, mathematics, or the bogus chronicles of
custody cultures at the government school.

He was almost an orphan, almost anonymous in the ruins of
native culture, in the same way as so many other native children
who never quite related to an actual father.

Bunker Boy was alone with only wispy shadows and traces of
snow ghosts that seduce lonesome natives to rest forever on a cold
night or bear the winter lures in any season of suicide.

GERALD VIZENOR
Waiting for Wovoka

Perhaps they have said me already, perhaps they have carried
me to the threshold of my story, before the door that opens on my
story, that would surprise me, if it opens, it will be I, it will be the
silence, where I am, I don't know, I'll never know, in the silence
you don't know, you must go on, I can't go on, I'll go on.

SAMUEL BECKETT
The Unnamable

CONTENTS

Hand Puppet Parleys / xi

1 Doyenne of Silence / 1
2 Native Royalty / 8
3 Fugitive Puppets / 12
4 Mutable Nicknames / 21
5 Strange Harmony / 26
6 Tears of Grace / 36
7 Sovereign Reader / 43
8 Shamanic Silence / 52
9 Silk Memories / 58
10 Columbus Rumpus / 63
11 Existential Colony / 71
12 Gospel of Labor / 79
13 Academic Skinwalker / 84
14 Chance of Mercy / 92
15 Hearsay Man / 95
16 Tutelary Grace / 103
17 Cultural Casualties / 109
18 Hoedown Activists / 114
19 Mongrels of Merit / 121
20 Shame of Liberty / 132
21 Salutary Nicknames / 138
22 Barefoot Psychiatrist / 145
23 Paraday Custody / 154
24 Sue for Mockery / 162
25 Jour Éternel / 172
26 Funerary Mockery / 176
27 Rainbow Herbicides / 184
28 Native Watchwords / 193
29 Trickster of Hearsay / 199
30 Portage Stayaways / 205

HAND PUPPET PARLEYS

CHAPTER 8 Zenibaa and Doctor Samuel Wilde / 56

CHAPTER 10 Erik the Red and Cristóbal Colón / 66

CHAPTER 12 Mother Jones and Andrew Carnegie / 80

CHAPTER 13 Clyde Kluckhohn and Noah Bear / 88

CHAPTER 15 Chance and Ethos / 99

CHAPTER 19 Fidèle, Queena, Fala, and Dingleberry / 123

CHAPTER 20 Richard Nixon and Indian Agent / 134

CHAPTER 22 Doctor R. D. Laing as Barefoot, Director, Quilty, Heartthrob, Ordure, Hacksaw, and Chorus / 147

CHAPTER 24 Samuel Beckett, George Lincoln Rockwell, Gertrude Stein, Rachel Carson, J. Robert Oppenheimer, and Father Joseph Musch / 169

CHAPTER 27 Adolf Hitler and Docteur Appendice / 185

CHAPTER 28 Wilfred Burchett, President Lyndon Johnson, Hubert Humphrey, Ronald Reagan, General William Westmoreland, and Walter Cronkite / 197

THEATRE OF CHANCE

DOYENNE OF SILENCE

Dummy Trout, the mute puppeteer, leaned back on a rusty clamshell chair and soughed with the natural motion of the wind in the birch and white pine trees. She was honored as the native Doyenne of Silence, a shaman of silence, mockery, and liberty on a separatist reservation, and only the six loyal mongrels at her side that early summer morning heard the slight murmurs of pleasure with the sway of trees and the waves on Spirit Lake.

The mute puppeteer persisted in the tease and tacit artistry of silence for more than seventy years and praised in dream songs and heart stories the silence and spirit of hand puppets. Silence was a creative mode of resistance, a character of natural motion and the seasons, and the slight murmur of water may not have been the only sounds the mongrels heard on summer mornings near the shoreline. The sighs of enchantment and hesitations of temper were easily disguised as the wafts, waves, and whispers of natural motion.

The creative hearsay at the reservation post office revealed that the mute puppeteer might have faintly shouted brava, brava, brava more than thirty years ago during the Metropolitan Opera radio broadcasts of the great soprano divas and other memorable events at the Leecy Hotel on the White Earth Reservation.

"Dummy must have thought that only the mongrels could hear the slight soughs and faint sighs and hints of rapture," said the demure Poesy May Fairbanks.

"Poesy May is an intuitive stowaway, shaman and poet of soughs, sighs, and slight whispers, and she heard the faint pleas and reserved murmurs of burned books in the ruins of the Library of Nibwaakaa," said Bad Boy Aristotle. "Poesy May hears the tease of chance in natural motion, desire in the ashes of poetry books, and the soughs of native dream songs in the clouds."

"Books are never silent, the words forever sough, whisper, shout, and gasp near readers and create a natural undertone of presence and patience in libraries," said Poesy May.

"Dummy has heard the hearsay that she shouted hallelujah, hallelujah, hallelujah at ravens and sandhill cranes, but she never countered the pork barrel bullies of envy with more than ironic scenes in hand puppet parleys and silent gestures of mockery," said Master Jean Bonga. "The five stowaways and not even the toady mission nuns believed the hallelujah hearsay."

"Dummy is a shaman, and she heals natives with the spirit of puppet parleys," said Truman La Chance. "She turns the nasty hearsay into shuns of silence and mocks the weary predators of tradition and pork barrel bullies with their own words."

The mute puppeteer wrote dream songs about the wonders of silence and creation, totemic relations, and the migration of birds, but the stowaways never actually heard even the slightest soughs over the great spirit of totemic beaver. Some post office hearsay and sough stories were much easier to respect, that she swooned at dusk with the swoop of nighthawks, whirred with the murmuration of starlings, or a generation ago mocked with hushed tones the constant womanly chatter of outsiders in fancy outfits on horse carriages between the Ogema Train Station and the Leecy Hotel.

The stowaways learned to create stories that slighted the cultural poseurs, mocked the predators of tradition, teased the priests of penance and salvation, and overturned the customs of certainty. That was not an easy course of chance and confidence for the abandoned and abused natives who were counted as the loyal stowaways at the Theatre of Chance.

Native heart stories and dream songs were enactments of chance, irony, and liberty, and the native feats of survivance were always necessary in the ruins of native traditions and civilization. The puppet parleys, heart stories, dream songs of chance, and native nicknames of personal recognition easily reversed the course of churchy destiny and the outright miseries of separatism on a federal treaty reservation.

Native heart stories are the tributes of presence, the chance of remembrance, and the ironic hints, traces, silence, and lure of shadows in the dusty words of discoveries. The stories and creative hearsay of resistance and survivance lasted for more than three centuries, and then the bullies on reservations recounted predatory traditions of favors and blood counts, and the creative outcome was mockery and puppet parleys.

Birchy Iron Moccasin, a poseur, and many other envious crybullies renounced heart stories and abandoned the mutable nicknames that once promised an ironic tease of native presence and sense of recognition and liberty.

The mute puppeteer provoked, teased, and heartened the names of five stowaways, Big Rant Beaulieu, Bad Boy Aristotle, Poesy May Fairbanks, Truman La Chance, and Master Jean Bonga, to create catchy heart stories and dream songs with a sense of native presence and natural motion, and come what may to counter the sway of predatory traditions with spirited mockery recounted in puppet parleys. Mockery was a stray dare, and chance was creative resistance and the native sway of sovereignty that easily disrupted the poseurs, bullies of envy, and predators of traditions.

Dummy printed pithy messages and dream songs on two small chalkboards, and that morning over oatmeal and hard bread the stowaways read out loud the silent missives that were related and envisioned by chance. Some of the messages were later copied in a blank book bound in leather, one of several blank books that were stacked near a single bed and the potbelly stove in the Theatre of Chance.

"Native creation stories are stray sensations in theatres of chance and sometimes mockery of treaty deceit, separatism, and predatory traditions on reservations," shouted Big Rant Beaulieu.

"Catch black bears and elusive cedar waxwings in dream songs, bounce with the ravens and shamans, and then raise your hands and shout hallelujah, hallelujah, hallelujah for chance and the natural motion of liberty," whispered Poesy May.

"Predatory traditions are the treasons of native liberty, the seasons in natural motion are not bent to the bullies of traditions, and the mockery of puppet parleys is a ceremony of liberty," read Truman La Chance.

"Dream songs of black bears," said Master Jean.

"Dream songs of chance and liberty," shouted Big Rant.

"Dream songs of natural motion," whispered Poesy May.

Chance, not churchy destiny, was the creative character of native stories and dream songs, and chance was clever, chance was mercy, chance was enticement, chance was natural motion, chance was that great bounce of liberty, and chance was more than expectation or churchy pastime of suspense, speculation, sacrifice, or salvation.

The enigmatic spirit of hand puppet parleys conveyed native chance and character, and even with that easy course of hearsay chance advanced a sense of native presence and ethos for the five stowaways who shared two ramshackle cabins near Spirit Lake rightly named the Theatre of Chance.

The hand puppets were emissaries of native liberty, and the creative puppet parleys mocked, coaxed, teased, resisted, and conveyed the spirited sway and back talk of chance. That crucial sense of survivance and native recognition continued in the silent gestures, spirited manner, irony, and mercy of Dummy Trout.

"Dummy surprises the poseurs of native tradition and even the reservation deadheads who denounce opera music and the gestures of hand puppets," said By Now Rose Beaulieu.

By Now and her lover, Prometheus Postma, and Basile Hudon Beaulieu and his brother, Aloysius Hudon Beaulieu, were active in *La Résistance* during the Nazi Occupation of Paris. By Now is a nurse with a curious public health hospital birth name for a very late delivery. Prometheus is a raconteur and mime who escaped from the Frisian Islands. Basile is a critical writer, and Aloysius is an artist, a fauvist abstract painter.

Chance and character were obvious in the natural motion of the seasons, the great wonder of summers in the spring, the easy turn of autumn tributes, the echoes of bird migrations, the seductive blue shadows of winter ghosts, the magical bounce of ravens, the mournful sound of killdeer in the spring, and the great hesitations of lightning in every thunderstorm.

Heart stories were creative adventures of compassion and courage and the elusive ethos of chance. Heart stories were the natural tease of native creation, remembrance, and the favor of totemic associations. Heart stories were ironic and worth more than the customary forecasts of consent, courtesy, tradition, or cultural practices. Native heart stories simply sidetracked the backbiters, envious bullies, and predators of tradition, and the menace of treaty reservation separatists.

"The stowaway stories of the heart are scenes of chance and creation, the traces of the past in the natural motion of a native presence," said Master Jean.

"Natural motion is not a tradition," said Poesy May.

"Chance is liberty, not a tradition," shouted Big Rant.

Native shamans, ceremonial clowns, tricksters in creation stories, humane herbal healers, and puppeteers were never predators of tradition.

The poseurs and predators of tradition consent to the fur trade dominions of greed with the weary wails of monotheism, shame, separatism, and victimry. The poseurs of tradition are the cause of separatism, not the sources of chance and native liberty.

Dummy presented two scruffy hand puppets fashioned with refuse and debris and asked the stowaways to create a parley for the puppets. The most recent puppet parley focused on native survivance and the chance of new totemic associations with the easy motion and maneuvers of animals, birds, insects, and other creatures. The past parleys honored totems and other creative scenes at the Theatre of Chance.

"Loons are my cousins," shouted Big Rant Beaulieu.

"Dare to dive with a beaver," said Truman La Chance.

"Dance with the killdeer," said Bad Boy Aristotle

"Masturbate with the bears," said Master Jean Bonga.

"Tease me as a butterfly," said Poesy May Fairbanks.

Truman La Chance and the other stowaways counted the thunderstorms and daredevil flights of bald eagles that summer as premonitions. More than ever the trees pitched and twisted in the frightful wind, and the leaves shouted and shivered in wild bursts of lightning over Spirit Lake.

"Nothing, not the season, not the red pine, not the shoreline, not even our heart stories and totemic trust are the same after the rage of a thunderstorm," said Bad Boy.

La Chance considered the moments of silence between the flash of lightning and sound of thunder as natural hesitations, the tease of seasons and stories of creation, the evocative wavers of native irony and presence, and related them to the great silence of the mute puppeteer. The native stowaways practiced silence and the oral art of natural hesitations in puppet parleys.

Dummy Trout wrote dream songs with a clever sense of irony and quietly carved from fallen birch trees the distinctive faces of hand puppets. She envisioned the native caricatures of puppet parleys and concocted the gestures of a spirited presence with ironic scenes and slight hesitations that were related to the rare moments of silence in the natural world.

The mute puppeteer turned to silence almost seventy years ago during a firestorm, and there were no hesitations or silences in the recount of fearsome crown fires or the curves and wild roars of the deadly flames. The only silence was the heavy smoke and ashes that slowly covered the bodies of hundreds of humans and animals out of breath.

Dummy survived the fire by chance, not by native wisdom or dream songs, and not by hesitations, shamanic sleights, favor of traditions, or other causes. Only chance and the mercy of the wind suddenly turned the direction of the firestorm, and the outcome for hundreds of others was a ghastly bounty of native ashes and an eternal silence in the ruins of memory.

Dummy was eighteen years old that late summer of the Great Hinckley Fire in 1894. The fatal firestorm burned more than three hundred square miles of woodland and destroyed Hinckley, Sandstone, Mission Creek, and Bakegamaa Lake, a native community otherwise named Pokegama, and other places in northern Minnesota. She wandered in silence and misery for many days and nights coated with the ashes of the native dead and since then has never spoken a single word, never whispered a reverie, and never chanted out loud a dream song of chance.

Nookaa, her beloved lumberjack, and hundreds of other natives were burned to shadows of bone and mounds of ashes. The wild rush of animals, deer, black bears, bobcats, badgers, gray foxes, wolves, raccoons, porcupines, weasels, squirrels, rabbits, skunks, and mice rushed out of the course of the firestorm in the natural motion of survivance and a strange totemic unity with no sense of prey or predators. The great firestorm has never been forgotten in the historical chronicles of the state, but not many reports have mentioned the count of lost natives.

Dummy mourned the death of thousands of animals and birds, and many were honored as totemic relations. Later, the spirited and clever mute puppeteer cared for deserted animals and abused and abandoned children with a curious fusion of native mercy, tacit mockery, humane teases, dream songs of liberty, and heart stories of natural motion that she sometimes printed on two small chalkboards.

The stowaways were easily united in an ethos of natural motion, trust in the shamanic spirit of silence, and the creative parleys of many hand puppets in two drafty cabins with cracked windows celebrated as the Theatre of Chance.

Dummy reached to the natural motion of the clouds with great gestures, silent shouts, and dream songs, and she mocked the bullies of tradition and nasty hearsay in silence for almost seventy years. The silent gestures of brava, brava, brava for the great soprano divas of the opera, the silent hurrahs for the dream songs and heart stories of the native stowaways, and the silent salutes for the harmonious moans, melodic bays, and lively barks of the loyal mongrels were common themes of more generous hearsay at the reservation post office.

Several generations of natives remember the enchantment of the mute puppeteer, the gestures of silent mockery, the constant tease of hand puppets, and the steady taunts of haughty native leaders, mission priests, and mundane federal agents in puppet parleys.

Dummy was a silent poet of native survivance, a puppeteer, a teacher, and a storier, and she might have become an opera singer, a movie director, a theatre actor, a train conductor, an auctioneer, a nomadic raconteur, or a justice of totemic rights and liberty in federal courts.

\\\\\ 2 /////

Native Royalty

Dummy Trout was doubly silent about the absence of native words for the precise manner of shamanic silence, but she saluted a new nickname announced that summer by the stowaways. Big Rant praised the mute puppeteer with two native words, *manidoo biiwaabik,* a magnet or the silent spirit of a lodestone, since there were no certain native words for hush or shamanic silence and only *bangan,* peace or quiet, and *awibaa,* calm, or *goshkwaawaadizi,* for a quiet manner in Anishinaabe. The dead, *nibo,* an eternal silence, and *nibooke,* a death in the family, were never considered as dares or teases of silence at the Theatre of Chance.

Yet there were many native words for the discrete spirit of speech and the manner of speaking, *giizhiiwe,* speak loudly, *wiinigiizhwe,* speak nastily, *gwayakowe,* speak correctly, but not a single native word to portray the natural tease of silence and the marvelous spirit of the mute puppeteer.

"Chance is silence, a shamanic silence," said Big Rant.

"Silent dream songs in the clouds," said Poesy May.

"Silence is the hesitation of creation," said La Chance.

"Natural motion is never silent," said Bad Boy.

"Every spoken word is ironic, a chase of meaning in every sentence of names and play on the page," said Master Jean. "Puppet parleys are ironic, the nature of conversations, and a mockery of every word in a colloquy."

Manidoo Biiwaabik, the spirited puppeteer, was honored by the stowaways in heart stories, seasons of dream songs, and hand puppet parleys and always by the barks, bays, moans, and gentle nudges of the loyal mongrels, George Eliot, a gracious greyhound and retriever, Trophy Bay, a mongrel coon hound with a baritone bay, Tallulah, a bold mongrel beagle with a contralto bay, Hail Mary, a spaniel and husky, Dingleberry, a spotted black and white terrier with a lively yodel, and Daniel, a black spaniel. Manidoo Biiwaabik was soon shortened to Manidoo, a silent spirit, and Manidooke, spiritual power and ceremony.

Later the stowaways staged an ironic puppet parley that mocked with great devotion the slight hesitations, the silent gestures of brava, brava, brava for the soprano divas, and the concise declarations and dream songs that the mute puppeteer printed at least once a day on two handy chalkboards.

birch leaves
natural motion on spirit lake
hesitations of thunder
manidoo biiwaabik
adrift in shamanic silence

Manidoo celebrated silence as an ironic native heart story and recently wrote on a chalkboard, "Clever creation stories are hesitations of silence, and every creation story mocks the ghosts of envy that haunt the deals of the predators and separatists." Once or twice a month the stowaways related in heart stories the chance of presence and liberty at the Theatre of Chance.

"Manidoo and the mongrels rescued me at least twice a day from the memories of my drunken uncle," said Bad Boy Aristotle.

"Manidoo saved me from the absence of a father and the misery and remorse of my unknown mother, who abandoned me as an infant in a rickety basket at the door of the mission," said Big Rant Beaulieu.

"Manidoo teased me as an orphan to create stories of natural motion with my hesitations," said Truman La Chance. "Silent shadows of a moccasin flower and a wary otter on a riverbank are silent hesitation in my heart stories."

"Manidoo smiled and gestured in silence that my murmurs were the natural motion of native dream songs, soughs, and whispers of poetry," said Poesy May Fairbanks.

"Manidoo teased me as a lonesome boy from the mission school, the descendant of a fur trade slave, and together we carried out the art of meditation and mockery of targets in native archery," said Master Jean Bonga.

Manidoo Biiwaabik was a shaman of silence and easily overcame the native nickname *bagwanawizi*, dumb or ignorant, and other curses and hearsay that she was nothing more than a "witless birch bark puppet with stringy white hair." The mute puppeteer outwitted the backbiters as the only steadfast native Doyenne of Silence on the reservation, the envisioned maestra of opera arias and great sopranos Renata Tebaldi, Geraldine Farrar, and Alma Gluck.

Manidoo countered derisive nicknames with hand puppets that teased and mocked the bullies, braggarts, and bigots of contrived traditions with strategic silence and witty parleys. "Hand puppets are much more clever than native bullies in fake cowboy boots and camouflage coats," she printed on a hand chalkboard.

Postcard Mary, the native manager of the reservation post office created ironic postcard stories that favored the spirit and surprise of the mute puppeteer and countered the nasty hearsay of the pork barrel bully boys.

The mute puppeteer cared mainly for the spirit of native children, mongrels, soprano divas, puppets carved from fallen birch trees, the beaver, and other animal and bird totems, and she was never tempted to shout into panic holes or scare a lonesome child with the curse of pious pity, monotheistic shame, or scary scenes of salvation.

"Manidoo is a dream song," said Master Jean.

"Manidoo is a silent poet," said Poesy May.

"Manidoo is a great hesitation," said La Chance.

"Manidoo is a parley in the clouds," said Big Rant.

"Manidoo is forever in a book," said Bad Boy.

The mute puppeteer was more curious, creative, mysterious, and memorable in silence than other natives who carved out their patchy presence with pouts, shouts, groans, grumbles, slights, trivial misfortunes, and getaway liquor, and she was certainly more native by spirit than the bullies that boasted about traditions, birthrights, and quantum blood sports on a treaty reservation.

Manidoo Biiwaabik printed a declaration on the chalkboard that "the federal crazy count of our ancient native blood could only mean that we are royalty, regal blood down to the very last stain, and the obvious outcome of our bloody royalty is that we inherited the native blood rights and titles of kingly, queenly, and princely sovereignty, and that favors the mongrels and entitles me to be the Queen of Spirit Lake and the Doyenne of Silence."

Master Jean mounted the royal decree over the wash basin, and the five sovereign stowaways mocked each other with the native peerage of Baron Bad Boy, Grand Duke La Chance, Marquis Master Jean, Princess Poesy

May, and Duchess Big Rant at the Royal Theatre of Chance near Spirit Lake. Royalty was the ironic outcome of the federal crazy quantum count of blood and reservation names.

The creation of native royalty was a necessary tease and mockery of treaty bloodlines on the reservation, and the miseries of abandoned and abused native children were bearable in the ironic puppet parleys of liberty. The mongrels nudged the five runaways to stay as stowaways at the Theatre of Chance. Truman La Chance, a contrary heir of the continental fur trade, created dream songs about totemic animals, and he was an orphan in the ruins of civilization at the government school. Poesy May Fairbanks was a clever native poet and whisperer, and she was sensitive to the signature voices of authors in libraries. Master Jean Bonga, a runaway from the mission school with the ironic name of a slave in the fur trade, was nudged to stay with his black mongrel named Daniel. Big Rant Beaulieu was abandoned as an infant at the mission and shouted out every word when she learned to read in the library. Bad Boy Aristotle was abused by a drunken uncle and touched with favor by the mongrels to stay as a stowaway, and he rightly earned the nickname of a curious disciple of classical poetics at the Theatre of Chance.

\\\\\ 3 /////

FUGITIVE PUPPETS

Truman La Chance, an orphan at five, Big Rant Beaulieu, abandoned at birth, and Bad Boy Aristotle, shamed and abused by a drunken uncle, were the first runaways surrounded by the mongrels and nosed with favor to stay as stowaways.

Master Jean Bonga, an audacious child of convictions and visionary justice with the ironic first name of a slaver, lord, and master of the ancient fur trade, and Poesy May Fairbanks, the gentle poet of marvelous whispers, were the last native runaways favored to stay by the loyal mongrels at the two ramshackle cabins near Spirit Lake.

The five mongrels, Hail Mary, an elusive spaniel, Trophy Bay, a mongrel coonhound, Tallulah, the beagle and husky with a contralto bay, George Eliot, a racy mongrel with the blood of a greyhound and retriever, and Dingleberry, a dinky, fidgety, black and white smooth fox terrier mongrel, snuffled the runaways that crossed the threshold of chance, and then one by one the mongrels bumped and nudged with favor each of the natives selected to stay as stowaways.

Master Jean arrived at the Theatre of Chance with Daniel, a loyal black spaniel mongrel with the first name of Captain Daniel Robertson, a slaver and officer in the British Army. During the colonial wars in the late eighteenth century, the colonial slaver was named commander of Fort Michilimackinac in the Province of Canada. The captain owned slaves that were emancipated at his death, including Jean Bonga, once a surname of servitude in Martinique. Master Jean was told by a priest at the mission school that the word *bonga* in Zulu, a Bantu language of southern Africa, could be translated as praise or gratitude.

Nagamo Trotterchaud, a tiny native woman, was born in a cold wigwam on the Ash River Trail near Sullivan Bay. She met George Bonga at a Métis summer dance, and they were married a few months later at the mission on the White Earth Reservation. Nagamo craved for the mere native favor of more time to praise and tease her only child Master Jean Bonga, but slowly she lost her strength and withered with fevers, fatigue, and slight chest and body pains, and after several years of disguised misery she was diagnosed with tuberculosis. Nagamo was sent straight away to the Ahgwahching State Sanitorium near Walker, Minnesota, and the Leech Lake Reservation.

George Bonga had enlisted in the United States Army and served in a segregated company as a truck driver for the Red Ball Express during the Second World War. He was not aware of the ancient disease, *ozosodam-waapinewin*, or the curse of tuberculosis in the language of the Anishinaabe.

Master Jean was a solitary child and desolate without his gentle mother. He was alone for more than a month that summer of his sixth birthday and always hungry, and in that lonesome time he learned how to carve the perfect curve of a bow from green ash and fashion arrows from a juneberry bush. Day after day he prepared to be a native hunter, but the wait in the brush to sacrifice an animal for his survival was cocky and clumsy, and wisely he recast the chase to honor animals and birds as native totems.

Master Jean never forgot the lovely voice of his mother as she sang "Only Forever" and "I'll Never Smile Again" every morning as the sun slowly moved through the great maple tree near the tiny cabin. She had learned by heart the popular songs of Bing Crosby and Frank Sinatra. Nagamo, a visionary native name, means "she sings" in the language of the Anishinaabe.

Bad Boy, Big Rant, Poesy May, and Master Jean first met at the mission school and later became close friends in the ruins of the Library of Nibwaakaa. The reservation library was burned to the ground by an arsonist and the books smoldered for several days, and then faint soughs and murmurs were heard from the gray hazy residue of the library, the sound of wounded words at the scene of a despicable crime against literature and survivance in the ruins of civilization.

Bad Boy shoveled through the smoldering ashes of the library and found burned copies of *King Lear, Hamlet,* and other tragedies by William Shakespeare, *Poetics* by Aristotle, and the brilliant essays of Michel de Montaigne. Big Rant sifted the ruins and recovered *The Whale* by Herman Melville, *Light in August* by William Faulkner, *Look Homeward Angel* by Thomas Wolfe, and other novels. Poesy May waded in the ashes and found poetry books by Robert Frost, Carl Sandburg, John Keats, and Walt Whitman. Master Jean grazed in the ruins for several days and rescued two partly burned books about the coureurs de bois of the fur trade, *Caesars of the Wilderness* and *The Voyageur* by Grace Lee Nute, a badly charred copy of the *History of the Ojibway Nation* by William Whipple Warren, and a scorched edition of *Hiroshima* by John Hersey.

Bad Boy arrived at the Theatre of Chance with body bruises and a camouflage backpack that contained two shirts, a pair of black socks, one silver dollar, a pocket watch, a small jackknife, and burned books. Even as a child he resisted the notions of native tragedy, and as a grateful stowaway he created scenes from the burned pages of *Poetics* by Aristotle and imagined that natural motion was the *instinct of imitation* in native trickster stories and irony was the *difference between him and the other animals* in a scene he created from the margin of the burned pages.

Later he created a distinct scene of native presence with a few burned pages from the chapter "Of Fear" in the *Essays of Montaigne* by Michel de Montaigne. The stowaway created stories and ironic scenes from the burned margins of the book and then interrelated the created scenes with the actual remains on the printed page.

Bad Boy read the selected scene out loud that night at the Theatre of Chance. *Such as have been well rubbed* in native trickster stories *may yet, all wounded and bloody as* the beaver in the fur trade *brought on again the next day to charge* in the ancient tease of shamans *as have once conceived a good sound* of a demonic curse and fury of the *enemy, will never be made so much as* the last traces of temper and fear *in the face. Such as are the immediate* causes of native chance and misery *losing their estates, of banishment, or* the cruel separation of treaty reservations, *live in perpetual anguish, and lose all* native memories of natural motion, heart stories, and dream songs, and *repose, whereas such as are actually poor* ironic banishment of natives *or exiles, ofttimes live as merrily as other* deserted cultures of resistance. *And the many people who impatient* turned to provocateurs of the enemy way with *perpetual alarms of fear, have hanged or* pretended to ridicule and punish *themselves, or dashed themselves to pieces* only later to rage and then convince *us sufficiently to understand that fear* of old churchy promises of salvation are more *importunate and insupportable than death* of the crafty poseurs of the future.

Master Jean created the necessary heart stories about his ancestors and more from the burned pages of the *History of the Ojibway Nation* by William Warren. The author, a descendant of natives active in the fur trade, was born at La Pointe, Madeline Island, Wisconsin Territory, in 1825. He died at age fifty-three and more than thirty years before the first publication of his book by the Minnesota Historical Society in 1885. Warren was a fluent speaker of French, English, and Anishinaabe and served with distinction as an interpreter for explorers and federal agents during the late fur trade, and later he was named a member of the Legislative Assembly of the Minnesota Territory.

Master Jean leaned forward and read out loud the ironic episodes that he had created and then cleverly related the scenes to the remains of the original pages of the *History of the Ojibway Nation*. Take notice that the explorer Jacques Cartier Bonga *first made his appearance* as a bold native of two continents in the early sixteenth century, and that *occurred in the third generation*, and after many adventures *had passed away since that* great union of native liberty in *their history*. The elderly native *was about sixty years of age at the* time he properly celebrated *this plate of copper, which he said had* been given to him by a shaman of the natives and slaves, *direct through a long line of ancestors*. Then, after many *years since, and his death has added the* secret of the copper plate *indentation thereon; making, at this point, nine* native scenes and stories of liberty *since the Ojibways first resided at La Pointe*, and many other heart stories of native totemic *generations since their first intercourse with the* first continental slavers after the royal calculations and obscure navigation of Christopher Columbus. The Indians of the East Indies were more than nine thousand nautical miles from the island named *Guanahani* by the native Taino of the West Indies.

Master Jean continued his heart stories with the familiar name of Jacques Cartier, the predatory explorer of preposterous conceit who claimed North America and thousands of native cultures and native mappery of rivers, trade routes, and the entirety of the continent in the name of La France.

Master Jean was the master of mockery and satirical stories about the barren chronicles of discoveries and the natural motion of continental liberty. Nagamo recorded the birth names Master Jean Bonga with a sense of historical favor and native romance, and in turn the master storier continued the native favor and irony with the name of Jacques Cartier Bonga, a second surname of ancient slavery in Nouvelle France.

"The French and Zulu explorer in my native heart stories might have celebrated the natural motion of the continent with the word *Bonga*, a place of honor, gratitude, and reverence, and with the daily tributes of native liberty," declared Master Jean Bonga.

Jean Bonga and Marie Jeanne Bonga were emancipated by the death of Captain Daniel Robertson at Michilimackinac in 1787. France allowed colonial agents, priests, military officers, and many other outliers of treachery to liberate their slaves. Jean and Marie Jeanne married and later established the first hotel and tavern and raised four children, Pierre, Etienne, Rosalie, and Charlotte, on Mackinac Island.

Etienne was a voyageur in the fur trade for the North West Company and later for the American Fur Company. Pierre was a fur trader and a translator at Fond du Lac and was named *makade wiiyaas*, a black person, by some of the natives. He was a fluent speaker of Anishinaabe, or Ojibwe in colonial nominations, and easily understood that *makade* was the word for black, *wiiyass* was meat, and *makwa* was bear. His wife was native, and his son George was educated in Montreal, and Stephen studied for the ministry in Albany, New York.

George Bonga was a translator for Louis Cass, the Brigadier General, noted Freemason, politician, slave owner, graduate of Phillips Exeter Academy in New Hampshire, and governor of Michigan Territory. Stephen Bonga was the primary interpreter for federal agents and Wisconsin Territorial Governor Henry Dodge at Fort Snelling.

George and his Anishinaabe wife lived near Leech Lake in Minnesota and established a hotel after the decline of the fur trade. The beaver, muskrat, marten, and many other totemic animals were close to extinction as mere peltry after more than a century of greedy hunters and traders. The voyageurs carried out the custom of camp songs and erotic stories about native women after the daily decimation of totemic animals.

George, the amateur hotelier, was a memorable storier, and his twentieth century namesake, the decorated veteran of the Red Ball Express in the Second World War and distant descendant of slaves, had inherited nothing more than the easy cut and run stories of native traders and a perceptive and estranged son who became a stowaway and puppeteer at the Theatre of Chance.

"Jean Bonga was a domestic slave, and there would be no me without slavery," said Master Jean. "Curious, strange, even spectacular that a successor of colonial slavery becomes a native stowaway and puppeteer with a military bugle on a segregated treaty reservation."

"Marquis *Makade Wiiyaas*," shouted Duchess Big Rant.

"Captain Daniel was a slaver and would never know there would never be an ironic me, a puppeteer of chance, without his death and the curious catch and release of slaves at Mackinac Island," said Marquis Master Jean.

"Slave master of irony," said Grand Duke La Chance.

"French Jesuits were crafty slavers," said Baron Bad Boy.

Master Jean wrote to his mother once or twice a week with lively stories about the nuns and students at the mission school and told her in every letter how much he was touched as a child by the sound of her beautiful voice every morning. Nagamo responded to every letter from her son with memories of their time together and never once mentioned her condition or deadly disease. Master Jean received a short notice that winter from the Ahgwahching State Sanitorium that Nagamo Trotterchaud died peacefully in her sleep on Sunday, January 7, 1945.

"Colonial tuberculosis is not peace," shouted Big Rant.

Master Jean wrote only four letters to his father in the past twenty years. The first letter, short and printed on the side of a brown paper bag, was about his hunger, but the letter was never delivered during the Second World War.

The second letter was written on lined paper and posted from the mission boarding school. "Good place with new friends, and every meal is a celebration of food and piety, and the big priest wants me to become an archer and take part in state competition as a mission student, but the practice targets are not for me because nothing anchored or permanent is ever real to me. My heartbeat is a natural motion, and everything in the natural world is in motion, but history, social studies, sermons, and targets are printed on dead paper and with no natural motion. The nuns at the mission school tried to distract me from the natural motion of my heart."

Master Jean wrote a third letter to his father when he quit the mission school and became a runaway and then a stowaway at the Theatre of Chance. "My letter is chance in natural motion, you know, the same as the seasons, and yet never the same. My good thoughts about chance and motion were not accepted at the mission school, and then the priest told me that hand puppets and parleys are wicked, as wicked as my thoughts about chance. So, the reason for my escape from the mission school was the easy stories and teases of chance in the company of other stowaways.

"The Theatre of Chance is now my heart story, and the wild puppet parleys are the most creative mockery of the old mission play of providence. That probably bothers you, but chance is my time, my place, and my adventure of natural motion, and chance saved me from the fakery of piety and the politics of confessions as the way to salvation."

Master Jean wrote the last letter to his father George Bonga from the converted school bus that was parked near the Iron Pergola at Pioneer Square. The stowaways had traveled on the *Theatre of Chance* to the Seattle World's Fair in the late summer of 1962. George was always on the move, but no one considered the moves of his father to be natural motion in a native heart story. He married a Japanese nurse, and they moved to Los Angeles, California.

The last letter was written on proper stationary with the faint watermark pattern of natural scenes. "The Second World War lingers here, and everywhere, and with every raspy sigh and overnight shouts and nightmares of wounded, lost, and deserted veterans. They barely sleep under threadbare military blankets, and some veterans are covered with nothing more than a few pages of a newspaper in abandoned buildings and shiver in every den and doorway near Pioneer Square.

"Atomic 16, a wounded veteran and new friend of the stowaways, has taken part in the puppet parleys. Combat soldiers gave him the deadly nickname for the scent of sulfur because he was exposed to radiation during military clean up duties at Hiroshima, Japan.

"Yesterday we presented a puppet parley between Edward Teller, the physicist who created the horror of the thermonuclear bomb named Castle Bravo, and the Japanese survivors on a fishing boat named the Lucky Dragon. The hand puppets played out the irony of the lucky tuna boat sailors and a nuclear disaster that destroyed Bikini Atoll.

"Why would anyone want to test the most wicked and deadly weapon in human history? Why? The war was over, Teller lied about Robert Oppenheimer, and now he is honored as the evil genius of Castle Bravo. Does that mean that nuclear poison is the deadly outcome of science and civilization? You were lucky as a truck driver during the war, and by chance, even though your unit was segregated. You only had to worry about the cannons, machine guns, enemy aircraft, and not about a slow and miserable death caused by the exposure to nuclear radiation from Little Boy detonated over Hiroshima.

"Dummy Trout and the stowaways return to the reservation in about two weeks, after a puppet parley between Samuel Beckett, the French playwright, and Sitting Bull, the Lakota visionary. We plan to stage the parley on a crowded street in San Francisco and then on the campus of the University of California at Berkeley. The title of the puppet parley is *Waiting for Wovoka*, an ironic native version of *Waiting for Godot* by Samuel Beckett."

George Bonga received the last letter from his son and a few months later responded with a short note on a postcard, "Moved to Kyoto, Japan. Noriko, my wife, is a nurse at a medical clinic." Master Jean could barely imagine the scene with nothing more than an exotic name and place, which was a common style of his father.

Postcard Mary, the manager of the post office, created a marvelous version of the postcard note, a hearsay story that Noriko was born in Tokyo and named in honor of the sensational soprano diva Noriko Awaya, who was born in Aomori Prefecture in 1907. The hearsay was traded and enhanced throughout the reservation and existential colony that George Bonga had married Noriko Awaya, the famous diva, not a nurse, and became the personal manager of the soprano who was celebrated as the Japanese Queen of the Blues.

Manidoo Biiwaabik carved distinctive hand puppets only from fallen birch trees and created punchy and ironic parleys, and her singular experiences, courage, and mercy, were a native sense of presence in every season and parley. She endured the seclusion of two world wars, separatism on a treaty reservation, predatory traditions, the bullies of torment, and the Great Depression. She perceived, at the same time, a sense of solace and survivance in sounds of natural motion, and once a week she listened to the broadcasts of glorious arias of soprano divas from the New York Metropolitan Opera on the console radio at the Leecy Hotel.

Last summer the mute puppeteer traveled thousands of miles on a bouncy seat in a converted school bus christened the *Theatre of Chance* with five stowaways, six loyal mongrels, and four relations and confidants who survived the Nazi Occupation of Paris. Basile Hudon Beaulieu, native author who wrote fifty letters during the war that were published and distributed on the reservation, and his brother Aloysius Hudon Beaulieu, the fauvist and expressionist painter whose work has been exhibited at the Galerie de la Danse des Esprits, or Galerie Ghost Dance, By Now Rose Beaulieu, a nurse, and her marvelous lover Prometheus Postma, a Frisian raconteur, served together in *La Résistance* in France.

Manidoo Biiwaabik wrote on a hand chalkboard that she might have been "a nurse, a diva, a virtuosa of the opera, a radio news reporter, an oboe player in an orchestra," and with other native cues and virtues she would have "served as a silent warrior with fugitive puppets in *La Résistance* alongside my native relations during the Nazi Occupation of France."

MUTABLE NICKNAMES

Postcard Mary, the stout and sturdy manager and postal envoy of good cheer at the cozy reservation post office, was teased by the callous bullies several times a week with tiresome nicknames, Postage Due, Picture Postcard, Sticky Stamp, Late Delivery, Wrong Address, and Dead Letter Lady. Despite the steady slights, the post office was a persistent center of creative, ironic, and spectacular hearsay that circulated more widely than the boasts of predatory hunters or boring blabber of the pork barrel bully boys.

Postcard Mary created and enhanced ironic postcard stories that circulated for several weeks, or until the nasty strains of envy and other rumors were favored once more over the creative and lively scenes of hearsay. The frightful rumors of the reservation bullies were easily sidestepped and then overcome with native irony, teases, and customary mockery.

Dummy Trout and the lurid tales of the mongrels were the common themes of malicious rumors, and later the stowaways were merged into the repugnant stories about wild sex with dummies and hand puppets in the ramshackle cabins of masturbation and harlotry. The nasty bully boys never uttered the nickname Manido Biiwaabik, but they doubled the stories about magnetic attraction, masturbation, and *mazhi*, or sex, with the mongrels, stowaways, and Dummy Trout at the Theatre of Mazhi.

Postcard Mary created two memorable stories about the birth and sway of the mute puppeteer and the ironic source of the freshwater surname to counter the derogatory nickname Dummy Trout. The hearsay stories related at the post office were ironic, spirited, humane, reverential, and outrageous, but the variations were motivated by envy, resentment, and forecasts of misery and victimry. The favors of hearsay and ironic heart stories were only heard with pleasure at the post office and always at the Theatre of Chance.

Manidoo Biiwaabik printed a dream song on a chalkboard, leaned back in the huge wooden chair near the stove, and teased the loyal mongrels with shreds of pemmican. George Eliot raised a paw and soughed, and Dingleberry pranced around the wood stove and faintly bayed.

hand puppets
gesture to the clouds
mock the masturbation bullies
handy turns of hearsay
native harmony astray

Dummy Trout, and later Manidoo Biiwaabik, was commonly honored with the creative hearsay of a recent postcard, and even the loyal mongrels were devoted listeners as they waited for thin shreds of pemmican behind the potbelly stove. George Eliot was the most devoted mongrel at the post office, but she was never given more pemmican than the other loyal mongrels. Clearly the favors of dried meat would have been earned for the fancy dance of Dingleberry.

The federal government once threatened to terminate treaty reservations and assimilate natives with no recognition of bloody royalty. The creative post office hearsay countered the rush of remorse, crazy and berserk rumors that became more elaborate and strategic since the political threats of the termination of treaty reservations. The memories, regrets, nostalgia, and generous hearsay were cautious and slowly eroded the nasty rumors of revenge booty and bloodline charter rights.

The malicious turn of rumors probably started at the blind pig saloons about the same time that thousands of natives moved away from reservations at the end of the First World War and during the desperate years of the Great Depression, and then more natives relocated for education, job training, and work in small towns and cities after military service in the Second World War.

Manidoo Biiwaabik was silent about more than eighty years of rich memories of the coureurs des bois and the fur trade and lived with loyal mongrels and related some exotic experiences only in the lively parleys of hand puppets and the emotive arias of soprano opera divas. Puppetry was popular in many other countries, but the creative sentiments and delights of the magical gestures of hand puppets were sidelined by jealousy, hearsay, the predators of dubious traditions, and the creases of segregation on treaty reservations.

Native nicknames at the end of the fur trade were transient and sometimes cursory translations that became the entitlement of a surname in the strange chase of woeful missionaries and despotic colonial agents. Postcard Mary mocked the missions of epithets and created several nicknames for the mute puppeteer who was born near French Portage Narrows on Lake of the Woods.

Truite de Lac, a lake trout, and La Taquine, the teaser, were, in French, nicknames in the original hearsay. Postcard Mary created sensational stories with each situational nickname, and the stowaways once considered the name La Taquine as a given name and surname in stories, and the name circulated in native communities and much later became hearsay for a short time on the existential native colony in Minneapolis.

Postcard Mary created the first hearsay story that Truite de Lac was born at Lake of the Woods at the end of the fur trade and start of separatism on treaty reservations and reserves. She was the doyenne of totemic dream songs and the sovereign of fur trade stories. La Taquine, the teaser, created buoyant heart stories of native chance, resistance, and every ironic scene provoked the coureurs des bois and voyageurs of the colonial fur trade.

"La Taquine the voyageur of teases," said Poesy May.

"Doyenne of puppet parley teases," said Bad Boy.

La Taquine was only sixteen years old when she first created stories with totemic trust and a sense of native liberty, and her heart stories were the primary sources of native recognition in the fur trade at the time, but the dithery missions and the eternal trade of high wine, rum, and brandy became the mercenary course of the fur trade and the outright massacre of totemic animals.

Monotheism, greedy hunters, and the high wine culture of the fur trade almost caused the extinction of the beaver, marten, mink, otter, muskrat, and many other animals, and the spirited stories of totemic animals were almost gone.

"Beaver heart stories never end," said Big Rant.

"Beaver never turned nostalgic," said Master Jean.

"Beaver created sanctuaries," said Bad Boy.

"Beaver dams are cathedrals," said Poesy May.

"Beaver fedoras are criminal," said La Chance.

La Taquine turned the demise of totemic animals into the chance of shamanic heart stories, cultural irony, and deceptive praise and almost reversed the withered craves of the fur trade with the strange shamanic sounds of animals that mocked the coureurs des bois late at night. The alcohol traders were bedeviled by the strange sounds, whispers in the trees, steady gasps of shame near shore, and heavy groans of misery at every portage.

La Taquine tormented the alcohol traders on the lakes and rivers near the international borders and sabotaged the birchbark canoes loaded with rum and high wine, and over the next two years the stories of a shaman of liberty, a giant lake trout, became more believable as the teaser wrecked the entire subversive trade of moonshine on Lake of the Woods.

The stowaways were captivated by the original hearsay stories that the mute puppeteer had sabotaged the high wine trade, and together they declared a native resistance movement to disrupt and terminate *ishkode waaboo*, alcohol drink, and end the primary sources of drunken envy and hearsay by the pork barrel bullies on the reservation.

The Bureau of Indian Affairs established the Special Office for the Suppression of Liquor fifty years earlier, but reservation agents could not overcome the political power of saloon owners and the economy of serious native drinkers. Alf Oftedal, a federal agent at the time, warned about the moral dangers of saloons in Walker, Park Rapids, Bena, Mahnomen, and other small towns on and near reservations, and agent John Hinton reported that there were blind pigs, or unlawful saloons, and native bootleggers on the White Earth Reservation.

A dedicated troupe of native citizens once petitioned the government to terminate the sale of liquor on the reservation, but petitions were nothing more than parchment teases because the elusive bootleggers supplied the blind pigs and at the same time mobsters secretly transported alcohol across the international border and safely through native reservations to Saint Paul and Minneapolis during enforcement of the Eighteenth Amendment on Prohibition.

Postcard Mary revealed in the second hearsay story that Truite de Lac captured François de Noyon, a short, muscular, and bold coureur des bois at French Portage Narrows and teased the adventurer to mourn the massacre of totemic animals. Truite de Lac and François recast the fur trade and persuaded hundreds of other coureurs des bois and lonesome colonial adventurers to gather on Massacre Island in Lake of the Woods for a late summer celebration to honor the bear, beaver, bobcat, marten, otter, and lake trout totems and the shamanic sway and spiritual power of totemic creatures. The younger coureurs des bois were in heavy debt, lonesome, and disenchanted with the constant demands for the scarce beaver, and they were eager to find a native woman and renounce the mercenary trade.

Truite de Lac mocked the colonial agents of the continental fur trade, and at the same time she maneuvered to alter the name of Massacre Island, rightly commemorated for the massacre of the Jesuit missionary Jean-Pierre Aulneau, Jean Baptiste de La Vérendrye, and nineteen French explorers, to Jiibay Minisaabik, or Rocky Ghost Island, Lake of the Woods.

Postcard Mary continued the creative hearsay at the post office, three or four new stories a month, and the ironic stories of mercy and redemption became even more wild mutations that lasted for several years on the reservation. La Taquine scouted out the old portages in one story and stole birch bark canoes and convinced the greedy coureurs des bois with steady erotic teases to liberate the last bundles of beaver peltry on Jiibay Minisaabik. She sang dream songs about totemic liberty as the fur traders slowly untied the bundles, stretched out the beaver pelts on the rocky shoreline, and then appealed to the ghosts of more than a hundred million animals that were slaughtered in the fur trade for some recognition of mercy and absolution for the massacre of totemic animals and crimes against the natural world.

5

STRANGE HARMONY

By Now Rose Beaulieu and her giant lover, Prometheus Postma, the raconteur and libertarian mime from the Frisian Islands, moved early last spring from Bad Boy Lake on the White Earth Reservation to a Murphy bed apartment on LaSalle Avenue near Loring Park in Minneapolis. By Now was hired as a nurse at a medical clinic near Mount Sinai Hospital. Prometheus founded an escort and tour service for international visitors interested in the Guthrie Theater, the Minneapolis Institute of Art, the Walker Art Center, and the University of Minnesota.

Basile Hudon Beaulieu and his brother Aloysius Hudon Beaulieu rented an apartment in a converted mansion a few blocks from Elliot Park and three widely known native hangouts, Little Judge's Liquor Store with the huge red neon sign, Hello Dolly's, a notorious bar, and the Band Box Diner near Chicago Avenue.

Basile had written more than fifty letters to Dummy Trout during the Nazi Occupation of Paris and continued to write long letters to the mute puppeteer from the existential native colony in Minneapolis. He was a contract writer for magazines and weekly newspapers and published critical articles about the politics of poverty on reservations, treacherous federal agents, predatory traditions, and the retraction of services to natives in urban areas and critical editorials that compared the police violence against natives with the violence against various labor unions in Minneapolis.

Basile continued the research on an article he read by Gerald Vizenor, staff writer with the *Minneapolis Tribune*, that revealed the actual location of the Central Intelligence Agency disguised as a general law office in the Midland Bank Building in downtown Minneapolis. The names of four lawyers were posted at the entrance, but only a secretary was present in the small office. One name was entered in a directory of lawyers, and a short biography indicated that he was a friend of Vice President Hubert Humphrey, and the lawyer was an intelligence officer during the Second World War. The maintenance supervisor in the basement of the bank building provided the ordinary evidence from a register that the rent for the office was paid by the Central Intelligence Agency.

The Agency spied on citizens at home in the United States, an unambiguous violation of the charter that established the intelligence service at the end of the Second World War. The agents ordered the removal of every trace of the covert bank office and seized copies of the article from the newspaper library and from the apartment of the journalist, an obvious search and seizure without a legal warrant that was an apparent violation of the original charter of the Central Intelligence Agency, and the agents apparently breached the protection of the Fourth Amendment of the United States Constitution.

"The Central Intelligence Agency is obsessed with keeping secrets. Paul Hendrickson, the local keeper of secrets, demanded that his arcane telephone number not be published," Vizenor wrote in the *Minneapolis Tribune*. "The agency has at least two local telephone numbers. One is listed in the directory without an address, and the other is a secret. The person who answers the calls to both numbers will not reveal the location of the office. Both numbers are listed as regular business accounts with the telephone company in the name of Hendrickson."

Basile considered the critical information in the report by a native journalist and continued to investigate for a magazine article the double violations of a domestic search and seizure without a warrant. He eventually located other secret locations that contravened the charter of the Central Intelligence Agency.

Basile was under surveillance by domestic agents and other covert envoys from several federal agencies, and the stowaways were enraged by similar fascist strategies of federal agents on reservations and decided to become domestic counterspies, creating an ironic network of deception by posting hand printed posters on stores, doors, and polls in the existential colony that revealed the daily activities of the agents. The mimeographed posters were secretly removed every night, and a few days later the stowaways posted caricatures of the agents by Aloysius Hudon Beaulieu on the inside windows of the Band Box Diner and Hello Dolly's.

Basile slighted the domestic criminal agents in a magazine article and then turned to a series of critical essays about the demon core and plutonium scientists, atomic veterans, and the soldiers who were exposed to nuclear radiation during the military occupation at Hiroshima and Nagasaki and the thousands of soldiers and downwind citizens who were later exposed to high levels of radiation from atmospheric tests at the Nevada Test Sites.

Aloysius, the painter, created shadowy fauvist scenes of abstract totemic animals and birds, the buoyant contours and traces of beaver, otter, bear, marten, muskrat, loon, golden eagle, and sandhill cranes in natural motion. The enigmatic contours were painted over light gray shadows and faint outlines of abandoned buildings, a library, hospital, hotel, factory, tenement, and a railroad depot. Many of the slight structures that were depicted in his paintings had been razed in the mercenary maneuvers of urban renewal in downtown Minneapolis.

Aloysius created the abstract presence of deformed birds and animals that migrated from predatory hunters and agrarian poisons in northern lakes and rivers, a migration from the deadly chemical pollution of fields, forests, and lakes. The expressionist scenes were not respected on the reservation and shunned at museums because the abstract fauvist images were not considered by curators as traditional native artistic themes.

Basile wrote a critical letter to the museum curator and never mentioned the artistic stature of Aloysius Hudon Beaulieu at galleries in Paris. "The mercenary fur trade is over but the escape of totemic animals and birds from deadly chemicals and extinction is a crucial abstract conception of native art, and the existential migration of natives from the predatory traditions and cultural ruins of treaty reservations is a necessary expression of creative native survivance."

By Now and Prometheus lived next door to Alice Beaulieu Vizenor, a close relation, and her blind husband, Earl Restdorf, who collected clocks and somehow repaired vacuum tube radios for friends and neighbors. The many mechanical clocks ticked, ticked, ticked, clucked, chimed, and bonged over and over in a strange harmony, and only one clock was set to Central Standard Time.

Alice recognized a few exotic and mellow ticks and clucks of the clocks in the same way she regarded native hearsay, and yet she seldom noticed the time on any clock. Rather, she decided on the necessary hours of the day by the season and slant of the sun and by natural motion, not by the hands of a clock. Even so, she teased anyone who noticed that the actual weather forecasts were decided by the appearance of a disfigured witch that waited in a Hansel and Gretel Weather House mounted on the window sill over the kitchen sink.

Alice first moved to the existential colony about thirty years earlier during the Great Depression and then returned to the reservation for a few years when two of her five sons were murdered by mobsters who were secretly protected by the police and the Citizens' Alliance, a posse of greedy business owners and politicians worried about socialists and communists in local trade unions. The members of labor unions embraced the ethos of a socialist democracy, and the delusions of third rail reactionary conspiracies in the state of ten thousand lakes was nothing more than greed and fanciful speculation by the posse of merchants and mercenaries. The Law and Order Committee of the Citizens' Alliance, or The Low and Odor Committee, the sardonic name circulated by labor unions, was obsessed with the preposterous political threats of a Soviet Communist Republic in Minneapolis.

"Cops Fire on Unarmed Pickets" was the banner headline of *The Militant*, the Weekly Organ of the Communist League, on July 21, 1934. Police Chief Michael Johannes authorized some officers to carry shotguns and shoot unarmed members of the local union of truck drivers during an organized strike in the Produce Market District of Minneapolis.

Henry Ness, John Belor, and other union members were shot by the police. Ness was shot in the back and died that muggy afternoon. The emergency doctor removed more than thirty shotgun pellets from his back. Ness, a veteran of the First World War and father of four children, was an active member of the Minneapolis Teamsters Local 574. He was a union striker for a basic living wage as a truck driver. More than forty thousand citizens and union members honored the loyal truck driver in a funeral procession.

"Workers Blood Is Shed, Johannes, the Butcher Uses Shotguns to Mow Down 48 Unarmed Workingmen" was the headline of *The Organizer* on Saturday, July 21, 1934. The newspaper was published by the local union of the Minneapolis Teamsters. "The blood of workers ran freely in the streets of Minneapolis yesterday. They were shot down and wounded by the uniformed thugs commanded by Police Chief Michael Johannes, by Johannes the Murderer, in the name of the city administration and at the behest of its master, the Citizens' Alliance. Forty-eight sons of the working class were mowed down by shot guns in the hands of the police. They were shot down though they were defenseless and unarmed, like animals in a trap. They were shot in the back by base cowards who dared not look them in the face."

Meridel Le Sueur, a resistance writer for the working class, witnessed the police violence on Bloody Friday. As the strikers turned "instinctively for cover they were shot in the back. And into that continued fire flowed the next line of picketers to pick up their wounded. They flowed directly into that buckshot fire, inevitably, without hesitation as one wave follows another. And the cops let them have it as they picked up their wounded. Lines of living, solid men, fell, broke, wavering, flinging up, breaking over with the curious and awful abandon of despairing gestures, a man stepping on his own intestines bright, bursting in the street, another holding his severed arm in his other hand. . . . The wounded were arrested for being shot. They were searched. Not a picket was armed with so much as a toothpick."

More than sixty union strikers were wounded during the police assault, and fifteen wounded strikers were arrested and denied medical care, including Emanuel Happy Holstein, a truck driver and loyal member of the Minneapolis Teamsters Local 574. Jacques Dazhim La Roque, another native unionist, drove a truck for the Indianhead Truck Lines, and later he was an over road trucker. Dazhim, a contrary nickname, means gossip or hearsay in Anishinaabe. Happy and Dazhim were active union truck drivers and natives from the White Earth Reservation.

Eric Sevareid, the twenty-two year old journalist at the *Minneapolis Daily Star*, reported that the police set "a deliberate trap" and "nearly all the injured strikers had wounds in the backs of their heads, arms, legs, and shoulders: they had been shot while trying to run out of the ambush."

The *Minneapolis Daily Star* was founded fourteen years earlier by the lefty Nonpartisan League, and for a few years the newspaper was sponsored by Thomas Van Lear, the first socialist mayor of Minneapolis, and Herbert Gaston, who was once a newspaper editor and later served as an Assistant Secretary of the Treasury under Henry Morgenthau during the presidency of Franklin Delano Roosevelt. The liberal newspaper continued to lose advertisers and readers and was bought by an executive of the *New York Times* and competed with the *Minneapolis Times* and the *Minneapolis Daily Tribune*.

THEATRE OF CHANCE 31

Isadore Blumenfeld, or Kid Cann, a clever, persistent, and punchy immigrant child from a shtetl in Romania, and his brother Jacob Blumenfeld, or Yiddy Bloom, became prominent mobsters in Minneapolis. Kid Cann no doubt wore his signature maroon suit, bright yellow shirt, and narrow suede shoes when he shot and killed Charles Goldberg, a taxicab driver, murdered an investigative journalist named Walter Liggett, and shot and killed James Trepanier, a police officer, and others, yet the mobster was never convicted of murder, despite the testimony of several sworn eyewitnesses. Kid Cann served only four years in federal prison for jury tampering and for violations of the Mann Act.

"Mann actor in a maroon suit," said La Chance.

"White slaver in a yellow shirt," said Master Jean.

"Kid Cann killed our relatives," shouted Big Rant.

"Clement Vizenor was a dancer," said Bad Boy.

"Truman Vizenor was a storier," said Big Rant.

"Kid Cann derailed the street cars," said La Chance.

"Mobsters never shout in panic holes," said Poesy May.

Kid Cann and his henchmen were probably involved in the calculated murders of Clement William Vizenor and Truman Paul Vizenor, sons of Alice Beaulieu Vizenor. The native brothers were house painters from the White Earth Reservation. They told ironic heart stories at night about their young sons, wore cheap wool fedoras on the weekends, and were active in the historic 1934 Truckers' Strike and other protests that were organized by the International Brotherhood of Teamsters in Minneapolis.

Basile wrote an essay for a magazine and a letter to the mute puppeteer about the desolate natives in the urban reservation or existential colony. He declared that natives were unseeable, only shadows, cultural fugitives with barely a sense of presence or human recognition in the easy street scenes of other citizens. Native fugitives in a city of mobsters, menace, savage police, deceptive politicians, and there were always poseurs and predators of native traditions.

WEDNESDAY, 23 OCTOBER 1963.

Manidoo Biiwaabik,

Yesterday was Freedom Day in Chicago, and more than two hundred thousand students skipped classes and protested the cruelty of segregation in the public schools. No native liberty days on a federal reservation or here in the existential colony, only our heart stories and mockery of bigotry, treaty separatism, and the constant abuse of natives by the police on Franklin Avenue. Puppet parleys are necessary on this existential urban reservation to mock the autocrats and mercenaries of renewal, the outside promises of social services, the back talkers, traitors, and betrayals of native liberty.

The Theatre of Chance and puppet parleys must move to this existential colony and establish a new native socialism. The noises and rush of ordinary time are serious distractions, but the thunderstorms and natural motion of the seasons are spectacular on the streets and city parks and especially along the Mississippi River, and there are great opera productions.

Reservations are federal treaties of removal and predatory capitalism and, at the same time, the termination of the communal sentiments of natives. Yes, the native heart stories of socialism, the uneasy sentiments of individuality, recognition, communal equity, and liberty, are strange slants of natural motion in this existential colony.

The unusual entanglements of natives and others in the ruins of so many cultures, as we learned so many years ago in Paris, were always the creative start of ironic heart stories. New stories of survivance and existential socialism but without the mark of fugitive blood rights and never the absurd course of separatism on a treaty reservation.

Aloysius created several puppet parleys for the existential colony with Arthur Naftalin, the Jewish mayor of Minneapolis, and Kidd Cann, the natty Jewish mobster from Romania. Lillian Smith, who wrote *Killers of the Dream*, and James Baldwin, the author of *Nobody Knows My Name*. Eric Hoffer, the San Francisco longshoreman and author of *The True Believers*, and Hush Browne, the prime native organizer of the *Biibaagi* Résistance Movement. Eleanor Roosevelt, the First Lady of the United States, and Gracia Alta Countryman, the first woman director of the Minneapolis Public Library. Aloysius is bursting with artistic energy and maybe he has created the scenes of too many puppet parleys, but the stowaways should consider at least one or two parleys to present in this existential colony.

Natives are in misery, broken bones, children with serious infections, and older natives with ancient sores, cancers, and wounded hearts are refused admission to the Hennepin County General Hospital. Natives are told they must return to public health clinics and hospitals on the reservation or return to the federal policies of fugitive separatism.

The Bureau of Indian Affairs area office on Lake Street spends more money on salaries and the maintenance of a huge building than on the actual urgent medical services of natives in Minneapolis. An outrage that natives are unseeable even at the very center of a federal agency created with the invented name of Indian. Federal agents are separatists, cursory moles, and many times removed from native experiences, and yet they might pretend over casual backyard beer and burgers to provide basic changes about race and poverty on reservations, only separatist treaty reservations, and not in an existential colony.

The Orpheum Theater, that majestic dominion of murmurs and recitations, has not been razed by the corrupt ministers of progress. The Minneapolis Central Library has been deserted in the rage of urban redevelopment. The Metropolitan Building, West Hotel, Hotel Vendome, and other hotels and grand old stone buildings that we first visited more than fifty years ago were destroyed in the name of urban renewal, a devious manner to terminate the memories of the past generations of construction workers and the heart stories of laborers and their families in the city.

The modernist buildings are the absence of memory, the evidence of greedy corporate shareholders that scarcely consider labor or the community. There are no memorable stories in the steel beams and flash of metal, and the vacuous rectangular buildings will never replace the grandeur of granite and marble. We can never forget our first visit to the city and the great curved bay windows and cozy corners of books at the old Minneapolis Public Library.

Kid Cann, the same mobster who murdered our relatives and a journalist and, with impunity, was named as the gangster who menaced public officials and seized control of the Twin Cities Rapid Transit Company. The air is already poisoned by industry, and more than a thousand electric street cars and five hundred miles of steel tracks were replaced with noisy buses that befoul the entire city, and corruptible politicians and greedy oil companies got rich while ordinary citizens lost forever a great system of direct, reliable, and inexpensive public transportation.

By Now is a very popular nurse, of course, and patients at the community medical clinic demand to hear stories about her experience in *La Résistance* during the Nazi Occupation of France. As usual, most of the patients are amused by the story of her names and can hardly believe that By Now was recorded as her first name on a reservation birth certificate.

Prometheus visits the clinic two or three times a week and with his signature white gloves and the gestures of a mime convinced only a few children that he was not a clown of classical literature. By Now and Prometheus, in other words, my dear puppeteer of native chance, continue as healers with ironic heart storiers. All of this means that you, the stowaways, and mongrels should escape from the predators of tradition and move to this existential colony.

Aloysius has a new fauvist creative style, as you know, and next year our friend Nathan Crémieux will exhibit his paintings at the *Galerie de la Danse des Esprits*, the Galerie Ghost Dance in Paris.

> *Good cheer and puppet parleys,*
> *Basile*

Big Rant slowly read out loud the letter from Basile as the stowaways finished an early dinner of sunfish, baked beans, rice, fresh spinach, and delicious cornbread prepared by La Chance. The conversations turned to the miseries of fugitive natives on separatist treaty reservations compared to natives on urban reservations or existential colonies.

Manidoo Biiwaabik printed on the chalkboard, "Natives outwit speculators, federal agents, bullies, spies, and outlive the misery of capitalism. Separatist reservations are a great sorrow, and our puppet parleys are necessary everywhere in the world after the fur trade and the ruins of civilization to mock the predators of traditions and greedy merchants of culture."

Master Jean worried about the contests of political power on the reservation and wondered about a native audience for puppet parleys in an existential colony, but the other stowaways were silent and either not interested or not ready to move the Theatre of Chance to Minneapolis.

The mute puppeteer leaned back in the wide wooden chair and, with the loyal mongrels at her side, wrote another message in a notebook that was read out loud by Big Rant. "The Theatre of Chance is the tease of chance, a celebration of nothing, and the puppet parleys of chance are more than heart stories, more than our stories on a treaty reservation. No one can hold back native liberty and the ironic play and mockery of puppet parleys.

"Our puppet parleys have mocked the notorious nuclear physicist Edward Teller in front of the United States Science Pavilion at the Seattle World's Fair, and our best puppet parley teased the great Samuel Beckett and changed the title of his play *Waiting for Godot* to *Waiting for Wovoka*. Our puppet parleys are always at hand and ready to be heard around the world, and why not in an existential colony in Minneapolis."

‖‖‖ 6 ‖‖‖

Tears of Grace

Manidoo Biiwaabik was melancholy, uncertain, and evasive that summer of her eighty-seventh birthday. The heart stories of the stowaways and generous post office hearsay revealed that she was born at first light, a child of summer, and her native descent had been observed only as a season. The exact date of her birth was never recorded at French Portage Narrows. There was no history of dates or given names, and for that reason the eternal spirit of the mute puppeteer has been celebrated during the entire summer at the Theatre of Chance.

The stowaways and mongrels were uneasy that summer of her birthday, and months later in the autumn they were worried even more about the strange torment of her silence, the hesitant gestures, the evasive smiles, the peculiar sense of distance, and the nostalgic dream song she printed on the hand chalkboard.

memory undone
shamans at the treeline
reverse our days
summer nights of dismay
last stay of chance

The stowaways were troubled by the wistful moods and absence of irony in the dream song, and then she seemed to recover the usual silent gestures, but later she turned even more melancholy with a curious absence, and the familiar gestures withered once more overnight. The mongrels were restless as they waited for the return of the spirited presence and necessary teases and mockery of the mute puppeteer.

Manidoo Biiwaabik listened to the radio report that cold and windy night about the assassination of President John Kennedy by Lee Harvey Oswald on Friday, November 22, 1963. She turned away and wept silently over every radio broadcast and eyewitness account of the political murder at Dealey Plaza in Dallas, Texas.

The Theatre of Chance became unearthly, almost haunted with the solemn radio reports. The mute puppeteer printed a strange notice on a chalkboard, "Chase away your worries and hide your fears, the wicked *wiindigoo* waits in every scene and season of violence and steals native heart stories at night." The *wiindigoo*, a ghastly cannibal monster in native stories, lurks in the shadows of misery and sentiments of death.

The mute puppeteer became doubly silent once again and seemed to lean into darker moods with only the slightest sense of presence and stay, and the stowaways were worried over the turn of spirits, the severe sorrow, and the absence of ordinary gestures, irony, mercy, and play. The six mongrels were shied and slowly bumped each other in silence that week of national misery and unsure celebrations of the season.

Manidoo Biiwaaabik shunned the morning light, and the usual wild shimmer of her tousled white hair wilted with every somber recount of the three shots and bloody head wounds that caused the death of the president. George Eliot licked the hands of the mute puppeteer, and the other mongrels leaned closer, much closer, moaned, and rested their heads on her thighs as a promise to stay.

Chronicles of the gruesome assassination of the spirited and buoyant president lasted for weeks in radio news, investigative reports, political commentary, and familiar stories of the heart. The ordinary native tease and trust of silence was never quite the same at the Theatre of Chance.

The *Minneapolis Tribune* reported on Saturday, November 23, 1963, under a huge banner headline that a "hidden gunman shot President Kennedy to death with a high-powered rifle Friday. Three shots reverberated and blood sprang from the President's face. He fell face downward. His wife clutched his head crying, Oh, no!"

Big Rant read out loud the front page newspaper report at the reservation post office, and there were no customary stories or creative hearsay by Postcard Mary. The mongrels were hesitant and waited for the slightest reason to moan or bay. The mute puppeteer was withdrawn and distant, and she seemed more silent than she had ever been since the great firestorm almost seventy years ago.

The entire native community was distraught and moody and almost lost without the customary course of hearsay, envy, tease of mongrels, and the ironic promises of salvation on a separatist reservation. Postcard Mary neglected the mail and the usual treats of pemmican for the post office mongrels on that cold and windy week of misery.

"Within half an hour, John F. Kennedy was dead, and the United States had a new president, Lyndon B. Johnson. The assassination occurred just as the President's motorcade was leaving downtown Dallas at the end of a triumphal tour through the city's streets. His special car—with the protective bubble down—was moving down an incline into an underpass that leads to a freeway route to the Dallas Trade Mart, where he was to speak. Witnesses heard three shots. Two hit the President, one in the head and one in the neck."

"President Kennedy honored natives," said Bad Boy.

"Kennedy never posed in feathers," said Poesy May.

"He donated his salary to charity," said La Chance.

"Great memories died with the president," said Big Rant.

"Politics will never be the same," declared Master Jean.

"Manidoo will never be the same," said Bad Boy.

"Manidoo is our only chance," whispered Poesy May.

The mute puppeteer gestured to the clouds one morning a few days later and then smiled, pointed at each of the loyal mongrels, shouted hallelujah, hallelujah, hallelujah in silence, and that night the stowaways celebrated the comeback with a meal of baked walleye and listened to opera music until sunrise.

A few days later the mute puppeteer printed on the hand chalkboard that she was ready to create a puppet parley between John F. Kennedy and Lee Harvey Oswald. Big Rant and the other stowaways were dumbfounded by the announcement and turned away in silence. The puppet parleys had never been censored, but the rush to tease conspiracy theories about the assassination of the president was unbearable and not the nature of native irony or mockery. The tease of a conspiracy parley was uncertain and never mentioned again, and about six months later the mute puppeteer created a puppet parley that rightly mocked the Civil Rights Act.

President Lyndon B. Johnson signed into law the Civil Rights Act on July 2, 1964. The bold legislation would outlaw discrimination based on race, color, religion, and national origin. I want to "talk to you about what that law means to every American," said President Johnson during a radio broadcast. "One hundred and eighty-eight years ago this week a small band of valiant men, began a long struggle for freedom. They pledged their lives, their fortunes, and their sacred honor, not only to found a nation, but to forge an ideal of freedom. Not only for political independence, but for personal liberty. Not only to eliminate foreign rule, but to establish the rule of justice and the affairs of men. That struggle was a turning point in our history."

Manidoo Biiwaabik raised one hand in silence, wagged a few fingers, a determined gesture of disdain. Hail Mary sighed and George Eliot moaned and Dingleberry barked at the strange voice of President Johnson. "Americans of every race and color have died in battle to protect our freedom." Trophy Bay and Tallulah cocked their heads to the side and delivered wavering moans with every slow word in the distinctive drawl of the presidential cowboy from Texas.

"The purpose of this law is simple," recited the president. "It does not restrict the freedom of any American, so long as he respects the rights of others. It does not give special treatment to any citizen. It does say the only limit to a man's hope for happiness and for the future of his children shall be his own ability."

Once again the mute puppeteer wagged several fingers to mock the serious tone and folksy presidential turnaround and absence of natives on the continent. That warm summer night she printed a message on a chalkboard, "Big talk presidents are only newcomers to this continent, and the federal government betrayed natives with treaties of separatism in a constitutional democracy, and presidents of greed forget that natives created cultural irony, mapped ancient trade routes, and carried out continental liberty, and native dreams songs are forever in the clouds and never in the gadabout politics of civil rights."

"Natives created our liberty," shouted Big Rant.

"Long before the empire slavers," said Master Jean.

"Politicians reversed native liberty," said La Chance.

"Savants created native races," whispered Poesy May.

"Race is an empire concoction," shouted Master Jean.

"Big ironies of colonial enlightenment," said Big Rant.

"Cultures of betrayal and slavery," shouted Master Jean.

"Empire diseases and the fur trade," said Bad Boy.

Manidoo Biiwaabik printed on the second chalkboard a dream song about totemic silence in the clouds and the natural motion of creative heart stories and native liberty.

tears of grace
shimmer on spirit lake
heart stories of native liberty
hearsay and puppet parleys
silent in the clouds

The mute puppeteer placed her favorite phonograph record on the Silvertone hand crank player and leaned back in the giant wooden chair near the stove. She listened at full volume to the soprano Renata Tebaldi sing the arias "Sì mi chiamano Mimì" and "Quando me'n vó" from the opera *La Bohème* by Giacomo Puccini. The sublime soprano voice of the great diva resonated in the birch and white pine trees and over the slight waves on Spirit Lake.

She played the two arias a second time and gestured to each of the loyal mongrels. Trophy Bay and Tallulah leaned closer and moaned and bayed in harmony with Renata Tebaldi. Hail Mary and George Eliot softly bayed, a mongrel chorus with the arias. Dingleberry pouted and then danced around the chair on her back legs.

Manidoo Biiwaabik was fast asleep when Renata Tebaldi sang the line "Da me tanto rifuggi," you shrink from me, near the end of the aria. The hand crank record player had not been wound for the second round of arias, and the clear soprano timbre slowed down to mere moans and groans. Tallulah and Trophy Bay turned their heads and gently bayed, and the other mongrels moaned with the last slow sound of the soprano diva.

That the mute puppeteer was asleep at the end of the aria was not unusual, and she never twitched or wheezed, and several hours later George Eliot howled, and the other mongrels circled the wooden chair and nosed the mute puppeteer. Later, the stowaways noticed that she might have lost consciousness for several hours.

Big Rant was in tears as she ran to the public health hospital, and early that morning the mute puppeteer was carried away by ambulance on the Fourth of July, 1964. Bad Boy was allowed to use the hospital telephone to contact Basile and By Now in Minneapolis. Basile talked with the public health doctor and arranged for the mute puppeteer to be transported immediately by ambulance to Mount Sinai Hospital in Minneapolis.

Two years ago, the stowaways were worried for the same reason at the Seattle World's Fair. The mute puppeteer was apparently unconscious in a camp chair near the Iron Pergola at Pioneer Square in Seattle, Washington. She wound the record player only once, and the loyal mongrels moaned as usual when the sound slowed down. The last aria turned to groans and then silence under the streetlights.

The mute puppeteer was doubly silent when a vagrant veteran found her hunched over in a camp chair at the Iron Pergola. The mongrels circled the chair and bumped her thighs and arms, but there was no response. The stowaways raised her head and shouted out several times the name of Renata Tebaldi and then shouted out the names of the six mongrels, Tallulah, Trophy Bay, Hail Mary, Dingleberry, George Eliot, and Daniel to reach her silent memory. Master Jean played a rousing version of military reveille on the bugle, but the mute puppeteer never blinked, winked, or moved a finger.

Poesy May felt a slow heartbeat but could not hear the breath of the mute puppeteer, and her hands were cold and pale. The stowaways were scared by the strange silence, an absence of spirit, and then suddenly she blinked, smiled, almost sighed, and slowly raised a finger, a hand, an arm, and then reached out to touch the loyal mongrels.

"Silence is the great diva of silence," said Bad Boy.

"Silence is not a want or absence," said La Chance.

"Silence is the spirit of the puppets," said Bad Boy.

"Silence is a natural distance," said Master Jean.

"Silence is a dream song in the clouds," said Big Rant.

Poesy May wrote a dream song to honor the mute puppeteer, and the following day the stowaways played the same two arias from *La Bohème*. They raised their arms and shouted in silence, brava, brava, brava, and the loyal mongrels raised their heads and moaned, groaned, and bayed in perfect harmony.

theatre of chance
dream songs of spirit lake
silence and memory

manidoo in the clouds
forever in natural motion

Master Jean loaded the converted bus with hand puppets, books, chalk-boards, clothes, and kitchenware, and four mongrels rushed to occupy the front row seats for the ride to Minneapolis. The bus had been christened the *Theatre of Chance* and the *Célébrité de Rien*, or Celebrity of Nothing, two years earlier for the journey to the World's Fair in Seattle. Since then, the bus was used only a few times a month for short journeys to the discount food markets in Detroit Lakes and Mahnomen and for an occasional overnight at Bad Medicine Lake to catch the spirited bass in the cold water.

Tallulah and Trophy Bay turned away and ran together into the woods when the stowaways carried the camp chairs to the *Theatre of Chance*. Bad Boy shouted out their names several times, but the two mongrels balked at leaving the cozy hearsay of the post office and the pemmican favors of Post-card Mary. The four loyal mongrels were already seated in the front rows of the bus, and the stowaways were packed and prepared to visit the mute puppeteer at Mount Sinai Hospital. The stowaways had planned to return a week or two later to Spirit Lake.

The mission priest, reservation politicians, and federal agents waited for the mute puppeteer and stowaways to leave the reservation, and then they removed the personal possessions to storage and razed the two ramshackle cabins. The Theatre of Chance was terminated on the White Earth Reservation, but the heart stories, puppet parleys, and hearsay of envy about the diva of silence would last forever.

The natural shoreline of Spirit Lake was covered with white sand, and the landscape was prepared for the lease and construction of modern vacation cabins. Six miniature grave houses had been erected to honor the memory of the loyal mongrels of the Theatre of Chance. Fidèle, the first loyal mongrel from the fur trade, and Papa Pius, Queena, Makwa, Miinan, and Snatch were enclosed in a newly painted log fence and declared a traditional native grave site for tourists.

7

SOVEREIGN READER

By Now Rose Beaulieu related easy stories about the mute puppeteer. She was born in a domed wigwam in the summer of 1876, the only child of native fishers and traders, near French Portage Narrows on Lake of the Woods, or *Lac des Bois*, Canada.

"The coureurs des bois that camped at the narrows and traded beads and calico for lake trout celebrated the birth of the child, and in the same concert of recognition the traders were rightly shamed for the decimation of animals in the fur trade," declared By Now. "The coureurs des bois worried that deadly diseases were the revenge of the animals."

Natives and their families were sometimes separated by the chase and enterprise of the fur trade and the dominion of distant outposts, and the international border agents were not expected to be amiable or patient. The Jay Treaty of 1794, an agreement between Great Britain and the United States, granted natives, the coureurs des bois, and métis traders to easily travel across the border without restrictions.

By Now told the stowaways that the mute puppeteer had earned many nicknames as the outcome of curious encounters and adventures at French Portage Narrows. The solitary native learned how to imitate the wail, waver, and yodel of loons, the guttural groan of great blue herons, and teased the other birds to haunt the coureurs des bois and traders at portages. *Maang*, the word for the common loon in Anishinaabe, was the first nickname the mute puppeteer could remember, but that lasted only a few summers.

Maang was a thirteen year old spontaneous reader when she first envisioned the natural motion of native dream songs and heart stories. She was never tutored or removed to a government or mission boarding school, and with an outright sense of native liberty she discovered the tolerant manner of portage barters, the cultural teases and worthy gestures, and favored the stories of remorse that were told by the lonesome coureurs des bois at the portage.

By Now related that Miikindizi, the teaser, was probably the second

44 GERALD VIZENOR

nickname earned at the portage, but she rightly countered the epithet with silence, not even with a gesture. Two years later, in the desolate ruins of the colonial fur trade, she shouted bravas at the autumn clouds for the comeback of the beaver and chanted the eternal hurrah for the eternity of totemic animals, and then she envisioned scenes of natural motion in native heart stories.

Mazina was the third native nickname of recognition at the narrows, a favor of the word *mazinaigan*, a book or document, in the language of the Anishinaabe. She learned to read from books that had been forgotten or abandoned by missionaries, federal agents, and the coureurs des bois at trading posts and portages. The hearsay and teases that she was a sovereign native reader reached the traders at nearby posts, and every lost book was delivered to the portage. The fur traders were generous storiers at overnight campsites, but not many of the lonesome predators of the fur trade were readers.

Mazina was heard reading words and phrases out loud at the narrows in the early morning, surrounded by the sounds of natural motion, waves on the bright stones, and bird songs in flight, and in that intuitive situation she pretended to catch the tones, traces, teases of manners, and the easy gestures of strange characters with a secure dialogue of accents in the novel *Pride and Prejudice* by Jane Austen.

The eager portage reader selected and separated names and envisioned particular words in *A Christmas Carol* by Charles Dickens. Mazina shouted out curious phrases, *Scrooge and Marley, chief mourner, unhallowed hands, bestow a trifle, hand at the grindstone, blind men's dogs, chink and keyhole,* and *dingy cloud*. She learned to tether the causes of motion and maneuvers in scenes and sentences and then created dream songs and depictions that would suggest a version of scenes in the novel.

Ebenezer Scrooge was stingy, spiteful, and distant, clearly the consequence of a boarding school, not a winter cannibal. His face was cold and blue, but the ghosts in the memory of the miser were not the ghostly blue of a *wiindigoo*, the monster of winter that would never become a generous native in the stories of any season.

Mazina might have envisioned Scrooge as a voyageur or *mangeur de lard*, a pork eater, the miser that transported the precious bundles of beaver, otter, marten, and mink peltry on *canots de maître*, or huge canoes, to

Montreal. Scrooge might have been conjured in overnight portage stories as a greedy missionary or a predatory colonial agent on the possessive treaty circuit in the grandiose cause of civilization.

Mazina never returned to the same portage in native stories, or even with the close turn of seasons, pitch of cascades, heave of a canoe, or the customary versions of natural motion, since she read at age sixteen the stained and tattered three volumes of the novel *The Whale* by Herman Melville, published in London in 1851. The native visionary reader at the portage was nurtured by totemic animals and the steady motion of water near the narrows, the migration of birds, and the crack of ice in the spring, and she easily sensed the great reach of natural motion in every chapter of the novel. Ishmael carried her to the ocean on a whaleboat and told stories that became the second great sense of native liberty in the discontent of monotheism and betrayal of totemic animals in the fur trade.

Great canoes loaded with beaver and the savagery of the fur trade were recounted in native stories and somehow comparable to the obsessions and moral tease of the great white whale in the novel. Captain Ahab of the *Pequod* was tormented and beset with vengeance for the secretive motions of the white whale, and in the wild hearsay at French Portage Narrows and Lake of the Woods, the entire mean and motion of the beaver and totemic animals became the obsession of the furrier John Jacob Astor. Ahab lost a leg to the white whale and hobbled on deck with an ivory prosthesis. Astor never ranted about an elusive white whale, but instead, as a mercenary merchant, he was obsessed with the beaver, totemic peltry, and the criminal trade of opium in China.

Prometheus, the mime and raconteur, read out loud three quotations about the artistic perception of motion and whales that were printed on a chalkboard and then transcribed in a blank leather bound book of the mute puppeteer. He read the short narratives on a clear and windy night. Mazina had secured the novel in a leather pouch, but the three volumes of *The Whale* were burned to ashes in the Great Hinckley Fire. The second copy of the novel was a present from a native admirer, John Clement Beaulieu, during a radio broadcast of the Metropolitan Opera at the Leecy Hotel. She has carried three memorable notations in silence for more than seventy years and was almost in tears last year when she heard the words and pictured the scenes from the novel that night at the Theatre of Chance.

Prometheus envisioned the steady tone and gestures of the narrator, Ishmael. "The more I consider this mighty tail, the more do I deplore my inability to express it. At times there are gestures in it, which, though they would well grace the hand of man, remain wholly inexplicable. In an extensive herd, so remarkable, occasionally, are these mystic gestures, that I have heard hunters who have declared them akin to Free-Mason signs and symbols; that the whale, indeed, by these methods intelligently conversed with the world.

"The French are the lads for painting action. Go and gaze upon all the paintings of Europe, and where will you find such a gallery of living and breathing commotion on canvas, as in the triumphant hall at Versailles."

Prometheus continued, "The natural aptitude of the French for seizing the picturesqueness of things seems to be particularly evinced in what paintings and engravings they have of their whaling scenes. With not one tenth of England's experience in the fishery, and not the thousandth part of that of the Americans, they have nevertheless furnished both nations with the only finished sketches at all capable of conveying the real spirit of the whale hunt. For the most part, the English and American whale draughtsmen seem entirely content with presenting the mechanical outline of things, such as the vacant profile of the whale; which, so far as picturesqueness of effect is concerned, is about tantamount to sketching the profile of a pyramid."

"Mazina would never paint the beaver," said Bad Boy.

"Mazina is a storier of natural motion," said Poesy May.

"Mazina envisioned the natural motion of the entire world of whales, beavers, the natural motion of native heart stories, and the novels she read from French Portage Narrows to Spirit Lake," said Big Rant.

"Mazina earned hundreds of nicknames," said Bad Boy.

"Mazina was born that same summer of the Battle of the Greasy Grass in Montana," said La Chance. "Surely she shouted out loud the first great bravas and hurrahs with the Lakota and Northern Cheyenne over the combat death of the demon General George Armstrong Custer."

Mazina, the sublime emissary of seasons at the portage, the generous teaser of the coureurs des bois, and the scenes of a great novel, were envisioned in silence by the mute puppeteer, and later the pork barrel bully

THEATRE OF CHANCE

boys shamed the silence of a sovereign native and shaman with the nickname Dummy Trout.

La Taquine, the teaser, Truite de Lac, the lake trout, were once hearsay nicknames at the post office and the stories continued as mutations for several months. The teaser as a nickname in stories soon became Taunter, and trout became a common carp. Truite de Lac withered away in the hearsay of the stupid freshwater trout. La Taquine was the most persuasive nickname because of the ironic stories and tease of puppet parleys at the Theatre of Chance.

"She was the diva of secrets on those lonesome portage nights," said By Now. "No one in seventy years has heard the seductive voice that once teased the coureurs des bois at the narrows and portages of Lake of the Woods."

Mazina revealed a few scenes of the nickname stories on a chalkboard, how she paddled a birchbark canoe across the international border of Lake of the Woods and landed at age eighteen in the late spring with two small bundles, a leather pouch with *The Whale* and other books, and a loyal fur trade mongrel named Fidèle at Muskeg Bay, a native community near Warroad, Minnesota.

The Jay Treaty, an agreement between Great Britain and the United States, allowed natives to travel across the border. The treaty, signed more than a century earlier, had become one of the few reliable stories at the time. The mute puppeteer was born near French Portage Narrows in Canada. The actual date of her birth was never recorded, but she and other natives with no birth records were allowed to cross the border, an unusual recognition of natives in a territorial and colonial treaty.

By Now celebrated the name Fidèle, a loyal, faithful, and devoted mongrel of the coureurs des bois that had located by scent the last beaver dams near *Lac des Bois*, and then the loyal mongrel with a distinctive accent and fur trade bark from the bows of a canoe was deserted near French Portage Narrows.

Zenibaa was a nickname introduced later, a shortened version of *zenibaawegin*, the word for silk in Anishinaabe. She had earned, endured, and abandoned several portage nicknames, but when she denounced the coureurs des bois and celebrated the new fashion of silk as the banderole of survivance and liberty for the beaver and other animals in the fur trade, she could not have envisioned a more relevant name. The nickname was directly related to the actual gift of a silk cloche hat, and she wore that silk hat every day for several years.

Zenibaa was always silent about personal experiences, and no one ever persuaded the native resistance reader of natural motion and sovereignty at the portage to reminisce about the fur trade, relate stories about the silk hat, restate or even tease with epithets the mutable hearsay of nicknames in the past. She was content with the stories of the ironic nicknames and concert of loyal mongrels, and the new teases of the stowaway turned out to be a sense of *just now* and evoked the marvelous chance of the silk trade that saved the beaver.

By Now related a memorable story at the post office about John Ka Ka Geesick, as he was known in Warroad, Minnesota, or Gaagige Giizhig an intuitive native shaman and healer who lived near Muskeg Bay on Lake of the Woods. Zenibaa was never at ease in the presence of traders or native healers who recounted the hearsay of a native migrant in a radiant silk hat.

Zenibaa smiled and then teased the nickname of the old shaman, *Gaagige*, forever, and *Giizhig*, day or sky, in the language of the Anishinaabe. That generous native tease of a never ending day and gentle nudge of the mongrel Fidèle delighted the old man named the Everlasting Sky. He welcomed the silk woman and the loyal mongrel to stay at his cabin. The free and easy shaman created stories for several days about the presence of natives in every turn of the seasons, tease of natural motion, and visionary scenes of liberty. Gaagige Giizhig recognized the courage of native chance, the nature of silence, and the sway of shadows and stories with no poses, pronouns, or mastery. He created elusive heart stories with scenes of natural motion, the totemic dance of sandhill cranes, the play of otters on a riverbank, and the sublime summer concerts at beaver dams enhanced with silk banners of liberty.

Gaagige Giizhig related the desperate retreat of the coureurs des bois and the courageous beaver that returned to build new dams from the memories of survivance. The coureurs des bois were boasters, not builders, and worried about the vengeance of the animals and later turned to some other predatory course in the mercenary enterprises of colonial empires.

Zenibaa and Fidèle walked more than a hundred miles that late autumn to Bakegamaa Lake, an easy native community about twenty miles south of Hinckley, Minnesota, where she met her only lover, Nookaa, a tender, ironic, and generous lumberjack.

"Nookaa and hundreds of other natives were burned to ashes, entire families vanished in a massive forest fire," related By Now.

Zenibaa survived with Fidèle, and the silk cloche hat was covered with gray ashes. The chance, romance, resistance, gratitude, irony, and creative heart stories were common sources of native wisdom but not earned altogether in just eighteen years. The outcome of chance, heart stories, and the nicknames of a native reader in the ruins of the fur trade has remained in silence for almost seventy years since the Great Hinckley Fire.

Zenibaa and Fidèle meandered in silence for more than a month, and then by chance they were allowed to live in a small abandoned ramshackle cabin near Spirit Lake, and there she became a silent native citizen of the White Earth Reservation. She smiled and gestured with care but was resolute about silence and never articulated the sound of a single word, not even literary whispers to the loyal mongrel, Fidèle.

The mute puppeteer was teased and debased by the pork barrel bullies as a dummy, a dunce, a simpleton, and a witless moron, and then she was demeaned and tormented with the nickname Dummy Trout. The spiteful surname was contrived by the bullies as an allusion to a stupid fish, the freshwater trout.

She presented puppet parleys about shamanic silence, the fur trade massacre of beaver and totemic animals, and the outrage over the custody of predatory traditions that hinder native art and literature on the reservation, but she has been secretive about the teases and associations with the coureurs des bois and voyageurs.

"The pork barrel bullies were envious and ridiculed the mute puppeteer with nasty stories about the fairy silk hat traders in China, France, and Lake of the Woods," whispered Poesy May.

The stowaways heard the usual prurient fur trade stories about erotic rendezvous with the coureurs des bois, and versions of the stories that were repeated over and over as native envy, but nothing more was revealed about the curious surname, Trout, until the recent stories of By Now. Even so, the wobbly rumors and stories about the actual origins of native surnames were never certain. Some native surnames were bad translations of nicknames by missionaries and at federal boarding schools, and other nicknames were created by relations and ironic teases of experience, and some nicknames were visionary secrets. The colonial surnames of fur trade marriages and country wives of traders were obvious in French and English.

Big Rant enhanced the patchy rumors with stories that the mute puppeteer was directly related to the ancient shamans of lake trout and salmon. The stories were ironic, overstated in hearsay, and more elaborate renditions of other totems as surnames were circulated at events on the reservation. Dummy never confirmed or denied that she was a silent heir of the lake trout or shamans.

The beaver, marten, muskrat, otter, fox, and other fur trade animals and birds were rescued from extinction by chance, the chance of the silk trade, the chance of silk moths from China, and the frivolous turn of fashions from beaver felt hats and furry coats to the light, bright, exotic touch of woven silk fabrics. Silk became the craze of the bourgeoisie, and the new fashion inadvertently saved the beaver from extermination in the fur trade.

Zenibaa wore a silk cloche hat to celebrate the liberation of fur trade animals from extinction. She wore the silk hat every day and in every season, even in the heat, smoke, and ashes of the Great Hinckley Fire. The bright silk was clouded by the ashes, and then the larvae of moths devoured the fibers.

Zenibaa had never been in a hospital, and certainly not with a new nickname. The mute puppeteer was a spirited child with mighty fur trade and portage immunities to diseases. She was treated only once by a medical doctor who prescribed opium, willow bark, and sweat baths to remedy a fever, diarrhea, and a short breath caused by the noxious ashes of pine trees, and nothing more than a whisper of care for the silent heartache caused by the death of her lover Nookaa in the Great Hinckley Fire.

The only doctors she heard about as a child were native healers, *nenaandawiiwed*, the inscrutable shamans and spirited singers, and most conditions of the head and heart were treated outright with shamanic visionary hearsay. Sore throats, head and body aches and pains, and other minor maladies were cured with the inner bark of the willow and the secret concoctions of plants, bark, roots, and totemic bones by the obscure native healers of the Midewiwin or the Grand Medicine Society.

Deadly diseases were transmitted for centuries by colonial explorers, missionaries, high wine traders, voyageurs, and the coureurs des bois of the continental fur trade. Native shamans and herbal healers died with other natives from the same colonial diseases, smallpox, tuberculosis, influenza, bubonic plague, cholera, measles, scarlet fever, typhoid, chickenpox, and more, and many traditional native burials were abandoned because there were so many deaths in families. There were no natural or medical cures for the colonial diseases that caused the miserable deaths of millions of natives in the Americas.

"Old World diseases decimated our native ancestors by the millions even before the contagious missionaries and strange stories of providence and salvation, and natives turned to the clouds and totemic associations with no stories of the cause, no evidence of medicine traders or sickly animals, only the usual relations of natives on the continental trade routes," said Basile Hudon Beaulieu.

ⅠⅠⅠⅠⅠ 8 ⅠⅠⅠⅠⅠ

SHAMANIC SILENCE

By Now, Basile, Aloysius, and Prometheus worried about the mute puppeteer and waited for her to arrive by ambulance early that morning from the White Earth Reservation.

Mount Sinai Hospital was a theatre of care, comfort, sovereignty, and personal recognition by perceptive doctors and nurses in private rooms, a curious sensation of peace with no sense of chance, and yet somewhere in that marvelous theatre of care were shouts of pain, broken bones, surgery, and diseases that were discovered, examined, and treated in every touch, crease, and concern of medical custody.

Mount Sinai Hospital was the first medical center in the city to admit natives for necessary examinations and critical treatment without consideration of religion, race, or residence. The hospital opened about thirteen years earlier, and since then the doctors and nurses have practiced medicine without the encounters of bigotry, after many decades of antisemitism in medical schools and health centers. Jewish doctors and nurses have never denied medical services to natives, compared to the county hospital that directed natives to return to reservations for medical care.

Hubert Humphrey was the mayor of Minneapolis when he reported the antisemitism and racism documented at local hospitals, an obvious condition that natives endured for decades. Moses Baron, a medical doctor, revealed the very same conclusions of bigotry, that Jewish medical doctors and minority citizens were excluded from hospitals. Baron and others created a community foundation and established Mount Sinai Hospital in Minneapolis.

Dummy Trout, the reservation nickname of the pork barrel bully boys, was forever silent, a curse of envy that ended in the easy overnight motion of an ambulance, and she was registered at the hospital with only one name, Zenibaa. The mute puppeteer of silk and silence smiled whenever the doctors, nurses, orderlies, and hospital custodians pronounced her native nickname.

THEATRE OF CHANCE

Zenibaa easily mocked the big practice of medicine because she had no traces of disease or medical history. The doctors and nurses had nothing critical to review of her past and presence but great wrinkles, white hair, thick toe nails, bent fingers, and the enigma of shamanic silence. She was saluted every day as a native elder of the silk and in return she mocked the nurses with very slow responses to examinations and even with ironic messages slowly printed on a hand chalkboard.

"My shamanic meditation is a theatre of silence, a native opera and eternal hush, not a disease or malady. Edward Teller, that nuclear bomb monster, and Senator Joseph McCarthy, that pious predator of the Red Scare are the deadly causes of head diseases, not my heart, not my belly, not my memory, not my hands or breasts, not my ironic heart stories, and not any parts of my native brain or lovely native body."

Doctor Samuel Wilde, a consultant cardiologist, and several other medical specialists examined the heart, head, throat, lungs, eyes, and ears, and tested the native blood, bones, urine, hair, fingernails, and cognitive functions of the mute puppeteer, and there were no traces or evidence of any underlying medical or psychological conditions that would explain the bouts of silence or hearsay of unconscious states and could only report that the patient was in good health even when she was reported to be unconscious for several hours at a time.

Doctor Wilde compared the silence and perceptions of the mute puppeteer to modes of spiritual concentration, astral projections, meditation mantras, slow heart rates, visionary memories, or transmotion, and the singular practices of a native shaman. The mute puppeteer revealed in a clearly printed note to the doctor that seventy years ago she faced the fear of certain death with a glorious native lover and turned to silence and heart stories as a shelter of memory and resistance to the conventions of shame, grievance, and victimry.

"Silence is the natural motion of native memories, not some strange revision of absence, and my hush is a season, a tease of presence in visionary heart stories, and how could anyone forget the rush of hundreds of animals, predators and easy prey, that escaped in a totemic silence of unity from the terror of the firestorm," wrote the mute puppeteer. "Nookaa, a beloved lumberjack, was the last person who heard my reveries, and his silent visionary presence is forever in my heart stories." The mute puppeteer smiled as she watched the doctor read the printed message on hospital stationery, and then she printed a second note. "No surprise that the spirit of hand puppet parleys, the stowaways, and loyal mongrels favor my silence and heart stories as native sovereignty."

Zenibaa learned how to slow the beat of her heart with arias of the opera, the perception of natural motion, sway of summer willows, dart of hummingbirds in the red columbine, the totemic dance of sandhill cranes, easy float of autumn birch leaves, and the shamanic silence of heart stories since the death of her lover Nookaa in the Great Hinckley Fire.

Natural motion was more easily perceived in moments of meditation and silence, as an unnamable sense of chance and presence. The mongrels were enticed with the silent gestures of the heart, not the stern sound of directions or reactions, and the sense of silence has become the ironic character of hand puppets. The mute puppeteer conceived of silence as a shamanic reverie, a meditation of native creation, and the sublime sound of soprano divas of the opera became her visionary sense of native presence.

"The death of Nookaa was the start of an eternal meditation of silence, a theatre of silence," she wrote later that night in the hushed sovereignty of a private hospital room. Doctor Wilde read the note early the next morning. "The silence of native shamans in a world of poseurs, deceit, and trickery, the shamanic silence that gave me the confidence to mock the lure of *nisidizo*, the catch of suicide, and the torment of snow ghosts, and the meditation of natural motion and silence slows my heartbeat, so slow, as you know, that the loyal mongrels moan and the stowaways worry about my strange distance."

Doctor Wilde copied in a notebook the comments that she had printed overnight on hospital stationery and on two hand chalkboards. "My silence is meditation and the native tease of a shaman, the old shamans of the tent shaker stories, who were clever healers with hushed tones and silence, and when you listen to my heart and my heart stories you must be healed with the hush of peace, not the curse and temper of hearsay," wrote Zenibaa.

"I was born in the silence of natural motion, that moment of silence in a thunderstorm, the autumn shimmer of trees, the winter sighs of menace, the nostalgic sound of loons in the spring, and always my visionary memory of the seductive hush of French Portage Narrows and Lake of the Woods." The mute puppeteer easily charmed the doctor with silence and concise notes of wit and wisdom on hospital stationery and two chalkboards, and as he copied the transcriptions he smiled and gestured the words brava, brava, brava, in silence.

Zenibaa motioned with her hands that the doctor should not leave as she erased a chalkboard and printed one more message. "Silence is a heart story, the hush of memories, and my words are in the clouds."

Doctor Wilde was curious about how the mute puppeteer had acquired such a strong appreciation for classical opera music. She smiled, turned away, and after a long pause printed on the chalkboard, "The New York Metropolitan Opera radio broadcast of *Hänsel und Gretel* on December 25, 1931, at the Leecy Hotel on the White Earth Reservation."

The good doctor was surprised by her precise response and to learn that natives experienced a cosmopolitan world of opera on a federal reservation and heard radio opera broadcasts announced by Milton Cross. "The Leecy Hotel, of course, and now a native puppeteer and Jewish doctor share the same great pleasure of opera music," said Doctor Wilde. "So, what is your favorite opera music?"

The mute puppeteer smiled once more and slowly printed on the chalkboard, "*La Bohème* by Giacomo Puccini, and my favorite aria is 'Sì mi chiamano Mimì' by Renata Tebaldi."

Doctor Wilde raised a hand and smiled with delight, and the mute puppeteer reminded the good doctor on a chalkboard that *La Bohème* was on the hand crank record player when the loyal stowaways reported that she was unconscious or, more precisely, in a perfect state of shamanic silence and the mistaken reason that she was transported by ambulance from the Theatre of Chance near Spirit Lake to the theatre of medicine and sovereignty at Mount Sinai Hospital.

Zenibaa was completely surprised by Doctor Wilde, two nurses, and an orderly, who arrived early the next morning with an original hand puppet parley about a native woman who was admitted to the hospital only because she was a shaman in the shadows of meditation and silence. The two hand puppets, a medical doctor and a native puppeteer, were portrayed with distinctive features on two white hospital slippers. The orderly with bright cheeks was the gentle voice of Doctor Wilde, and the second slipper, the silent shaman of native teases, was the voice of By Now Rose Beaulieu, who suggested the white slippers as puppets of a hospital parley.

WILDE: Silence, and no one hears your great stories.

ZENIBAA: Every native creation story starts in silence.

WILDE: Yes, and on a chalkboard of a fugitive celebrity.

ZENIBAA: Silence is the natural motion of the seasons.

WILDE: Even heartbeats have a sound and story.

ZENIBAA: Silence is a cure for slights and frights.

WILDE: Sometimes nickname teases are silent slights.

ZENIBAA: Hesitations of thunder after the lightning.

WILDE: Yes, mighty moments of silence in a storm.

ZENIBAA: Silence creates a sense of presence.

WILDE: Heart stories bounce back with no catch.

ZENIBAA: Silence is the shadow of natural motion.

WILDE: Chalkboard stories are silent giveaways.

ZENIBAA: Native silence is not an absence.

WILDE: Creative writers describe scenes, not silence.

ZENIBAA: Silent heart stories are worth the chance.

WILDE: Chance and chalkboard stories are erased.

ZENIBAA: Great novels are silent in a library.

WILDE: Great operas are more than elusive silence.

ZENIBAA: Silence counters the predators of traditions.

WILDE: Silent stories stand alone at night.

ZENIBAA: Silence is my presence, not my absence.

WILDE: Silence and words are dust on a chalkboard.

ZENIBAA: Silence is the tease of every heart story.

WILDE: Silence has no tease of native hearsay.

ZENIBAA: Silence is the rest in music and lightning.

WILDE: Yes, the rests enhance the sorrows of an aria.

ZENIBAA: My silence is an opera of hesitations.

WILDE: Remembrance is more than silent moments.

ZENIBAA: Silence is the elusive manner of memory.

WILDE: Memories must be the best heart stories.

ZENIBAA: Heart stories are memories of natural motion.

WILDE: Yes, memory is a heart story, not a show.

ZENIBAA: Some doctors hear heartbeats not stories.

WILDE: Meditation and stories of the morning light.

ZENIBAA: Native silence is a dream song in the clouds.

WILDE: Yes, you convinced me that silence is a season.

ZENIBAA: Silence is the heart story of survivance.

Zenibaa raised her hands, waved, and shouted in silence, brava, brava, brava, and the doctors and nurses laughed and bowed in silence, and a short time after a memorable puppet parley of healers, the doctor, nurses, and orderlies responded to the code of an emergency on the hospital loudspeakers, and the room was suddenly deserted and a silent place.

||||| 9 |||||

SILK MEMORIES

Master Jean Bonga parked the *Theatre of Chance* near Peavey Park and the Waite Neighborhood House, a community center, on Park Avenue. The four mongrels rushed out of the bus and chased every scent and shadow in the park. The mongrels tumbled in the grass and then sniffed around the trees, light poles, and benches for the nature of the mute puppeteer.

Archie Goldman, director of the Waite House, greeted the stowaways and saluted the catchy names on the sides of the bus, *Theatre of Chance* and *Célébrité de Rien,* or Celebrity of Nothing. He expressed concern about the mute puppeteer, praised the doctors at Mount Sinai Hospital, and, in the same breath, invited the stowaways to park the bus in the driveway overnight for several days and to use the kitchen and toilets in the community center.

Goldman reminisced about the enchantment of hand puppets and marionette shows as a child, and he was delighted that the stowaways were dedicated to the spirit of puppetry. Big Rant promised the director an invitation to the first native puppet parley in Minneapolis. The director was personal and generous, but not comfortable with the four mongrels, and rather dismissive until he listened to a perfect melodic bay by George Eliot and was enchanted by the circle dance of Dingleberry.

By Now and Prometheus surprised the stowaways with a house they had rented nearby. They named the spacious house the Oshki Theatre of Chance. The word *oshki* was translated as new, young, or natural in the language of the Anishinaabe. The stowaways were more bewildered than surprised by the sudden decision to relocate the great puppet parleys to a house on the urban reservation, or existential colony, but the confusion was easily overcome once the stowaways visited the craftsman style house in a native neighborhood near Franklin Avenue, close to Peavey Park, Mount Sinai Hospital, and the Waite Neighborhood House and across the street from Den Norske Lutherske Mindekirke.

The mute puppeteer worried about the mongrels and the chickens at the cabins near Spirit Lake as she waited that early morning with clean chalkboards on her lap to be discharged from the hospital and return to the Theatre of Chance on the White Earth Reservation.

Doctor Samuel Wilde, the cardiologist, was about fifteen minutes late for the final examination of the silent patient, and naturally he was hesitant to convey a native tease for the delay, but that changed quickly when the mute puppeteer printed a message on hospital stationery. "No one is ever late, native time is natural motion, and motion is never late, clocks are never the time or the season."

Doctor Wilde saluted the mute puppeteer in silence, an unusual gesture for a medical doctor. She was pleased, and printed one more note on hospital stationery, the actual words of Ohiyesa, or Charles Alexander Eastman, the Dakota medical doctor. "Silence is the absolute poise or balance of body, mind, and spirit," and "silence is the cornerstone of character." Doctor Wilde proclaimed his medical endorsement of silence as the balance of character.

By Now was at her side on the way out of the hospital, and as she reached the exit the four loyal mongrels leaped, bounced, bumped, and bayed in natural harmony. The stowaways reached out to touch the mute puppeteer, and she was teary, an unusual response to the presence of the stowaways and loyal mongrels.

Later, she wrote on the chalkboard, "Natives are easy prey on the streets of a noisy city, far from the good cheer and ironic hearsay at the post office, and a native place of nicknames, and yet natives carry on with the ironic hearsay of creation on reservations and everywhere."

Poesy May and Big Rant presented a red and blue floral silk scarf to the mute puppeteer as she walked out of the hospital. Slowly she drew the wide scarf across her face and reached out with silk in hand to touch the others, a remembrance of the fur trade and portage liberty. The stowaways shouted hallelujah several times and the mongrels bounced and circled the mute puppeteer and bayed in harmony.

The native troupe walked a few blocks to the Oshki Theatre of Chance, a two story house on Tenth Avenue South with four bedrooms and a wide front porch surrounded by huge elm trees. The house was hastily furnished with tables, chairs, couches, bureaus, and beds from the Salvation Army. No one, not the mute puppeteer, stowaways, or mongrels had ever lived in a modern house with so much space and so many windows.

Aloysius painted a formal tablet, "Oshki Theatre of Chance, Zenibaa Residence," and with the names of the five stowaways, Big Rant Beaulieu, Master Jean Bonga, Poesy May Fairbanks, Bad Boy Aristotle, and Truman La Chance, and the mongrels, Hail Mary, George Eliot, Daniel, and Dingleberry. The wooden tablet of native recognition was mounted over the front door of the house.

The mongrels barked and bounced on the wide porch, and the mute puppeteer turned away to print a message on a chalkboard. "The Oshki Theatre of Chance is our new stage of puppet parleys and ironic heart stories."

Zenibaa, the nickname, was a native trace of distant fur trade memories, the glorious return of the beaver and other animals, and the chance of silk fashions and conversions, but never the desolate hearsay of separatism, envy, and the nasty reservation stories about Dummy Trout. Most native nicknames were related to experiences and never lasted more than a few years, unless, of course, a single nickname was translated by the missionaries or federal agents as a surname. The hearsay of the silk nickname was not directly related to the divas of the opera, shamanic silence, puppet parleys, the loyal mongrels, or the daily teases of the stowaways.

"Silk memories before silence," shouted Big Rant.

"Silk before the Great Hinckley Fire," said By Now.

"Silk has no reservation," said Poesy May.

"Silk chased the bullies away," said Bad Boy.

The Oshki Theatre of Chance was located directly across the street from a massive church, Den Norske Lutherske Mindekirke, and the distinctive name was carved in stone over the entrance. Bad Boy wondered if Sunday services at the Norwegian Lutheran Memorial Church were overheard on the street.

The mongrels circled the porch and barked at a distance, hesitant and curious, at a black cat perched on the inside sill of the bay window. The cat blinked once, nothing more, and the mongrels dared to nose the window. The black cat blinked twice with disdain, and the mongrels backed away from the window with muffled barks and waited for a familiar gesture from the mute puppeteer.

"The black cat is a stray, surely a stowaway, and she comes with the house," said By Now. "No name, but she has a natural presence and history in the house."

Zenibaa moved into the downstairs master bedroom with the mongrels, and the stowaways settled in the three bedrooms on the second floor. Big Rant and Poesy May moved into the front bedroom, and Bad Boy and La Chance shared the second bedroom. Master Jean was content with the cozy bedroom at the back of the house near the bathroom.

By Now, Prometheus, Basile, Aloysius, and the stowaways celebrated the good health and humor of the mute puppeteer that first night over dinner of baked walleye, wild rice, corn on the cob, tomatoes, and green beans with garlic, and everyone saluted the Oshki Theatre of Chance. The mongrels bayed at the right moments of heart stories and ironic native revelry. The black cat blinked at times and only moved from the cabinet room divider later that night for a few scraps of walleye.

The stowaways hardly slept that first night in the huge house. There were noisy cars, and the muted conversations on the street were distractions. The windows wheezed in the wind, and the hardwood floors creaked as the temperature changed overnight. Later, the black cat slowly climbed the stairs and moved silently through the bedrooms and calculated by stealth the presence of mongrels and strange newcomers. The mongrels were awake, nosed the night air, and remained silent and cautious as the cat prowled through every room of the house.

Zenibaa summoned the stowaways to create a nickname for the black cat that morning at breakfast. The cat waited on the oak cabinet room divider, the sentry of the house, for a name, any name that she could blink away. A few days later, when the mongrels were more at ease with the cat, the nominations for the nickname of the sentry started one afternoon on the porch. The mute puppeteer noted each name on a chalkboard, and later the stowaways voted on a nickname for the cat.

"Pensive, the cause of every cat, the pleasure of a silent cat with the virtues of meditation, and cats must be noticed every minute, day and night," said Bad Boy.

"Toupee, for perfect black hair," shouted Big Rant.

"Hilda, for Hilda Doolittle, who wrote more precious than a wet rose," said Poesy May. "The great poet and novelist died two years ago."

"Black Wet Rose," shouted Big Rant.

"Makade Norwindian," said Prometheus.

"Anishaa, no purpose, for nothing," said Bad Boy.

"Wink, for the blinks," said La Chance.

"Makade Bizhiins, a black cat," said By Now.

"High Brow," said Basile.

"Miikindizi, teases or provokes," said Aloysius.

"Pointe du Sable, for Jean Baptiste Pointe-du-Sable, the first black man in the fur trade, or Bonga, for Jean Bonga, a fur trade slave and my distant relative," said Master Jean.

"Mangizide, or Big Foot," wrote the mute puppeteer. "She saunters right past the worried mongrels at night, flicks her tail, and leaps on the bed and kneads my sacred belly."

The stowaways were convinced the cat, poised as usual on the cabinet room divider, blinked and purred over the ironic nickname Big Foot. She moved with the stealth of a panther on petite paws, not a monster with huge hairy feet, and kneaded the belly of the mute puppeteer every night.

"Big Foot shaman," shouted Big Rant.

Zenibaa created ironic puppet parleys about poseurs and resistance warriors, about the abuses of animals, the political cringes and slights of native continental liberty, and many other stories. She seldom complained about the weather, not even about hearsay, and never mentioned possessions, but she wrote several critical notes on chalkboards about books that afternoon and named the absent authors as characters. "Where is Michel de Montaigne, where are the books, the books, the books, where are the chickens, and where are the leather notebooks and wooden chair?"

10

COLUMBUS RUMPUS

Postcard Mary and Harmony Baswewe, the former librarian of the burned Library of Nibwaakaa, rescued the chair, books, and other personal property that had been removed from the two ramshackle cabins near Spirit Lake. The chickens were secure with the mission priest, and every book, metal dish, spoon, hand mirror, hand crank record player, opera album, canoe paddle, and four blocks of fallen birch to carve new puppets and other worldly goods were delivered with ironic gestures on Monday, October 12, 1964, Columbus Day.

Tallulah and Trophy Bay were lonesome for the other mongrels and arrived with the property from the Theatre of Chance. Tallulah leaped out of the car, raised her head with a wild contralto bay, and the other mongrels barked and chased each other around the grassy yard and house. That night the six mongrels gathered on the porch and bayed in harmony around the mute puppeteer in the great wooden chair. Aloysius painted the names of Tallulah and Trophy Bay on the outside tablet of the Oshki Theatre of Chance.

Corporal Harold Hutson, or Atomic 16, the peaky Second World War veteran who enlisted to serve in the puppet parleys at the Seattle World's Fair and at the Iron Pergola in Pioneer Square, surprised everyone that afternoon when he arrived with the two mongrels. Atomic 16 earned the curious nickname for the chemical element of sulfur because he was a combat soldier, and at the end of the war the army division was ordered to carry out cleanup duties in the radioactive ruins of Hiroshima, Japan.

Zenibaa and the stowaways saluted in silence and then embraced the bony veteran with shouts of care and favor and teased him as an overweight sulfur merchant. Master Jean played a few notes of "To the Colors," and everyone turned sentimental over the sound of a bugle and the presence of a close friend and an honorable soldier. Big Foot slowly blinked several times and purred in response to the pitch of the bugle, and the loyal mongrels

64   GERALD VIZENOR

bumped and nudged the veteran to stay as Hail Mary delivered a melodic bay.

Postcard Mary told the troupe that Atomic 16 hitchhiked across the country and arrived on the reservation a few days after the stowaways had departed for Mount Sinai Hospital. Corporal Hutson found the mongrel grave houses, but the two ramshackle cabins had already been removed, so he inquired about the mute puppeteer and stowaways at the post office.

Postcard Mary paused, smiled, and created a much more interesting postcard story about his adventure. "Atomic 16 was very surprised to learn that the stowaways and mute puppeteer were international celebrities in a movie about a native houseboat named the *Hearsay of Liberty* that sailed every night close to the international border of Lake of the Woods. The silent native captain of the boat created the overnight scripts of liberty, and the loyal crew of stowaways broadcast loud messages about predatory traditions, nasty priests, and the liberation of native students from mission schools."

"Tallulah and Trophy Bay liberated me," said Atomic 16.

Postcard Mary was persuasive and continued the hearsay and heart stories. "Atomic 16 mustered radioactive war veterans to surround the mission schools, double talked the priests with promises of absolution and nuclear salvation, and delivered the native students to native ports of liberty," said Postcard Mary.

Master Jean saluted the waves of irony on Columbus Day with puppet parleys and declared that his distant relations were among the first slaves in the colonial fur trade, and somehow they survived the deadly diseases delivered by the colonial explorers Erik the Red, Leif Erikson, Cristóbal Colón, and later the Knights of Columbus.

"Churchy handover of smallpox," shouted Big Rant.

"The Black Robes of measles," said La Chance.

"Columbus rumpus and syphilis," said Bad Boy.

"The Ku Klux Klan never teased the priests or told ironic stories about Catholics or Christopher Columbus," said Master Jean. "Columbus might have captured and changed the name of the Klan to the Klux Savages of Salvation."

Big Rant and Master Jean created the first puppet parley at the Oshki Theatre of Chance with the tricky hearsay of Cristóbal Colón and the mighty Norseman Erik the Red. The parley script was created with the ironic hearsay of his servant Diego de Salcedo, more than eighty other seamen, and some criminals with sovereign immunity for risky service on the Niña, Pinta, and Santa Maria, and most of the hearsay quotations were selected from the journal of the haughty colonial explorer and bewildered navigator.

Zenibaa and the stowaways invited Doctor Samuel Wilde, Archie Goldman, director of Waite House, two native advocates, Tedious Van Pelt and the mighty Hush Browne, Noah Bear, a native philosopher, Mitigomin Perrault, an existential healer, and Jacques Dashim La Roque, the buoyant native elder and retired trucker, to the inaugural hand puppet parley at the Oshki Theatre of Chance. Where Now Downwind, a professor of literature and author with a dedication to ironic stories that prune person, time, and place in the distinctive literary manner of Samuel Beckett, and Buoyant Fine Day, the heart dancer and native healer of stray women in the existential colony, were also invited to the parley.

Birchy Iron Moccasin, the stray poseur of nasty reservation hearsay, pressed her huge hands on the bay window and waited for an invitation to the parley. Tallulah and Trophy Bay growled at the stout woman at the window, and minutes later she waved the mongrels away with a fierce grimace, pushed past the shuns, and joined the others for the puppet parley in the living room.

"Counter name with no character," shouted Big Rant.

"Nasty character with a counter name," said Bad Boy.

"Godless daughter of an evangelist," whispered Poesy May.

"Birchy has outlived a thousand shuns," said Bad Boy.

"Double talk pretender," said Master Jean.

Gunnar Sandberg and Anders Bolstad, two thirteen-year-old Norwegian boys from Den Norske Lutherske Mindekirke arrived for the puppet parley and bravely announced to the stowaways and others that they were prepared to become proud American Indians.

"Columbus is your man, not natives," said Master Jean.

"Columbus captured the natives," teased Bad Boy.

"So, read the *Boy Scout Handbook*," shouted Big Rant.

"The primer for proud Indians," said La Chance.

"We read the book at scout camp," said Anders.

"Charles Alexander Eastman, Ohiyesa, the Santee Dakota medical doctor and author, was one of the founders of the Boy Scouts of America," said Bad Boy.

"Eastman created the Order of the Arrow," shouted Hush.

"Indians already, now what happens?" said Gunnar.

"Blood count of royalty and salvation," said Bad Boy.

"Boarding school and short hair," shouted Big Rant.

"Norwindian stowaways," said Tedious.

"Order of the Arrow mongrels," said Poesy May.

"Blood counts for nothing," said Birchy.

"Birchy blood counts of hearsay," said Tedious.

Hail Mary raised her head and delivered a melodic bay, and the other mongrels moaned in harmony and then bumped every visitor at the parley to stay, but not Birchy Iron Moccasin. Big Foot, the haughty black cat, was perched on the cabinet divider above the mongrels, as usual, and blinked several times with a curious sense of dominance and sovereignty.

The precise comeback comments of Erik the Red, the Norse adventurer, were ironic interpretations of medieval sagas, some close to historical rumors, poetic hearsay, and hunches about his son Leif Erikson. The distinctive portrayals of the two puppet explorers were caricatures painted by Aloysius Hudon Beaulieu on the converse sides of a huge brown paper bag mounted on a canoe paddle for the parley. La Chance calculated the turn of the paddle and changed the postures, expressions, and gestures of the two puppets in the discovery parley. Big Rant shouted the big voice of Cristóbal Colón, and Master Jean carried out the staunch and dominant voice of Erik the Red.

> ERIK THE RED: Who would concoct Columbus Day?
> CRISTÓBAL: Chancy sovereigns, slaves, and criminals.
> ERIK THE RED: The Norse knew where they were going.
> CRISTÓBAL: Christians out for greed, shame, and salvation.
> ERIK THE RED: Strange, you set sail for China and India.
> CRISTÓBAL: No one should fear to undertake any task.
> ERIK THE RED: You had no idea where you were going.
> CRISTÓBAL: Navigate in any direction and land in history.

ERIK THE RED: No Columbus Day in China or India.

CRISTÓBAL: The Captain of Chance is my nickname.

ERIK THE RED: Chance is not related to nautical stupidity.

CRISTÓBAL: My desire was to possess land anywhere.

ERIK THE RED: Predatory sailors invented the Indians.

CRISTÓBAL: My holy service continues without fear.

ERIK THE RED: The Taino were settled on Guanahani.

CRISTÓBAL: Taino natives were easily captured by force.

ERIK THE RED: Why capture slaves and then return?

CRISTÓBAL: Greed and gold change the world.

ERIK THE RED: The Taino feared your hairy crew.

CRISTÓBAL: These people were very unskilled in arms.

ERIK THE RED: Fake Christians and severe redemptions.

CRISTÓBAL: Norse sagas are about predators.

ERIK THE RED: Norse sagas endure with no shame.

CRISTÓBAL: Christian missions conquered the world.

ERIK THE RED: Leif Erikson, my son, was no conqueror.

CRISTÓBAL: The Norse raided and ruined other cultures.

ERIK THE RED: Leif the Lucky was a mariner of maturity.

CRISTÓBAL: And your father was banished for murder.

ERIK THE RED: Leif Erikson discovered Vinland.

CRISTÓBAL: Nothing more than grapes and pastures.

ERIK THE RED: Five hundred years before your mistake.

CRISTÓBAL: Blondes deserve to shiver in the north.

ERIK THE RED: Monarchs catch slaves to build churches.

CRISTÓBAL: The Norse were ponderous and ferocious.

ERIK THE RED: No one forgets the savage Black Robes.

CRISTÓBAL: Columbus Day honors my name forever.

ERIK THE RED: Fake Indian Day for a faulty navigation.

CRISTÓBAL: Knights of Columbus created my holy day.

ERIK THE RED: Norse mockery of a crude navigation.

CRISTÓBAL: Envy of the Knights of Norwindians.

ERIK THE RED: Norse sagas outwit the Knights of Fakery.

CRISTÓBAL: The Knights of Nothing create nothing.

ERIK THE RED: The Knights of Norse created a culture.

CRISTÓBAL: You were banished from Iceland.

ERIK THE RED: The Norse created great sagas, not Indians.

CRISTÓBAL: Columbus Day is not a celebration of Indians.

ERIK THE RED: Leif Erikson Day is every day in America.

Doctor Wilde raised his arms and shouted brava, brava, brava several times that night, and, at the same time, he gestured with favor and esteem to the mute puppeteer and stowaways for the phenomenal puppet parley. La Chance lowered the canoe paddle closer to the doctor and slowly turned the brown paper bag with the abstract faces of Cristóbal Colón and Erik the Red.

"Only fascists might concoct a national holiday to celebrate the absurd navigation of an amateur explorer and then honor a blunder and absurd name for millions of natives, and that crude irony has lasted for more than four centuries," said By Now.

"Cristóbal failed the course of navigation," said Bad Boy.

"Cristóbal was a colonial slaver," said Master Jean.

"Norse explorers were closer," shouted Big Rant.

"Norse sagas are never secure," said Poesy May.

"Erik the Red sails in the sagas of glory," said By Now.

"Indians are the charade of a blunder," said La Chance.

"Cristóbal was a colonial flasher," shouted Hush.

"Vinland on a reservation is mockery," said Tedious.

"Cristóbal gave us a good name," declared Birchy.

"Yes, Birchy Indians," shouted Big Rant.

"Good names last forever," said Birchy.

"Fakers find you and create a name," said Bad Boy.

"Cristóbal is our great discovery," said Birchy.

"Cristóbal craved to be a showstopper, greedy for fame and gold, and inadvertently created a miscellany of stopover cultures, and now a concoction of poseurs and outliers are forever on the road with contrived names and traditions," shouted Hush.

"Cristóbal holds a name in cock and bull stories as a stray minstrel of invention and inquisition and discovered nothing more than native hearsay, a slight touch of romance, a weary wait, and names of native absence in the chance of a presence and continues to relate continental discoveries, and maybe the stories were ours, the stance and stays of mere shadows, and at last we landed in a fake history as native tricksters much earlier and discovered ourselves with nothing more to say," said Where Now Downwind.

"Waiting for Godot," shouted Big Rant.

"Waiting for Wovoka," said Bad Boy.

"Stay and wait in a theatre of silence," said Poesy May.

"Samuel Beckett hears our stories," said Noah Bear.

"Samuel Beckett doubts the chance and turn of pronouns, and here he comes with an unnamable course with the tease of words as discoveries that we might have been already told in the stories of others, in the silence of absence, and maybe we have been said already, no we have never been lost or discovered or told by anyone, not yet, and what does yet, not yet, mean to the storiers of creation," said Where Now.

"Never, no one has said me already," said Birchy.

"Indian invention maybe, native never," said Bad Boy.

"Poseurs are never more than hearsay," shouted Hush.

Postcard Mary raised her voice and changed the ironic course of the Columbus Day puppet parley about the fakers of names and discovery and revealed that the song, "Do Wah Diddy Diddy" by Manfred Mann, a rock band, was the most popular song on the music charts, and after dinner the stowaways were prepared to mock the ironic sway of music and created a few new lines of the popular song. "Cristóbal Colón, there he was just a sailin' on the ocean in the wrong direction to China and India, singin' Do wah diddy diddy dum diddy do."

The mute puppeteer raised her hands and shouted out brava, brava, brava in silence to tease the poseur and explorer, the outright celebrity of nothing, and the loyal mongrels bayed in perfect harmony.

Gunnar and Anders traveled with other boys on a church bus through the village of Vinland to a campsite near Mille Lacs Lake and were reassured that they were American Indians. Leif Erikson, they reasoned, and without a doubt, clearly created the place name and the destiny of Norwindians. Vinland is located on the Mille Lacs Lake Reservation.

"Vinland is our blood story," said Gunnar.

"Vinland is our ancestry," said Anders.

"Place names are not heart stories," shouted Big Rant.

"But we want to be in heart stories," said Gunnar.

"Yes, in the old ways," said Anders.

"The *Boy Scout Handbook* is almost enough, but now you must cut away the margins of pages in the book and create new stories from the silence and absence of the cut away sentences," said Bad Boy.

"Pretend the edges of the book were burned, and then create your own poetic words for the burned pages. In other words, create the *Norwindian Boy Scout Handbook*," said Poesy May.

"Eastman would be honored," said Master Jean.

Harmony Baswewe admired the stowaways for their favor of books, the actual books on the sagging shelves of the library, and then for their eager search for burned books in the ashes after the arson that destroyed the library of Nibwaakaa. Harmony continued as the librarian of literary enchantment and generous hearsay, despite the criminal fire, and she continued to select books for the stowaways at least twice a year. She delivered a box of great books just as the *Theatre of Chance* was about to leave two years ago for puppet parleys at the Seattle World's Fair.

Harmony placed a selection of recently published books on the cabinet room divider. Big Foot slowly nosed each book and then blinked several times and walked away. Bad Boy Aristotle read a few pages of the novel *Catch 22* by Joseph Heller and then set aside *Lady Chatterley's Lover* by D. H. Lawrence.

Harmony was honored with heartfelt teases and salutes, and then the stowaways browsed *Profiles in Courage* by John F. Kennedy, *The Soul of an Indian* by Charles Alexander Eastman, *To Kill a Mocking Bird* by Harper Lee, *A Chippewa Speaks* by John Rogers, *The Myth of Sisyphus* by Albert Camus, *Tropic of Cancer* by Henry Miller, *A Stone, A Leaf, A Door* by Thomas Wolfe, *The Devil in France* by Lion Feuchtwanger, *The Heart is a Lonely Hunter* by Carson McCullers, *The Japanese Haiku* by Kenneth Yasuda, *No Longer Human* by Osamu Dazai, and the most pretentious and overstated sentiments of avarice, a cocky booklet of corporate greed and unintended irony, *The Gospel of Wealth* by Andrew Carnegie.

11

EXISTENTIAL COLONY

Tedious Van Pelt and Hush Browne, the dedicated native advocates in the existential colony, saluted the five stowaways and waited for the mute puppeteer to create puppet parleys that countered the cultural poseurs, predators of traditions, and mocked the deception of state and federal agencies.

The Bureau of Indian Affairs denied services to natives outside of treaty reservations, for a start, and that deserved protests and critical puppet parleys. Glenn Landbloom, the oblivious area director, declared that the exclusion policy was legislation enacted by the United States Congress. Hush Browne shouted past the obtuse federal agents and with the support of the local congressman revealed the deceit, "There was no record of congressional legislation or intent to provide federal services only to natives on reservations."

Panic Radio, a covert station in a camper van, broadcast radical native news and created a chance to shout out about misery and overcome hesitations. "Panic Radio was my start as a strategic heart story shouter after my wild, bleak, and desolate teenage shouts," said Hush.

Hush shouted at politicians, social workers, newspaper editors, and city police, cursed and shamed the emergency services at the county hospital, and carried out more elusive teases, ironic stories, and literary shouts about the fainthearted faculty and administrators at the University of Minnesota.

Zenibaa was the Doyenne of Silence and puppet parleys, a generous manner and steady beat of mockery and mercy that were spectacles of liberty in the court of chance and irony. The five stowaways became the maestros of clever backtalk in puppet parleys and celebrated native chance, but they were hesitant newcomers in the existential colony.

"Later, teachers once shriveled over my mockery and curses," shouted Hush. "Hand puppets are condoned and pardoned for spirited blurts and curses, but not my strategic profanity at teachers, journalists, and politicians, and how else would teachers start to understand poverty, racism, and the fascists of separatism if they worry about shouts and a few curse words."

The stowaways were wistful about the old ramshackle cabins, the solitude of the seasons and natural motion of birch and maple trees near Spirit Lake, and the hearsay and good cheer at the post office, but after a few weeks in the existential colony they were ready to shout, fake a pout, and create lively puppet parleys with the native advocates.

Master Jean moved the *Theatre of Chance* from the driveway of the community center and parked the converted bus on Tenth Avenue across the street from Den Norske Lutherske Mindekirke. The Norwegian Lutheran Memorial Church was established more than forty years earlier, and natives from reservations rented most of the divided houses in the existential colony. Two polite envoys from the church asked the native newcomers to park the bus out of sight or in the driveway at the back of the Oshki Theatre of Chance.

"Norwindians worry about the name on the side of the bus, Celebrity of Nothing," said Bad Boy. "Maybe they worry even more whether this is a native cabal or a celebrity bus route to nowhere."

"Churchy evasions of chance," said La Chance.

"Norwindian heirs of the fur trade," said Master Jean.

"Celebrity of Nothing is the bother," said Prometheus.

"Eric the Red is a celebrity of nothing" shouted Big Rant.

Zenibaa moved the giant wooden chair to the front porch early that first Sunday morning and waved at the rosy children and distracted a few parishioners as they arrived for church services. Master Jean raised the military bugle and played a round of reveille that early morning. A few proud parishioners waved back just as the school bus was slowly driven out of sight.

The mute puppeteer and stowaways were strangers, scouts, and native fugitives in the tease and tumble of hearsay in the existential colony. The Band Box Diner, for instance, the favorite native restaurant near Elliot Park, served cheap burgers with the most steady and reliable colony hearsay. Hello Dolly's, on the other hand, was a sour and sticky native bar, a dark nasty harbor of envy, jealousy, tacky stories, malicious rumors, cultural drifts, boasts, traditions lost on others by poseurs at the end of the bar. Native heart stories in the existential colony were never as creative or timely as the post office hearsay on the White Earth Reservation.

The stowaways created ironic heart stories as usual about chance and native liberty, and the colony hearsay of existential socialism was burdened with more weary conferences of doubts and departures than irony. Big Rant teased that there were no federal agents to deride in the public parks or at city bus stops and no camouflaged native hunters or predatory traditions to mock in the existential colony. The cut and run rumors about treaties were extraneous, on the far side of reservations, and so the stowaways continued as usual to create puppet parleys of chance, mockery, and irony with new stories of native existential survivance and liberty.

The Waite House on Park Avenue was dedicated to serve the social and cultural situations of the diverse fugitives in the neighborhood. Plainly, the recognition and communal assistance programs favored the liberal sentiments and ethos of socialism, and with a generous manner, but the director of neighborhood programs could not easily prepare just strategies of service that represented several thousand native fugitives from several federal reservations. Some community services for émigrés, runaways, and natives were undermined by envy and malicious hearsay in the existential colony near Franklin Avenue and Elliot Park.

Even so, native existential socialism, that uneasy course of recognition, survivance, and liberal justice, was closer to the native course of chance and sense of liberty than to the unstable sentiments of social service agencies, conventions of liberal crusaders, and the literary romance of native victimry.

The obvious outcome of treaty separatism and the carceral modes of federal agents was a quirky evolution of resistance and native existential socialism. The cast, wavers, and mockery of existence were much easier to perceive in the spirit of puppet parleys. The removal of natives from homelands and then relocation by coercive treaties to separatist reservations favored only autocratic capitalism, land tenancy, and greedy exploitation of natural resources. The outcome of tenurable mercenaries over more than two centuries was creative mockery and puppet parleys.

"Treaty reservations were never considered the essential plot of democracy," said Basile. "Think back, there were no obvious conventions of owners and labor on reservations and no cause to establish trade unions to protest the harsh conditions of remote exclaves, and the outcome was extraordinary, the persecution of natives and discount of treaties was countered with mockery and existential socialism."

"Separatist treaty reservations were the trial run of native fugitives with no cause, literature, or future, a disenchantment, and everywhere greedy federal agents reigned over the resources and labor and faked government reports to document the great progress of civilization," declared By Now. "The puppet parleys are scenes of existential socialism and survivance, scenes of continental liberty and the necessary double duty mockery of the treaty makers and communal fakers," said By Now.

"Natives favor mockery, not misery," shouted Big Rant.

"America is a history of reservations," said Basile.

"Millions of natives died from colonial diseases, and then the fur trade sabotaged a vital association of totemic animals," said Aloysius. "The Midewiwin emerged with secret cures as natives searched for relations and at the same time envisioned heart stories of survivance."

"The Grand Medicine Society was a closed union of native healers that prepared and owned secret concoctions that were sold to natives," said By Now. "The Midewiwin, a society of mostly native men, carried out cures in secrecy to regulate the herbal remedies, not the mercy of native healers."

"Continental liberty and native justice were the casualties of treaty separatism and capitalism," said Basile. "Natives were not recognized as citizens in a constitutional democracy until June 2, 1924, when Congress granted Indians born within the territorial limits of the United States be, and they are hereby, declared to be citizens of the United States."

"Natives were existential outsiders in the deceptions of a constitutional democracy," shouted Big Rant. "But not without memories of summer puppet parleys, creative heart stories at wild rice camps, and the seductive lures of snow ghosts."

"The heartless hearsay on reservations has continued in the cold ghetto rentals," said By Now. "For some natives the colony is nothing more than a fugitive encampment, the tenements of poseurs, disguises, and diseases, and the deceit of federal service agencies continue with only slight policy changes."

"Native stories of deception," said Bad Boy.

"Feather, leather, and turquoise," said La Chance.

"The Waite House is our new post office, and the native hearsay is more communal than the arrogance of federal agents and the hearsay of bullies on the reservation," said Master Jean.

Tedious Van Pelt was the first community advocate for natives in the existential colony, and he shared the huge back room in Waite House on Park

Avenue with Hush Browne, the second advocate, a poet of wild shouts and visionary dream songs who earned an ironic nickname because of her curses of political and academic poseurs and spirited shouts for native liberty.

"Federal agents looked the other way and timber barons clear cut our cultures and country, fascist grave hunters stole the bones of our relations, and now stony anthropologists steal our dream songs and heart stories for academic promotion," shouted Hush Browne.

Tedious and Hush were amateur bowlers and met for the first time at the Bryant Lake Bowl. Hush was small and hardly weighed much more than five regular fifteen pound bowling balls, but the mighty shouts she directed at the pins and course of the ball down the polished lanes became a source of erotic hearsay in the existential colony. She was teased with envy and coaxed by bowlers to direct the path of their balls with a native shout.

Hush launched the *Biibaagi* Résistance Movement, the shouts of resistance, to counter the delusions about natives as an absence and not a presence, but most natives were hesitant to shout and curse in public. Once a week in the early summer mornings she taught natives to shout in Peavey Park. Last week more than seventeen natives, students and elders, gathered at dawn to practice shouts at trees, ravens, squirrels, and sober faces on city buses.

"Panic Radio was the start of native shouts to overcome dread and hesitations," said Tedious. "Hush overcame cringes with the nightly broadcast of precise shouts, and with more confidence as a shouter, she graduated from the university with an ironic nickname that lasted."

Overnight, the petite native advocate with a political science degree became the natural sovereign of shouts and curses at academic symposia, city and county events, corporate boardrooms, meetings with newspaper editors, churchy conventions, and abusive police in the existential colony, but she has never misused her mighty shouts of native liberty at staged political events, cultural spectacles, foundation cocktail parties, or righteous liberal protests.

"Federal agents on the reservation once counted on native shuns and passive silence, but now native resistance and liberty are revealed in strategic shouts, shouts, shouts," shouted Hush.

Tedious Van Pelt was born in a fur trade shanty near Federal Dam on the Leech Lake Reservation and ten years later moved with his family to a dilapidated duplex near the Waite House. Marvin Van Pelt and Medora Rock praised, encouraged, and teased their seven children to resist and outwit the wicked snow ghosts and the curse of suicide on the reservation and existential colony.

Marvin was a pinsetter and janitor at the Bryant Lake Bowl in the busy Uptown district of Minneapolis. Tedious revealed that his father was first hired as a manual pinsetter, along with several plucky teenagers, and a few months later the hazardous labor and low pay ended with the installation of automatic pinsetter machines. Marvin was rewarded for his loyalty and promoted to a contract janitorial and maintenance crew with a higher salary. Medora created and sold beaded medicine bundles and kitschy spirit catchers at native feasts and festivals.

"My mother never used the words existential socialism, but she always stared down any gestures that were not responsible for the care of others and at the same time respected our duties to other natives and the family," said Tedious.

Hush was abandoned at birth, a reservation orphan raised in several foster homes with other abandoned and fugitive children. She shamed most of the mercenary foster parents, easily learned to outface bullies twice her size with wild reactive shouts, and she could easily stand her ground with no trace of remorse or mercy.

Hush cursed the daily bus ride to a public high school near the reservation, shouted at the bullies, separatist teachers, and austere administrators, and wisely quit school at age sixteen. She moved to the existential colony and was shied by the anonymity and the liberal calculations of victimry. Panic Radio and precise shouts restored her sense of confidence, and six years later she earned an associate of arts degree with honors in literature at a community college, and several years later the scrupulous shouter earned a bachelor of arts degree in Political Science at the University of Minnesota.

"Bachelor of political science shouts," shouted Hush.

Hush never lost her sense of native chance, the spirit of crucial shouts, and the necessary existential socialism of survivance and liberty, but recently she was overcome with a curious sensation of ease and peace, the actual silence and serenity of meditation, when she first viewed the abstract paintings of George Morrison, the native artist from the Grand Portage Reservation who taught art at the University of Minnesota.

THEATRE OF CHANCE

Hush was invited with other natives to visit his studio in a converted church in Saint Paul, and, surrounded by expressionist creations, she discovered an incredible liberty in the silence and mastery of art. Hush was truly hushed by the scenes of natural motion, the spectacular rush of colors and contours, and the spirit of a native presence in every trace of a paint brush, the seductive unity of colors and shadows, the tease of natural motion, and the curve and shimmer of an abstract horizon over Lake Superior.

"George Morrison paints the native sense of motion, the natural dance and shimmer of seasons and horizons, the abstract traces of creation, ancestral memories, native heart stories, and the shamanic meditation of silence," she shouted out a few days later.

Hush returned to her signature gestures the next day at a state conference of public school teachers about the absence of native authors in libraries. "Only a few books by native authors are on the shelves of libraries, and that denies the presence of natives," shouted Hush. "This is the time for librarians to retire the colonial histories, romance novels about native victimry, and acquire original books by native novelists, poets, essayists, and historians."

Tedious was prepared for the conference and read out loud a few sentences from *The Surrounded,* a native novel by D'Arcy McNickle. His mother "wore a handkerchief around her head and her calico dress was long and full and held in at the waist by a beaded belt. Her buckskin moccasins gave off a pungent odor of smoke. Nothing was any different. He knew it without looking."

"Yes, the cultural tease of a calico dress," shouted Hush.

"Medora Rock, my mother, is short, neat, and wears saddle shoes, not smokey moccasins, and she teases me that my tedious manner might sidetrack the shamans, outwit the tricksters, and bewitch librarians," said Tedious. One school librarian shouted out praise of native resistance, and others in the audience chanted hurrah, hurrah, hurrah, the liberal pose of countenance.

Big Rant followed the triple hurrah with descriptive scenes from *A Chippewa Speaks* by John Rogers, who returned from a federal boarding school and wrote, "Mother was seated on the ground, working on some fish nets. She was heavy and broad, but her hands and feet were small. Her hair, straight and black, was tied with a red string. She wore a full-skirted blue calico dress, with long blousey sleeves, a low neck, and a tight-fitting waist. Her waist was encircled by a fringed belt with red, yellow, green, and blue figures on it."

Bad Boy read a short selection from *The Soul of the Indian* by Charles Alexander Eastman. "Our faith might not be formulated in creeds, nor forced upon any who were unwilling to receive it, hence there was no preaching, proselytizing, no persecution, neither were there any scoffers or atheists."

A librarian asked about the novel *Wynema: A Child of the Forest* by Sophia Alice Callahan, a teacher and novelist associated with the Muscogee Creek. Hush rushed to criticize the romantic scenes of native victimry, education, and assimilation in the novel. "Wynema is fluent in at least two native languages, one learned from an old woman, and there are too many papooses, dark figures, and some in the din of battles, but maybe that was native talk when the novel was published more than seventy years ago, the first novel by a native woman."

Bad Boy related a short section from the second chapter of *Wynema*. The teacher in the novel read from the gospel and raised her eyes in prayer, "asking that he open the hearts of the children, that they might be enabled to understand His word, and that He give her such great love for her dusky pupils." The "pupils understood no word of it, but the tone went straight to each one's heart and found lodgement there. At recess Wynema came and stood by her teacher's side with deep wonder in her great, black eyes."

The librarians were eager to present native literature, but there was a persistent romance about traditions lost in that rush of reservation separatism, and the commerce of novels on native victimry was much more popular.

Zenibaa moved the wooden chair outside near the bay window, wound the hand crank record player, leaned back on that balmy night at the Oshki Theatre of Chance, and listened to Renata Tebaldi sing the familiar arias from the opera *La Bohème* by Giacomo Puccini. The mongrels circled the chair, nosed the moist breeze, and cocked their ears to the soprano diva. Hail Mary delivered a hesitant bay, and the other mongrels leaned against the mute puppeteer on that sublime summer night in the existential colony.

12

GOSPEL OF LABOR

Zenibaa, Doctor Samuel Wilde, Archie Goldman, Tedious Van Pelt, Hush Browne, Noah Bear, Jacques Dazhim La Roque, Emanuel Happy Holstein, Where Now Downwind, Mitigomin Perrault, the native troupe of chance, Basile, Aloysius, By Now, Prometheus, five stowaways, six loyal mongrels, and more than thirty natives and several others in the existential colony were present for the first puppet parley at the Waite House on Park Avenue.

Bad Boy and Big Rant created a lively parley for two hand puppets, a socialist union organizer in a quirky conversation with a conspicuously rich industrialist. Hush Browne was the firm voice of the socialist Mother Jones, and Master Jean practiced the arrogant, ambiguous, and narcissistic voice of Andrew Carnegie, the plutocrat and sometimes an optimistic philanthropist.

The thoughts of Mother Jones, who was born Mary Harris in Cork, Ireland, were selected from newspaper stories about her unreserved support of labor and lasting disputes with employers, from several published interviews with the dressmaker, activist, and schoolteacher, and from *The Autobiography of Mother Jones*. The studied words of Andrew Carnegie were selected from his essay, *The Gospel of Wealth*, first published in the *North American Review*, June 1889.

Aloysius painted two abstract caricatures on opposite sides of a brown paper bag, Mother Jones on one side, with fat cheeks, a downturned mouth, wire rim glasses, and the eyes of resistance and mercy, and Andrew Carnegie on the other side, a caricature with fierce eyes, polished cheeks, and bowler hat. The paper bag puppets were mounted on a canoe paddle.

Zenibaa was not ready to carve hand puppets from fallen birch, and certainly not a birch block work of art for the caricature of Andrew Carnegie. Truman La Chance was the bearer of the paddle, and as expected he turned the caricatures in the perfect manner of a perfect parley.

MOTHER: Get it straight, I'm no humanist, I'm a hell-raiser.

ANDREW: The problem of our age is the proper administration of wealth, so that the ties of brotherhood may still bind together the rich and poor in harmonious relationship.

MOTHER: I do not care what political party you put in power because we are of the economic power. It is not the political party that gained the eight hour day for the railroad man.

ANDREW: The Indians are today where civilized man then was. When visiting the Sioux, I was led to the wigwam of the chief. It was just like the others in external appearance, and even within the differences was trifling between it and those of the poorest of his braves.

MOTHER: The old condition is passing away. The new dawn of another civilized nation is breaking into the lives of the human race.

ANDREW: The contrast between the palace of the millionaire and the cottage of the laborer with us today measures the change which has come with civilization.

MOTHER: If you ever saw a policeman with a club in his hand, I want to ask you, did you ever see that policeman club a millionaire? But it is, "Get out of here, damn you, go on to jail, damn you," if it is a working man.

ANDREW: The poor enjoy what the rich could not before afford. What were the luxuries have become the necessities of life. The laborer has now more comforts than the landlord had a generation ago.

MOTHER: Your organization is not a praying institution. It's a fighting institution. It's an educational institution along industrial lines. Pray for the dead, and fight like hell for the living.

ANDREW: The Socialist or Anarchist who seeks to overturn present conditions is to be regarded as attacking the foundation upon which civilization rests, for civilization took its start from the day that the capable, industrious workman said to his incompetent and lazy fellow, "If thou dost not sow, thou shalt not reap," and thus ended primitive Communism by separating the drones from the bees.

MOTHER: I refer to the United States, the union of all the states. I ask then, if in union there is strength for our nation, would there not be for labor. What one state could not get alone, what one miner against a powerful corporation would not achieve, can be achieved by the union. What is a good enough principle for an American citizen ought to be good enough for the working man to follow.

ANDREW: Not evil, but good, has come to the race from the accumulation of wealth by those who have the ability and energy that produce it.

MOTHER: The miners lost because they had only the constitution. The other side had bayonets. In the end, bayonets always win.

ANDREW: We might as well urge the destruction of the highest existing type of man because he failed to reach our ideal as favor the destruction of Individualism, Private Property, the Law of Accumulation of Wealth, and the Law of Competition; for these are the highest results of human experience, the soil in which society so far has produced the best fruit.

MOTHER: Human flesh, warm and soft and capable of being wounded, went naked up against steel; steel that is cold as old stars, and harder than death and incapable of pain. Bayonets and guns and steel rails and battleships, bombs and bullets are made of steel. And only babies are made of flesh. More babies grow up and work in steel, to hurl themselves against the bayonets, to know the tempered resistance of steel.

ANDREW: Poor and restricted are our opportunities in this life; narrow our horizons; our best work most imperfect; but rich men should be thankful for one inestimable boon. They have it in their power during their lives to busy themselves in organizing benefactions from which the masses of their fellows will derive lasting advantage, and thus dignify their own lives.

MOTHER: Christ himself would agitate against them. He would agitate against the plutocrats and hypocrites who tell workers to go down on their knees and get right with God. Christ, the carpenter's son, would tell them to stand up on their feet and fight for righteousness.

ANDREW: In bestowing charity, the main consideration should be to help those who will help themselves; to provide part of the means by which those who desire to improve may do so; to give those who desire to use the aids by which they may rise; to assist, but to rarely or never to do all. Neither the individual nor the race is improved by almsgiving.

82 GERALD VIZENOR

MOTHER: In spite of oppressors, in spite of false leaders, in spite of labor's own lack of understanding of its needs, the cause of the worker continues onward. Slowly his hours are shortened, giving him leisure to read and to think. Slowly, his standard of living rises to include some of the good and beautiful things of the world.

ANDREW: The man who dies thus rich dies disgraced.

MOTHER: The future is in labor's strong, rough hands.

The puppet parley ended with the nostalgia of riches and disgrace, and then the gesture of the strong and rough hands of labor. The audience applauded and shouted praise and favor for the worthy parley and then wanted to hear much more about the biography of Mother Jones.

"Mother Jones was thirty years old when her husband and four children died in an epidemic of yellow fever in 1867, and four years later her home and dress shop were destroyed in the Great Chicago Fire," said Where Now Downwind. "She was devastated, of course, and mourned in silence, and then she mustered the sovereignty of workers in the resolute manner of her voice and organized movements for coal miners and other hard laborers to protest the conditions of factories, and she shamed the exploitation of child labor. She was active in the Knights of Labor and the union of the United Mine Workers."

Zenibaa shouted brava, brava, brava in silence and printed a response on a chalkboard. Big Rant slowly read the words of the mute puppeteer. "Mother Jones shouted out the passion of resistance after the Great Chicago Fire, and my native counter to absolute misery was silence, the silent shouts of resistance after the Great Hinckley Fire."

"Shouts and silence are close relations," shouted Hush.

"Shouts and silence are the natural balance of great spirits," said Bad Boy. "Charles Alexander Eastman wrote that silence is the cornerstone of character."

Hush Browne raised her hands and shouted out sentences from *The Autobiography of Mother Jones*. "No matter what your fight, don't be ladylike. God almighty made women and the Rockefeller gang of thieves made the ladies. If they want to hang me, let them. And on the scaffold I would shout, Freedom for the working class."

Hush paused to catch her breath and then shouted out one more good thought by Mother Jones. "The miners lost because they had only the constitution. The other side had bayonets. In the end, bayonets always win. Organized labor should organize its women along industrial lines. Politics is only the servant of industry. The plutocrats have organized their women. They keep them busy with suffrage and prohibition and charity."

"Mother Jones was a native at heart," shouted Big Rant.

"Mother Jones of resistance," said Bad Boy.

"Mother Jones was generous with a great spirit, and when she declared, 'I'm not a humanist,' that was ironic native back talk and the clever ethos of an existential socialist," said Basile.

"The great gospel of labor not wealth," shouted Hush.

"Somehow the wordy debris of capitalists seems to count in the world, even the unintended irony of Andrew Carnegie as he compares a palace to the cottage of a laborer, a strange measure that comes with a culture of opulence," said Aloysius.

"Carnegie in the ruins of civilization," said Master Jean.

"Carnegie poses in an aesthetic wigwam," said Bad Boy.

"Carnegie favors a wigwam over a tipi," said By Now.

"Carnegie was the enemy of unions," said Dazhim.

Zenibaa printed a quotation on a chalkboard, "Pray for the dead, pray for the unions, and fight like hell for the living," and then raised her hands to shout in silence, brava, brava, brava.

"The diva of labor unions," shouted Hush.

Doctor Wilde shouted bravo, bravo, bravo to tease Zenibaa, and repeated a comment by Mother Jones, "What one state could not get alone, what one miner against a powerful corporation would not achieve, can be achieved by the union."

George Eliot, the racy greyhound and retriever mongrel, moved her head to the side and delivered a marvelous soprano bay, and the other mongrels united in a chorus of magical sighs and spiritual soughs that raised the hair on the arms of everyone that afternoon at the Waite Neighborhood House.

ııııı 13 ııııı

ACADEMIC SKINWALKER

Noah Bear started every lecture and most conversations with the word *wonder*, a gentle gesture that was intended to create a sense of curiosity about marvelous heart stories and native speculations about slipstream perceptions of natural motion, and the favors of native hearsay over erudite convictions and subscriptions of cultural and academic getaways. Naturally, the obscure philosopher was teased by his relations as the curious native of handy wonders and a hunger for cheese.

Curds, a nickname at the government school, was rightly deserved because he was obsessed with the taste of commodity cheese, the blocks of cheese that were distributed to schools and hungry natives on the White Earth Reservation.

Curds packed his canvas pockets with chunks of yellow processed cheese as a government student on commodity foods and was teased about the earthly odor he created in classrooms. He earned a high school diploma on the reservation and moved to the existential colony, studied native literature and linguistics at the university, and packed bricks of cheddar and hard bread in a beaded velvet pouch, a medicine bundle of cheese, and shared pieces of bread and cheese at the graduation ceremony eight years later.

Sunny Bracer, the tiny, boney native lover of the chubby medicine man of curds and wonder, calculated that he probably consumed more than two thousand pounds of cheese in the past decade, and she could easily track his presence on the campus, in seminar rooms, at carrels in the library, and at the faculty club by the sweet scent of cheddar.

The weighty speculator wondered out loud and swayed with hand gestures in the presence of students or any audience and constantly related a sense of motion, the just wonders of every moment of natural motion, as he revealed with slight hesitations last week at a seminar on native cultures, motion, literature, and epistemology at the University of Minnesota.

"The tease of wonder arouses the awe, muse, ponder, and surprise of natural motion, memory, and heart stories of liberty," he declared at the seminar. "The very glint of wonder evades the heavy load of grammar that diverts the natural course of creative hearsay and heart stories."

The philosopher wore a stained denim cowboy shirt with pearl snap buttons and very slowly carried out the customary gestures and surprise motions of a hand puppet. He waved one hand close to his mouth, a motion of equivocal punctuation, or a hint of bad breath, or a curious reach for the perfect words about a just wonder, or to ease the expected tease and mockery of his medicine bundle of cheddar bricks by the mute puppeteer and stowaways at the Oshki Theatre of Chance.

"Count the chance of wonders, as everyone wonders what happens to the marvelous perception of creation, visionary scenes of remembrance, the canny pitch of shamans, and the natural tease of totemic associations over the crude ethnographic models of culture," declared Noah Bear.

Noah waved his hands once more and then announced that the "catch of a vision hardly lingers after the heave of pedantic words on the page, and not much of a creation story remains after the weasel words, narcissistic pronouns, poseurs of chance, and the cuts and queues of precise punctuation, and the great scenes of wonder and splendor of native creation stories were hushed with tedious translations, academic recitations, and airy theories of getaway cultures."

Noah paused between sources and stories of just wonders, as hesitations of native chance, and then carried on with the hand gestures of puppetry. "The waves of wonder and catch of native recognition are rarely revealed on the printed page, and for that reason even the most creative translations by ethnographers turn natural motion into provisional models and notions of handover consumer cultures."

The students were silent and hesitant, of course, but the stowaways one by one mocked the easy sway and gestures of the native philosopher and at the same time teased the concepts of wonder and hesitations with concise declarations.

"Sometimes the gestures of hand puppet parleys are blunt, clever, and elusive, hardly the slights of an academic disguise, romantic blather, or the faulty hunches about native relations at dinner parties," shouted Big Rant.

"Wonder word bait in the clouds," said Big Rant.

"Cheesy hearsay of ethnography," shouted Hush.

"Wispy wonders of anthropology," said By Now.

"Dead end scenes of translation," said Master Jean.

"Wonder is a clever tease of creation," said Bad Boy.

"Chase chance and shout wonder," shouted Hush.

"Catch wonder in a dream song," said Poesy May.

"Wonder is the nature of hearsay," said Big Rant.

"Wonder waits in the dust of words," said Where Now.

"Wonder is a tease of hesitations," said La Chance.

"Wonder is a tease of eagerness," said Where Now.

Noah Bear, the native philosopher, waved both hands close to his mouth and was amused with the teases of the stowaways and paused over the character of the dust of words and related that "possessive pronouns are the dust of hearsay and creation stories, not the art of resistance and wonder in language."

The portly professor of wonder moved with a sense of ease, the natural stance and balance of a mariner on rough seas, and at the same time he recounted the great wonders of native presence in oral stories and the absence of wonder in translations and the first person. He related that "the translation of native stories hardly favors the visions of dream songs or the ironic play of hearsay, hesitations of nature, natural motion of the seasons, or the tease and bounce of chance and sudden turns of silence, shadows, and remembrance."

Noah Bear rightly earned several nicknames at school on the reservation, Curds, Hand to Mouth, Cheese Head, Chancy Pause, Mosey Hearsay, Hand Puppet, and Wonder Hunch. Most of the nicknames were signatures of wonder that easily turned to teases and mockery in native hearsay, and when the stowaways first heard about the steady rush of his series of native wonders they created a parley with two strange papier mâché puppet masks.

The Wonder mask was elongated and creased with broad wrinkles, nothing sinister, only casual smiles and puckers worthy of wonder and mockery. The Skinwalker, on the other hand, was a hideous papier mâché mask that portrayed hairy witches and fearsome shapeshifters or the lecherous creatures that stray in nightmares. The skinwalkers chase dreams, shadows, and bursts of wind to catch the bloated spirits of dread and sentiments of death, and then the witchy creatures turn nights into a menace of wild tremors, with no tease or touch of mercy.

Clyde Kluckhohn, the anthropologist, easily came to mind that blustery autumn as the stowaways created a puppet parley of the skinwalker in the existential colony. The anthropologist was a predator of witchcraft hearsay on the Navaho Nation, and the actual words of the skinwalker mask were selected from his *Navaho Witchcraft*, published about twenty years ago.

Zenibaa and the stowaways conceded that gawky and distorted papier mâché puppet masks were more dramatic, enigmatic, scary, and memorable than the puppet caricatures of cloth remnants, bottles, cans, debris, paper bags, and canoe paddles, but not the more expressive hand puppets carved from fallen birch trees. The reservation hand puppets were slow and tiresome and not considered as wild and sensational as the huge papier mâché masks of Wonder and the feral Skinwalker.

The clever gestures of native heart stories and hearsay on separatist reservations and the lively creation of hand puppet parleys were essential to perceive a native tease, irony, and mockery, but the menace of a skinwalker mask was obviously more spectacular and memorable in the existential colony of cultural anonymity.

Big Rant, Master Jean, Where Now Downwind, the teacher and maven of the unnamable, and Dazhim La Roque, the retired native truck driver, created the papier mâché masks with thick paper paste and fashioned the masks on chicken wire skeletons. Big Rant sculpted the caricature of Wonder and the hairy menace of the Skinwalker, and Aloysius painted gentle creases on the brow of Wonder and hideous features on the predatory mask of the Skinwalker.

Noah Bear convinced the stowaways that lures of wonder were catchy and more persuasive than the irony and mockery of hand puppet parleys on reservations. "The tease of wonder is much easier to imagine than native envy and ridicule because wonder is not a native tease of resentment, wonder is more muse, speculation, curiosity, and surprise than hearsay, and liberal students at the university were more prepared for dramatic puppet parley masks of native wonder over the predators of victimry," declared Noah Bear.

"Masks of native existential wonder," shouted Hush.

"Masks of wonder and hearsay," said Big Rant.

"Masks of wonder are unnamable," said Where Now.

"Masks of wonder are traces of native memories and heart stories, and skinwalkers represent only the missions of misery, death, shame, and victimry," said Master Jean.

The Wonder mask and the Skinwalker mask were created for the first puppet parley staged that autumn in the atrium of Coffman Memorial Union at the University of Minnesota. The Faculty Club was considered, "but the university police would surely remove outsiders with masks of wonder and menace that were not members." Skinwalker, a menace in any cultural scene, was sculpted with huge clumps of black hair and blotched with gray paint, an absolute menace in a parley with the mask of Wonder.

Master Jean and Where Now carried the papier mâché masks of wonder and menace across the campus. A crowd of curious students followed the masks into Walter Library, and the masks surprised and scared graduate students in the stacks and carrels and then menaced students across Northrup Plaza to Coffman Memorial Union.

The Wonder mask was the actual voice of wonder, Noah Bear. The sinister sneers and moans of the Skinwalker mask were shouted by Hush Browne. Tedious Van Pelt created the lively gestures of the Wonder mask, and Where Now balanced the sudden moves of the Skinwalker mask as the evil face shivered with menace and other ominous gestures.

"Wonder is another name of chance," said Tedious.

"Skinwalker is an unnamable menace," said Where Now.

The mask parley generated a strange silence, an evocative sense of fear and absence with moans and gasps near the end when the mask of the Skinwalker leaned closer to the audience and snarled, "Ordinary people become witches and roam at night in the body of coyotes and other animals to carry out vengeance." The masks swayed, wobbled, and shivered with the words of the parley, and slowly the spectacular gestures created a sense of menace. Two students and an older woman fainted when the Skinwalker mask turned, cocked his head, and stared in their direction.

CLYDE: The principal reason that so little is known of Navaho witchcraft is the extreme reluctance of the Indians to discuss the matter.

NOAH: Anthropologists are academic skinwalkers.

CLYDE: The witches are naked save for masks and many beads and other articles of jewelry.

NOAH: Natives probably thought you traveled with witches.

CLYDE: On the other hand, if the informant relates anecdotes referring to the supposed witchcraft activities of others, he becomes liable to their hatred and revenge.

NOAH: Not so fast with the academic other hands, you created the catch of witchery, a strange account of skinwalkers as dead words on the page.

CLYDE: If these persons really are witches, and they learn that someone has gossiped about them, they are, it is believed, certain to witch the gossiper and get him out of the way.

NOAH: The witches listen to the daily studies, strange notions, and separatist theories, and become coyote anthropologists to menace natives with academic hearsay on reservations.

CLYDE: According to Navaho belief, there are a number of distinct methods of carrying out malevolent activity.

NOAH: The methods and malevolence of anthropologists.

CLYDE: The classic Witchery Way technique is that mentioned in the emergence legend. A preparation is made of the flesh of corpses.

NOAH: Witchery Way is the emergence of anthropology.

CLYDE: The flesh of children and especially of twin children is preferred, and the bones at the back of the head and skin whorls are the prized ingredients.

NOAH: No wonder you are an academic witch.

CLYDE: When this "corpse poison" is ground into powder it "looks like pollen." It may be dropped into a hogan from the smoke hole, placed in the nose or mouth of a sleeping victim or blown from furrowed sticks into the face of someone in a large crowd.

NOAH: The witchery of anthropology is a corpse poison.

CLYDE: Witches are associated with death and the dead. They are likewise closely associated with incest.

NOAH: The lost spirits of the dead and skinwalkers wait in the medicine bundles stored in that small room near the entrance of your house on Camino Rancheros in Santa Fe, New Mexico.

CLYDE: Almost all the female witches mentioned in actual anecdotes are old women, some informants insisted that only childless women could be witches.

NOAH: Kluckhohn is the crossover name of a skinwalker.

CLYDE: Persons become Witches in order to wreak vengeance, in order to gain wealth or simply to injure wantonly—most often motivated by envy.

NOAH: The wanton culture and hearsay of envy.

CLYDE: Witches are active primarily at night, roaming about at great speed in skins of wolf, coyote and other animals.

NOAH: Natives must wonder if you are the witch who drives his car slowly around on the reservation at night, a lonesome coyote ready to pick up hitchhikers and ask them about witchery.

CLYDE: Witches as were-animals meet at night to plan concerted action against victims, to initiate new members, to have intercourse with dead women, to practice cannibalism, to kill victims at a distance by ritualized practices.

NOAH: The witches and skinwalkers touched every spirit in your house, and the visitors who walked past that tiny room of coyotes and animal skins of death howl with envy and terror at night in the dreams of overnight visitors.

CLYDE: The gall of eagle, bear, mountain lion and skunk are the most frequently mentioned ingredients, but wolf, badger, deer and sheep are also referred to.

NOAH: Native wonder is abused by your wicked hearsay.

CLYDE: The Witches are naked save for masks and many beads and other articles of jewelry.

NOAH: Where do you hide your beads and jewelry?

CLYDE: If a witch confesses, the victim will at once begin slowly to improve, and the witch will die within the year from the same symptoms which have been afflicting the victim. If a witch refused to confess within four days, he was most often killed.

NOAH: Anthropology was never a course of confessions.

CLYDE: Apart from the effects of confession, a diffuse supernatural sanction against witches exists in the form of a belief that a witch who escapes human detection will nevertheless eventually be struck down by lightning.

NOAH: Wonder of lightning and the end of anthropology.

CLYDE: The chants are instrumental of great power which are intended for good. But an evil singer can turn the power of the chants to evil ends.

NOAH: The mockery of academic models is a greater power.

CLYDE: Witchery started out under the ground. First Man, First Woman and Coyotes—these three started it.

NOAH: Marvelous, you were taken for a ride by a hitchhiker.

Several more students were weakened by the Skinwalker in the puppet parley and rushed outside of the student union to escape the torment of the papier mâché mask and the quotations selected from the pages of *Navaho Witchcraft* by Clyde Kluckhohn, the distinguished anthropologist from Princeton University. Two senior university professors declared their disgust over the crude parley and representations of anthropology. The Skinwalker cocked his head and slowly moved closer to the professors and shivered in silence.

⑴⑴ 14 ⑴⑴

CHANCE OF MERCY

Poesy May Fairbanks, the mute puppeteer, and the other stowaways were inspired by the "I Have a Dream" speech delivered by Martin Luther King Jr. to a diverse audience of more than two hundred thousand at the Lincoln Memorial on the National Mall, August 28, 1963.

Poesy May obtained a complete transcript of the emotive speech almost five years ago, and with the dedication of the other stowaways created a shorter native version of the speech as two native dream songs.

Reverend King started his momentous speech on the steps near the stone monument of President Abraham Lincoln. Master Jean pictured the moment and read out loud sections from several paragraphs. "Five score years ago, a great American, in whose symbolic shadow we stand today, signed the Emancipation Proclamation. This momentous decree came as a great beacon light of hope to millions of Negro slaves who had been seared in the flames of withering injustice. It came as a joyous daybreak to end the long night of their captivity. But one hundred years later, the Negro still is not free. One hundred years later, the life of the Negro is still sadly crippled by the manacles of segregation and the chains of discrimination. One hundred years later, the Negro lives on a lonely island of poverty in the midst of a vast ocean of material prosperity . . .

"I have a dream that one day this nation will rise up and live out the true meaning of its creed: We hold these truths to be self-evident: That all men are created equal. I have a dream that one day on the red hills of Georgia the sons of former slaves and the sons of former slave owners will be able to sit down together at the table of brotherhood," recited Martin Luther King Jr.

"The grace of equal rights," said Big Rant.

"The grace of memory and justice," said Bad Boy.

"Slavers and memory games," said Master Jean.

The mute puppeteer and stowaways envisioned native scenes and created two dream songs of liberty.

"The elation of chance at every turn of history, and we considered the natural motion of dreams and ironic scenes that evade the first person pronouns and the grammatical objects of meaning," explained Poesy May. "Count the memorable visions of native dreams, relations and elusive reveries, moods of seasons, wonder, lures, delights, and the persistent nudge of customary scenes and images to stay with the heart stories of chance on this continent of greedy discoveries, occupation cravers, and the deadly curse of enslavement." The stowaways created two native dream song tributes to the great orator.

natural motion of dreams
chance of presence
chase the winter shamans
late creases of reservation time
emissaries of segregation
plucked with irony
natives of a continental presence

natural motion of dreams
gestures of conventions
chance of mercy and liberty
lost at museum games
camouflage of the forsaken
slavers chase the silhouettes
natives heart stories of survivance

Martin Luther King Jr. was assassinated by James Earl Ray in Memphis, Tennessee, in the early evening on April 4, 1968, almost five years after his memorable speech, "I Have a Dream," at the Lincoln Memorial. "MEMPHIS SNIPER KILLS DR. KING" was the huge banner headline in *The Minneapolis Tribune*.

Zenibaa collapsed in tears on the coach that cold and rainy spring morning, and the loyal mongrels nudged each other as they moaned and circled the mute puppeteer. Poesy May wept and whispered phrases from "I Have a Dream" and then rushed upstairs to be alone in the bedroom. The stowaways shouted out with rage as they read more closely the details of his death, shot in the face with a high caliber rifle as he leaned on the rail of the balcony outside the room of the Lorraine Motel.

Zenibaa mourned in a shamanic silence for several days, a desolation that she endured several times in the past, and more since the assassination of President John Kennedy, but at her side that spring, to console the mute puppeteer of extreme sorrow and seclusion, was a native complement of silence, Dazhim La Roque.

15

HEARSAY MAN

Zenibaa and the stowaways were invited to present puppet parleys at Den Norske Lutherske Mindekirke. The formal letter was delivered shortly after the Norwindian boys, Gunner Sandberg and Anders Bolstad, told church elders about the native customs of the Order of the Arrow and the parley they had attended at the Oshki Theatre of Chance. The elders were no doubt surprised to hear that Charles Alexander Eastman, the native medical doctor and author, was one of the dedicated founders of the Boy Scouts of America.

The mute puppeteer brushed aside the invitation from the elders of the Norwegian Lutheran Memorial Church for obvious reasons, the loyal mongrels were not included in the invitation, an ironic slight of native character. She considered the letter as nothing more than the churchy summons to account for the caricature of the Norse and Vinland in an ironic parley between Erik the Red and Cristóbal Colón. "Puppet parleys are moments of chance, bother, mockery, and good cheer, and never the mercy trade of churchy liturgy," she printed on a chalkboard. "Listen to the stowaways, they never weigh the mockery of hand puppets for anyone."

"Parleys are chance," said La Chance.

"Parleys are ironic diversions" said Master Jean.

"Parleys are parodies," said Bad Boy.

"Parleys are spirit shadows," said Atomic 16.

"Parleys are swerves of presence," said Poesy May.

"Parleys are native liberty," said Big Rant.

"Parleys are the tease of good cheer," shouted Hush.

The church elders reached out once more to mitigate any concerns, misconceptions, or native resistance with a handwritten note that plainly invited the mute puppeteer and stowaways of the "Oshki Theatre of Chance to present an original puppet parley, but not necessarily with explanations or interpretations, however learned or enlightened."

"Truly, learned and enlightened," shouted Big Rant.

"Norwindian unintended irony," said Master Jean.

"Parleys and opera music at night," said La Chance.

"Churchy concerns over native spirits," said Poesy May.

"Native witches in the parleys," said Tedious.

"Mongrels cast aside in monotheism," said Bad Boy.

"Monotheism has no heart stories," shouted Hush.

Zenibaa slowly printed on the chalkboard a diversion in response to the church elders, and later the counter invitation was written on a plain post-card by Poesy May. "The stowaways and puppeteers invite church members and other good neighbors to a puppet parley of native mockery at the Waite House on Park Avenue."

The Mide Spirit, an ironic puppet parley, was created with two cloth hand puppets that counter, tease, taunt, and mock the obscure enticements, mysteries, consent, and enterprise of secret herbs and the inscrutable cures. The exact date was decided later for an early evening puppet parley about native healers.

The huge papier mâché masks were scary and cumbersome, and the ironic puppet parleys of good cheer were overcome with the menace of a skinwalker. The stowaways agreed that much larger hand puppets with distinctive clothes, facial features, and character were catchy and more reputable in a parley about the Mide Spirit.

The Midewiwin, or Grand Medicine Society, nominated native healers who created quaint tributes to the Way of the Heart, or the Path of Life, an abstract serpentine image that represented the seven tangents, or depictions of the temptations, native manner, and experience. The first tangent represented the desires and fancy of youth, and the last tangent represented the wisdom of old age. The outcome of the seven tangents of temptations was related to the course, not the chance, of native maturity.

The Mide Spirit puppet parley countered and mocked the obscure practices of healers, and the age related temptations with creative and ironic versions of seven existential enticements and evasions, such as chance over secrecy, courage over salvation, recognition over predatory traditions, native presence over absence, stray shadows over specters, mockery and irony over cultural deception, and the ethos of survivance over victimry and the dominion of herbal healers.

The Way of the Heart meditation, curative songs, spirit, and the seven

THEATRE OF CHANCE

temptations were much easier to perceive as chance, courage, recognition, a sense of presence, shadows, and native ethos than the obscure cures of predatory traditions. The lively puppet parleys of mockery and ironic revelations healed some patrons and spectators with crucial unease, counters of nostalgia, double entendre hearsay, and the great swerves of native chance, curiosity, artistry, good cheer, and the praise of liberty.

Tedious Van Pelt and Hush Browne carried out the original parley mockery of existential temptations with two large hand puppets about the stature of spaniel mongrels. Michel Handy Maiingan, the eager grandson of a native healer and singer of the Midewiwin, Jacques Dazhim La Roque, the retired trucker, and By Now Rose Beaulieu created the spirited satire and parleys of ironic temptations and evasions. Aloysius painted distinctive faces, and the stowaways fashioned the two grand and sturdy hand puppets with bright cloth remnants, ribbons, scraps of leather, and showy buttons from the Salvation Army.

Chance, the young and bright native woman hand puppet, was portrayed as eager, concise, and confident. Ethos, the old man hand puppet, was hunched over with stringy gray hair, and he wore the uniform of a decorated war veteran. Chance wore a green scarf, and her short hair was touched with red. Ethos was portrayed with heavy jowls, curves of facial wrinkles, and the old trustworthy puppet wore thin wire framed spectacles.

Archie Goldman, the director of Waite House, introduced Zenibaa, Aloysius Hudon Beaulieu, Basile Hudon Beaulieu, By Now Rose Beaulieu, Prometheus Postma, Corporal Samuel Hutson or Atomic 16, Noah Bear, Jacques Dazhim La Roque, Doctor Samuel Wilde, Hush Browne, Tedious Van Pelt, Michel Handy Maiingan, Where Now Downwind, and the five clever stowaways, Master Jean Bonga, Big Rant Beaulieu, Bad Boy Aristotle, Poesy May Fairbanks, Truman La Chance, and the seven loyal mongrels of the Oshki Theatre of Chance.

Handy Maiingan was given the workaday nickname by a witless social worker, in one early version of post office hearsay, because he was handed over as an orphan to seven foster homes in five years and, in other canards, he was teased as ready, near at hand, and eagerly awaited every day to become a handyman for loggers, federal survey teams, and the bootleggers that traveled though the reservation in the last year of the notorious Eighteenth Amendment on Prohibition.

Handy was rightly named and learned some healing songs from his grandfather, but the secrecy and solitude of the healers became disparate, other worldly, and distant from the ordinary sentiments on a separatist reservation in the ruins of the Way of the Heart. He was distracted by the poseurs of tradition and pretense of rank and lost a native sense of presence, irony, and survivance. Older natives endured with heart stories and situational humor, but every day he was tormented by disguises in a state of separatism and severe hunger. Handy decided to move with hundreds of other malnourished natives from the reservation to the existential colony at the end of the Great Depression.

Handy remembered some of the songs and stories of the Way of the Heart and easily converted the simplistic notions of native temptations, dissociation, and worn out traditions on the reservation to ironic scenes that revived the sense of chance and liberty.

Where Now Downwind, the clever author, was born in the back seat of a station wagon on the White Earth Reservation. The teenage parents were never revealed, and the unnamed child was rescued by native strangers at a resort near Bad Medicine Lake. Where Now, an ironic nickname, was derived from the mystery and absence of parents and later certified on a birth certificate and school documents.

Where Now was a second year student at a state university when a literature professor pointed out that the words of her given name were the first two words of a singular query in *The Unnamable*, a novel by Samuel Beckett. Where Now continues to be teased with the literary queries of the first six words of the novel, "Where now? Who now? When now?" Nine years later the outcome of tricky teases and literary queries became an outstanding doctoral dissertation, "The Stray First Person Trickster Diversions in *The Unnamable* by Samuel Beckett."

Jacques Dazhim La Roque was captivated by the native spirit, lively manner, and shamanic silence of the mute puppeteer. Zenibaa was not surprised that the retired trucker was given the contrary nickname Dazhim, the word for hearsay in the language of the Anishinaabe. The nickname was ironic because he was the opposite, discreet, considerate, and hesitant at times to comment on manners or moods, and he hardly ever recounted hearsay.

Zenibaa, the mute puppeteer, and Dazhim, a retired trucker, created a generous silence and marvelous sense of presence, and they sat close together on the porch every night that summer with the loyal mongrels at their side and listened to opera music.

Zenibaa bowed to the audience and then raised Chance, the shameless young hand puppet, on her right hand, and Ethos, the bent over elder and war veteran puppet, on her left hand and waved the blunt cloth hands of the two puppets at the start of the parley. The Waite House became an ironic theatre of chance and ethos with an audience of more than fifty people.

Hush Browne was the resolute, assertive, and cheeky voice of Chance, and Tedious Van Pelt was the solicitous, courteous, and hesitant voice of the mature native veteran, Ethos. Chance turned and bowed to each of the puppet narrators of the parley and to three church elders who were seated in the last row. Ethos saluted the puppeteer in a military manner and then turned toward the audience and in a steady baritone voice announced the start of stories about native temptations and survivance of the Mide Spirit.

> ETHOS: The Way of the Heart is a necessary native story.
> CHANCE: Maturity is only time, not a course of wisdom.
> ETHOS: The secrets of the healers undermine the cures.
> CHANCE: Chance is a better healer than secretive men.
> ETHOS: Truehearted healers were not secretive or solitary.
> CHANCE: The Way of the Heart died with their secrets.
> ETHOS: Chance is a scene, not a memorable native story.
> CHANCE: My heart stories are chance creations.
> ETHOS: Chance is only a moment of native fortuity.
> CHANCE: Stories of chance healed me and the world.
> ETHOS: Native secrets incite the poseurs and predators.
> CHANCE: My chance started with native conception.
> ETHOS: Heart stories are spirits, not tricks of conception.
> CHANCE: Trickster stories created natives by chance.
> ETHOS: The native wit of presence is not a trick of chance.
> CHANCE: Churchy destiny buried chance on reservations.
> ETHOS: Churchy shame and pity were never native stories.
> CHANCE: Puppets create new trickster stories of chance.

ETHOS: Parleys are ironic stories of chance and liberty.

CHANCE: Temptations and maturity are always chancy.

ETHOS: Chance and fancy are necessary lures of maturity.

Chance and Ethos raised their arms and shouted out brava, brava, brava in silence to honor the puppet parley of the mute puppeteer. The stowaways shouted another round of bravas in silence. George Eliot, the greyhound retriever, leaned toward the audience and presented a glorious soprano bay. Trophy Bay raised his head and with a melodious baritone moan created a catchy harmony.

Big Rant announced that the stowaways and anyone in the audience should shout out and become part of the puppet parley. Tallulah, Trophy Bay, and Hail Mary moaned, bayed, and barked in harmony. The two hand puppets pointed at each other, turned their heads from side to the side, and then nodded with favor to the mongrels and narrators, Tedious and Hush.

"Shout out loud the seven counter temptations of the heart, chance, courage, recognition, native presence, shadows, mockery, and the ethos of native survivance," shouted Hush.

"Chance is more than a promise," shouted Big Rant.

"Chance is my name," said La Chance.

"Ethos is our native survivance," said Poesy May.

"Chance is my tease of presence," shouted Bad Boy.

"Chance is my only tradition," said Atomic 16.

"Ethos is an existential dream song," shouted Hush.

"Chance is a slight hesitation," said Dazhim.

"Chance is my literary name," said Where Now.

CHANCE: Puppet parleys are the chance of liberty.

ETHOS: Silence is the tease of chance and native resistance.

HUSH: Shout out native resistance and scare the poseurs.

CHANCE: Predators of tradition wither away with chance.

ETHOS: Natural motion is our chance and courage.

HANDY: Name me a bear in the stories of native liberty.

CHANCE: Stray natives waited for the chance of hearsay.

ETHOS: Postcard Mary created the hearsay of liberty.

WHERE NOW: Nicknames are the favors of hearsay.

ETHOS: Poseurs create the hearsay of envy.

CHANCE: Native recognition is a chance of heart stories.

ETHOS: Chance is the enemy of poseurs.

NOAH: Presence is the wonder of native sovereignty.

CHANCE: Chance is my native name for sovereignty.

ETHOS: Resistance and recognition are native favors.

ARCHIE: Good cheer and mercy create a presence.

CHANCE: The shadows hear my name at night.

ETHOS: Shadows are the past and presence.

WHERE NOW: Shadows last in literary queries of now.

WILDE: The silence of meditation is a shamanic shadow.

WHERE NOW: Shadows go on no matter the now.

CHANCE: Mockery creates stories of native liberty.

ETHOS: Mock the poseurs with ironic parleys.

DAZHIM: Mock traditions and hear the silence.

CHANCE: Mockery is the way of heart stories.

ETHOS: Mock forever the separatism on reservations.

DAZHIM: Mockery bares the deceit of nasty hearsay.

CHANCE: Mockery is the elusive shadow of presence.

ETHOS: Mockery is the native heartbeat of liberty.

HANDY: Only mockery outlasts wonder and hearsay.

CHANCE: Clocks are the mockery of native time.

ETHOS: Mock the hearsay of enticements and maturity.

DAZHIM: Mockery is the source of counter nicknames.

WHERE NOW: Mock the unnamable queries of now.

CHANCE: Mockery is chance not a culture or season.

WHERE NOW: Monotheism is an unintended irony.

ETHOS: Chance and irony are native seasons.

CHANCE: Chance and heart stories outwit mockery.

ETHOS: The dance of cranes is a totemic heart story.

CHANCE: Chance is forever my heart story of liberty.

DAZHIM: Survivance stories are created in silence.

WILDE: Shamanic silence is a meditation of eternity.

CHANCE: Chance is the catch of silence and stories.

ETHOS: Midnight moths chance the light as my day.

WHERE NOW: The unnamable chance must go on.

ETHOS: Shamanic silence is our story and must go on.

Dingleberry danced in a circle and the other mongrels moaned, bayed, and barked in harmony at the end of the parley. The applause for the hand puppets and the mongrels lasted for several minutes. Chance was shied by the favor, cocked her head, bowed several times, and then stared at a few faces in the crowd. The dark, emotive eyes of the puppet were two shiny buttons, and yet some people in the audience were moved by the spirit and gestures of the puppet. Ethos slowly raised one hand and declared, "The last of the seven tangents of temptation were mocked in the light that was not our day."

Zenibaa smiled and the two puppets raised their arms and waved. The mute puppeteer seldom related to the audience at the end of a parley, but the mood of silence and social distance had changed since the troupe moved from a separatist reservation to the existential colony. Doctor Wilde and Dazhim La Roque were plainly the reasons she revived the favor of dream songs about totemic unions and waves of shamanic silence.

> *seasons of migration*
> *great dance of sandhill cranes*
> *enchant the doctors and truckers*
> *existential shamans of silence*
> *bravas of liberty*

Zenibaa blushed and the mongrels bayed when the trucker first arrived at the chancy theatre and participated in the puppet parleys. Silence seemed much easier and more creative in the existential colony as she revealed with teases and a sense of devotion, a distinctive sentiment with smiles and short notes on the chalkboard. For instance, late one night she declared in a printed message on a chalkboard, and with an obvious sense of irony and presence, "Dazhim La Roque is my Hearsay Man."

The Hearsay Man, who was consistent and demure, smiled over the slight pleasures and ironic situations and then reached out for the mongrels as a necessary distraction and subtle gesture of his affection for the mute puppeteer. The devoted manners and motions of the hearsay trucker over the glances, sways, and silent smiles of the mute puppeteer were easily perceived as devotion by the loyal mongrels and stowaways.

16

TUTELARY GRACE

Zenibaa, Hearsay Man, By Now, and Doctor Wilde led the troupe of puppeteers, the Norwindian boys, and a few church elders back to the Oshki Theatre of Chance after the puppet parley of Ethos and Chance at the Waite House. Red Wing beer and hefty finger foods were served on the front porch. Big Rant, Bad Boy, Master Jean, La Chance, and Poesy May conducted the entire troupe in three silent rounds of brava, brava, brava for the mute puppeteer that balmy night.

Doctor Wilde wound the Silvertone hand crank record player and dusted the record with a special cloth, a precise motion that was imitated later as a tease by the mute puppeteer and stowaways. The medical maestro raised his hands and conducted scenes from acts one and four of *La Juive*, a grand opera by Fromental Halévy. The French opera composer was born Elias Levy in Paris in 1799. He studied at the Conservatoire de Paris, and composed *La Juive*, The Jewess, in 1835, and since then the opera has been performed in repertoires for more than a century.

The Chorus of *La Juive* chanted a hymn of eternal exaltation, *Te deum laudámus, te Dominum confitémur, Te aetérnum Patrem omnis terra venerátur*. Doctor Wilde translated the hymn, "God, we praise you, we acknowledge you to be the Lord, all the earth worships you, the Father everlasting."

"God never perched on this porch," shouted Big Rant.

"Churchy exaltations turn existential," shouted Hush.

"Only chance and irony are everlasting," said La Chance.

"God holds court across the street," said Tedious.

"The mongrels hold back barks," said Master Jean.

The first scene of the opera was staged near the square and the active workshop of a goldsmith more than five centuries ago in La Ville de Constance. Eleazar, a Jewish goldsmith, lived with his daughter Rachel, a child rescued as an infant from a mob and house fire. Eleazar was working as usual on a Christian festival day, and that was declared a desecration by the magistrate, Ruggiero, who sang, *Eh mais, grand Dieu, qu'entends je, et d'ou provient ce bruit étranger? Quelle main sacrilège en ce jour de repos ose ainsi s'occuper de profanes travaux?* Doctor Wilde translated, "And now, great heavens, what strange noise is here? What cause or place, what profane hand, boldly dares to work?" The chorus incanted the betrayal, "A heretic, a wealthy jeweler, the Jew named Eleazar." Ruggiero, performed by the Austrian baritone Robert Leonhardt, continued in an operatic voice, "Then bring him hither, for such a crime needs chastisement."

"Profane hand and obscene gestures," said Bad Boy.

"Must be a reservation opera," shouted Big Rant.

"Eleazar could be a native," shouted Hush.

"Rachel survived the savage cavalry," said Poesy May.

"Jews, natives, slaves, the heretics," said Master Jean.

"Ruggiero is the fascist federal agent," said Tedious.

Doctor Wilde revealed that Enrico Caruso, the great Italian operatic tenor, played the character of Eleazar, and Rosa Ponselle was the soprano opera voice of Rachel in the Metropolitan Opera House production of *La Juive* on November 30, 1920. That same year Victrola, Victor Talking Machine, released a single of "*La Juive*, Rachel! Quand du Seigneur la grâce tutélaire," an aria by Enrico Caruso. The maestro of the recorded aria provided a translation with a slight tease of irony, "The Jewess, Rachel, the grace of the Lord entrusts you to me with a tutelary grace."

Doctor Wilde conducted the grand operatic aria of Eleazar by the tenor Enrico Caruso on the porch that night of the Oshki Theatre of Chance. *Rachel, quand du Seigneur la grâce tutélaire, à mes tremblantes mains, confia ton berceau, j'avais à ton bonheur voué ma vie entière.* "When the tutelary grace of the Lord entrusted your cradle to my trembling hands, I had devoted my whole life to your happiness."

Et c'est moi qui te livre au bourreau, mais j'entends une voix qui me crie, sauvez-moi de la mort qui m'attend, je suis jeune et je tiens à la vie, ô mon père, ô mon père, épargnez votre enfant, Rachel, quand du Seigneur la grâce tutélaire. "And it is I who delivered you to the executioner, but I hear a voice crying out to me, 'Save me from the death that awaits me, I am young, and I want to live.' Oh, my father, spare your child, Rachel, when from the Lord your tutelary grace."

Trophy Bay cocked his head and delivered a perfectly timed baritone bay, and the other mongrels moaned, bayed, and with muted barks created the harmony of a chorus, a loyal mongrel consonance that liberated native irony from the great tenor aria of operatic victimry. Tallulah continued with a contralto bay, and Hail Mary bounced and barked to the clouds with a courtly mongrel melody. Big Foot, the haughty black cat, purred loudly, flicked her tail at every bay and bark, and then meandered around the mongrels on the porch that night.

George Eliot moved closer to the hand crank phonograph and roused the puppeteers and visitors with her spirited soprano bays. The stowaways raised their hands and shouted brava, brava, brava, and the mute puppeteer smiled and then simulated in silence the sensuous gestures of a soprano diva. The maestro of the recorded opera pitched his head back and burst into wild laughter.

Doctor Wilde grasped the ironic moment, the grand mongrel opera, the bravas, and gestures, and hurriedly changed the recording of Enrico Caruso to "Il va venir," an aria by Rosa Ponselle, the coloratura soprano. "He will come," the aria by Rachel, was recorded during the same opera season as the dramatic production of the opera *La Juive* at the Metropolitan Opera House.

Doctor Wilde translated the libretto at the end of the Rachel aria by Rosa Ponselle. Zenibaa was ready for the grand soprano diva that night and wrote on a chalkboard, "Rosa Ponselle was not included in the Metropolitan Opera radio broadcasts every Saturday at the Leecy Hotel on the White Earth Reservation."

The Columbia Historical Series record of the aria was released four years after the opera was performed at the Metropolitan Opera House. The recorded aria was rare, an operatic treasure, and was presented to the mute puppeteer, and the entire operatic presentation that night on the porch was staged to honor Zenibaa.

Il va venir, et d'effroi je me sens frémir. Mon âme, hélas, est oppressée. Mon coeur bat, mais non de plaisir . . . Et cepedant, il va venir. "He will come, and with terror I feel myself shudder. My soul, alas, is oppressed. My heart beats, but not with pleasure. And yet, he will come."

La nuit et le silence, l'orage qui s'avance augmentent ma terreur. L'effroi, la défiance s'emparent de mon coeur. "The night and the silence, the advancing storm increase my terror. Fear, mistrust take hold of my heart."

Zenibaa never considered an electric record player, and certainly not as a gift or sympathetic gesture. The slow second rounds of arias on a hand crank player were necessary to rouse the loyal mongrels to imitate the slow moans of the great divas, an ironic and uncanny chorus as the mute puppeteer entered a shamanic silence. The steady sound of an electric record player would obstruct the crucial slow moans of great divas and the natural motion of shamanic meditation.

Lily Pons, the coloratura soprano, was the grand opera diva of meditation that night with the aria "The Bell Song," or "L'air des clochettes," from *Lakmé*, a three act opera by the composer Léo Delibes. The composer was born in Saint-Germain-du-Val, France, in 1936. Delibes studied and taught at the Conservatoire de Paris, and his opera *Lakmé* was first performed at the Opéra Comique in Paris in 1883. More than a thousand performances of the opera were conducted in repertoires over the following fifty years.

The French libretto was created by Edmond Gondinet and Philippe Gille. The opera takes place in a town square in India during the British Raj. Lakmé, the daughter of a Brahman priest, lures a trespasser, a soldier, who is revealed and wounded by Nilakantha. Lakmé cares for Gérald at a hideout in the forest. Odéon Records recorded "L'air des clochettes" by Lily Pons.

Où va la jeune Indoue, filles des Parias, quand la lune se joue, dans les grands mimosas? Elle court sur la mousse, et ne se souvient pas, que partout on repousse, l'enfant des Parias, le long des lauriers roses, rêvant de douces choses, Ah! Elle passe sans bruit, et riant à la nuit.

"Where does the young Indian girl, daughter of the pariahs, go when the moon plays in the large mimosa trees? She runs on the moss and does not remember that she is rejected. The child of outcasts, along the oleanders, dreaming of sweet things, Ah! She passes without a sound and laughs at the night."

Là-bas dans la forêt plus sombre, quel est ce voyageur perdu? Autour de lui, des yeux brillent dans l'ombre, il marche encore au hasard, et perdu! Les fauves rugissent de joie, ils vont se jeter sur leur proie, la jeune fille accourt et brave leurs fureurs. Elle a dans sa main la baguette, où tinte la clochette des charmeurs. L'étranger la regarde, elle reste éblouie. Il est plus beau que les Rajahs!

"Down in the dark forest, who is this lost traveler? Around him, eyes shine in the shadows. He wanders aimless and lost. The wild beasts roar with joy. They will pounce on their prey. The girl runs to him and braves their fury. She has the wand, and the tinkle of the little bells. The stranger looks at her and remains dazzled. He is more handsome than the Rajahs."

Dazhim La Roque sat very close to the mute puppeteer on the coach, and, as the record player slowed down, the mongrels heard him whisper a line of the aria, *Elle passe sans bruit, et riant à la nuit.* "She passes without a sound and laughs at the night."

The second round of the aria was slower and slower, and when the mute puppeteer entered that shamanic silence and meditation, the mongrels raised their heads and moaned softly. The Hearsay Man leaned closer, muted his clear tenor voice, and slowly crooned lines near the end of the aria, *Elle a dans sa main la baguette, où tinte la clochette des charmeurs.* "She had the wand, and the tinkle of the little bells."

Trophy Bay moved closer to the mute puppeteer, bumped her legs, and then delivered a slow baritone moan, and Tallulah continued with a contralto bay, slower, and slower. The other mongrels moaned and bayed in the same slow, wistful, and easy harmony that night at the Oshki Theatre of Chance.

Zenibaa heard the news report on radio the next morning that Robert Kennedy had been shot and died later at a hospital in Los Angeles. "Kennedy Remains Near Death From Bullet Wound in Brain," was the main headline of the *Minneapolis Tribune* on June 6, 1968. Most of the stories on the front page were about the assassination of the senator from Massachusetts. "Jordanian Identified as Suspect" was the second headline, and the article continued, "The man who shot Sen. Robert F. Kennedy was identified Wednesday as Sirhan Bashara Sirhan, 24, a Jordanian from Jerusalem who recently has been living in Pasadena."

Zenibaa sat in the giant wooden chair on the front porch the entire day. The loyal mongrels were at her side and nudged the mute puppeteer once again to stay. The scenes of deep despair, agony, and shamanic silence were similar to other episodes, and there were no easy responses to touch or sound in the last passage of strange consciousness when Martin Luther King Jr. was assassinated in Memphis, Tennessee, and about five years ago on the reservation after the radio reports of the assassination of President John F. Kennedy in Dallas, Texas.

Doctor Samuel Wilde was summoned that afternoon, and he listened to heartbeats, closely measured the vital signs of the mute puppeteer, and declared that once more she had entered an enigmatic state of shamanic silence. Big Rant speculated that the death of a person the mute puppeteer considered special, loved, or deeply respected might reach to the first absolute silence she entered in response to the death of her lover Nookaa more than seventy years ago in the Great Hinckley Fire.

"Nookaa is a shadow of eternal silence," said Poesy May.

Dazhim La Roque, By Now, and the stowaways were at her side that night. The loyal mongrels leaned against the legs of the mute puppeteer, and later Poesy May wound the hand crank record player and played the arias of Renata Tebaldi in the opera *La Bohème* by Giacomo Puccini.

17

CULTURAL CASUALTIES

Birchy Iron Moccasin, the moody poseur and convenient conservative, scorned native dream songs and heart stories and denounced puppet parleys as counterfeit, and at the same time she favored the freaky hearsay and sentiments of abuse, misery, and victimry as a source of native character.

Birchy was shunned on the reservation as a brazen poseur and emerged later at churchy events as a casualty of culture, a showy witness of native wounds, and posed from time to time as an ironic native celebrity of torment and misery in the existential colony.

She wore a leather vest with simulated Indian head nickel buttons, and the stowaways never hesitated to tease and mock the conceit and furor of the edgy poseur. The contradictions of native experience, the wily manner, posture, sway, sectarian certainties, and feigned maneuvers of sorrow, shame, and victimry, emerged with the paternal service of evangelism, bearing godly witness, and the reactionary censure of native socialism.

Birchy and Snivel were nicknames earned at a church camp where she practiced withers, snivels, and protests several times a day for more food that summer. Later, she eluded the dietary restrictions with pouts, shouts, and stealth in every season as an apostle of hunger and outright misery. She countered the ironic teases as a slender birch by creating nasty hearsay about the Oshki Theatre of Chance.

The ironic compound nickname lasted, and twenty years later she learned to bear the great bulk of her early snivels and buffet binges with a thrust of broad shoulders, heavy arms, stout thighs, and a throaty voice that elevated the contrived witness scenes of casualty and confidence only to become a stalwart lackey of the John Birch Society.

Birchy held back her usual cruise of cultural casualties and boasts of godly witness last week and concocted spiteful hearsay that Zenibaa, the mute puppeteer, Jacques Dazhim La Roque, a retired trucker, Doctor Samuel Wilde, the singular cardiologist, Noah Bear, the shaman of wonder, Where Now Downwind, the native author of unnamable literary maneuvers, and the five stowaways, Master Jean Bonga, Bad Boy Beaulieu, Truman La Chance, Poesy May Fairbanks, and Big Rant Beaulieu, were "seditious agents that manipulated ungodly puppet parleys only to broadcast the communist subversion and ridicule of capitalism, evangelism, and monotheism at the Waite Neighborhood House and Oshki Theatre of Chance."

"Birchy is on a cruise of resentments," shouted Big Rant.

"Birchy is a storier of distemper," said Tedious.

"Birchy is the trace of deceptions," said Poesy May.

"Birchy lost her heart as a witness," said Master Jean.

Birchy was on a reactionary cruise of native deception when she warned several hundred public school teachers at a convention last month that Brooke Medicine Eagle, Iron Eyes Cody, Grey Owl, Hyemeyohsts Storm, and hundreds of other poseurs and bogus shamans were more trustworthy natives than the puppeteer socialists at the Oshki Theatre of Chance.

"Birchy cruises with Cristóbal Colón," said Bad Boy.

"Birchy cruises with the poseurs," shouted Big Rant.

"Rouse the passive and conservative public school teachers to honor eminent native artists and authors, Sacagawea, Hole in the Day, William Apess, Sarah Winnemucca, Standing Bear, Chief Joseph, Crazy Horse, Geronimo, Sitting Bull, Cochise, Red Cloud, Pontiac, and Maria Martinez, George Morrison, Leslie Silko, Vine Deloria, Oscar Howe, Charles Alexander Eastman, D'Arcy McNickle, John Joseph Mathews, N. Scott Momaday, and hundreds of others in every classroom in the country," shouted Hush.

Brooke Medicine Eagle was a poseur of Dakota and Nez Perce ancestry. She was not a native citizen but originated a fancy presence as an author and agent of spirituality. Espera Oscar de Corti was a poseur who created the character Iron Eyes Cody and contrived a native presence in western movies. Grey Owl was born Archibald Stansfeld Belaney in Sussex, England, and became a persuasive pretend native, legacy trapper of the fur trade, and habitat activist in Canada. He was featured in several films and published five books, including *The Men of the Last Frontier* and *Pilgrims of the Wild*. Hyemeyohsts Storm was born Charles or Arthur Storm and posed as a native of several cultures, Dakota, Cheyenne, Crow, and was teased as a plastic shaman. His book *Seven Arrows* was a simulation of native traditions that was later published as fiction.

"Birchy shouted out the names of charlatans, pretenders, poseurs, and deceivers as a righteous union of natives only to convince the school teachers that the poseurs were persecuted for their achievements and celebrity, a common vindictive maneuver in the theatre of fascist politics," said Basile. "George Wallace wailed at a campaign event that his right to speak was denied, and the good liberals that were not present rushed to honor the constitutional rights of a racist and fascist."

"Academic liberals reach out to represent the rights of every citizen and for righteous reasons the absolute rights of fascists to shout down a constitutional democracy," shouted Hush.

"*Oshki* is a native word for abuse and perversion, and chance is the devil, not a theatre. Puppet parleys are not native traditions, and the puppet dummies are given the words of communist agents, so get ready in the classroom for more subversive parleys of native socialism," shouted Birchy.

"Birchy was spurned on a native cruise," said Bad Boy.

"Hearsay envy by a mingy poseur," said Master Jean.

"Birchy needs a huge panic hole," shouted Big Rant.

"Hearsay abuser of hand puppets," said La Chance.

"Birchy is the truant of a tragic poem," said Poesy May.

"Hearsay outlier, peevish and cocky, and grouses about being shunned on the reservation, and that amounts to nothing more than the tedious contentions of a native pretender," said Where Now.

Birchy mistrusted most men and favored only her father, Asa Randolph, a poseur and cocksure evangelical preacher, for his churchy stature and courage and honored the hesitations and privacy of her mother, Caitlin Nelson, who taught lonesome farm girls how to embroider and crochet. These two cultural poachers, the skinny father of godly dreads, shame, witness resolves, and consecration stories and the bulky daughter of buffet dinners, cultural separatism, communist conspiracies, and victimry, were never counted nor considered as native citizens of the White Earth Reservation.

Astrid Randolph delivered her son Asa in a cold shanty close to the railroad switchyard just outside the treaty boundary of the reservation on Armistice Day of the First World War, November 11, 1918. Asa was pale, weak, and withered at birth and barely survived that first winter, and he has associated forever the harsh sound of trains, the click, clack, high hiss of steam engines, whistles, steady squeaks, and the heavy metal clunk of coupled cars with a drafty and unheated shanty, severe shivers, and grave hunger that called for extreme measures to outlive the sense of exclusion and contrition of a single mother and her tuckaway son.

Astrid was sixteen years old that late autumn, the outcast daughter of an immigrant farmer family, and she lived alone with a newborn son, or, in the cast of hearsay at the time, two outcast children were banished at a railroad switchyard on the border of the reservation.

Asa heard the stories many years later that his father was a casualty of the war, and yet his mother never revealed the name of the man she loved at least for one night. Astrid easily poached a memorable native surname to formally register her son as Asa Randolph Iron Moccasin so he could attend school on the White Earth Reservation.

Birchy Iron Moccasin was born on a treaty reservation, the second casualty of poseurs with a poached name, and the hearsay that her relations were migrant farmers, not natives, encouraged the ironic stories about the stolen surname, Iron Moccasin. The everyday hearsay and teases continued in the absence of a native bloodline, and then the stories decreased when the entire family with only a souvenir surname moved to a cold red brick derelict apartment near Hennepin General Hospital on Chicago Avenue in downtown Minneapolis.

"The sentiments of poseurs are dopey tropes, nothing much to respect, and the brazen maneuvers of poseurs are never dream songs or the heart stories of native survivance," said Master Jean. "Birchy could easily convert the colonial slavery of the fur trade into a conceited homily of churchy rapture and devotion."

Birchy arrived with craves for food and notice at a church camp and could never evade a signature nickname. Ten years later she craved the sensations of nicotine and almost earned a new nickname for loose tobacco, Bully Durham. The constant craves for nicotine and recognition continued as casual gestures and became more obvious when she slowly rolled a cigarette by hand with Bull Durham smoking tobacco.

The Band Box Diner near Elliot Park and Chicago Avenue was a common place to tease the old men with cheap burgers and the fragrant smoke of a cocky woman perched on a black stool at the red counter. One man with a crooked neck slowly raised a stained finger to ponder the unsteady turns of native traditions in the existential colony and then related combat scenes as a native scout in the Second World War.

"The old men bear the wounds of war and native traditions and search for heart stories and mercy, and the heavy shadows of unforgiven scenes and memories became the disguised gestures of petulance, rage, and remorse but never shame," said Basile.

"Birchy cruises in customary native places in the existential colony with an arrogant mission to ease her craves and celebrate the most notable native poseurs, and for that she teases and bothers the old men of tricky reveries," said Poesy May.

"Birchy is more at ease in the presence of Bat Tremain, a blunt, fleshy, sweaty soulmate with a heavy beard and steady boasts, doubts, and obsessions for recognition as a native and college student. They first met at the Minneapolis Community College and a year later became interns at the Bureau of Indian Affairs," said Where Now.

"Christopher Columbus misread the compass and sailed in the wrong direction and captured the wrong natives, and since then the Bureau of Indian Affairs continues to invent and then employ the native poseurs as interns to document services and resources on federal reservations," shouted Big Rant.

18

HOEDOWN ACTIVISTS

George Wallace, the haughty presidential candidate and former governor of Alabama, scheduled a major campaign speech at the Minneapolis Auditorium on Grant Street. More than four thousand people gathered to cheer the signature rants of racial exclusion, the southern scorn of liberal politics, and the curse of civil rights by the candidate on July 3, 1968. Once elected governor as a Southern Democrat he became a turncoat politician and then founded the American Independent Party only to challenge the Democrat Vice President, Hubert Humphrey, and the Republican candidate, Richard Nixon.

Birchy and Bat Tremain boasted about destiny, or at least fate, but never chance, that they were seated near the front of the auditorium next to Leo Landsberger, the prairie conservative candidate for governor of North Dakota. Birchy revealed later at an education conference that "Landsberger leaned closer, touched my arm, gestured with a hesitant smile, and said he wanted to smoke a cigarette with me, and that was a moment of great honor because he was a steadfast member of the John Birch Society."

A country music band enlivened the conservative audience with "Happy Days Are Here Again." Bat was excited and leaped out of the seat, distracted from his ordinary torments of identity, and from memory and in a spirited tenor voice, he was heard in the entire auditorium. He sang, "The skies above are clear again, let us sing a song of cheer again, happy days are here again, altogether shout it now, there's no one who can doubt it now, happy days are here again . . ."

"Bat was moved by music and envy," said Big Rant.

"Birchy lost her voice to envy," said Bad Boy.

"Bat was in the clouds that night," said Poesy May.

"Birchy has dreamed every night since the convention about sharing cigarettes with the prairie conservative Leo Landsberger," shouted Hush. "Not much chance a liberal doctor could ever talk her out of smoking."

Most of the elders in the audience were aware that "Happy Days Are

Here Again," with music created by Milton Ager and lyrics by Jack Yellin, was a presidential campaign song and political anthem of Franklin Delano Roosevelt in 1932.

Basile, By Now, Prometheus, Hush, Tedious, Where Now, and the stowaways were observers at the back of the auditorium and ready to document, photograph, and relate stories about George Wallace, the reactionary and segregationist candidate for president who defied the federal desegregation of schools and opposed the Civil Rights Act of 1964.

More than thirty spirited activists entered the auditorium and cavorted down the center aisle and then started to square dance. Most of the dancers were descendants of slaves, and the dance clothes were bright, coarse, and ironic for the demonstration. The allemandes, circles, do-si-dos, promenades, and honors were heartfelt movements of freedom in the segregated political haunt of the demonic racialist from Alabama.

The Minneapolis police were armed for combat and waited backstage and, with the malicious private security agents of the presidential candidate, assaulted the square dancers of good cheer with chemical sprays and truncheons and forced the ironic hoedown activists out of the auditorium. They then promptly arrested the dedicated civil rights organizers, Matthew Eubanks and John Cann.

"Police riot, riot, riot," shouted Hush.

"Police deceit and no surprise," said Master Jean.

"Eubanks should have been honored," said Big Rant.

"Negro and white protesters scuffled with security men for George C. Wallace, and others in the hall, Wednesday night, delaying the presidential candidate's Minneapolis speech one hour and thirty-five minutes," wrote Bernie Shellum, the stodgy and blunt political reporter for the *Minneapolis Tribune*. The front page story continued, "A Negro jumped to the platform and attempted to address the audience . . . Another Negro became involved in a tug-of-war with a security man who fell from the platform."

Shellum must have been obsessed, maybe haunted, with the word *Negro* and focused more on the delay and time lost that night than on the ironic square dance, and he never mentioned the maneuvers and brutal assault of the police force and security agents that lurked in the wings of the stage and surprised the audience.

The dancers were removed, and there were no reasons that George

Wallace could not have delivered his entire reactionary speech that night. Instead, he mounted the stage and declared, "These are the folks that America is sick and tired of." Later, at a hotel press conference he asserted, "I can assure you that if I'm elected president, I'll show you how to keep law and order."

"Politicians are coached to be elusive, a necessary practice of most elections, even in the course of obvious facts and recorded situations, and only to preserve the perfect moment to enhance their standing as astute and reasonable," said Basile.

"George Wallace was devious and manipulated the entire scene at the auditorium, of course, and once more he outwitted the liberals and then waited for apologies from the Democrats," said By Now.

The *Minneapolis Star* reported a day later, July 4, 1968, that "Minneapolis Mayor Arthur Naftalin apologized publicly today to George Wallace for the actions of demonstrators who heckled the former Alabama governor as he tried to speak at a rally in the Minneapolis Auditorium." The mayor stated that he disagreed with the "political and social views" of the candidate, but he has the "right to speak and to be heard," and then referred to "this kind of mob action" that denied the freedom of speech. "I was dismayed and saddened by the behavior of those misguided persons who protested," and they "dishonored our city and our long record of respect for basic liberties."

"Never, the mayor was outwitted," said Prometheus.

"The dancers honored Minneapolis," shouted Hush.

"Mayor Naftalin would never declare that the protest was caused by the police, not by the square dancers, or that respect and basic human liberties would never describe the way police treated labor unions in the past, or how the police cover their names and badges and assault natives as a midnight game in the existential colony," said Basile.

The Minnesota Civil Liberties Union board of directors was eager to release an official statement that George Wallace was denied the right to speak. The only rights that were abridged that night were those of the square dancers and creative descendants of slaves in southern states.

Gerald Vizenor, a member of the Minnesota Civil Liberties Union board of directors and a staff writer for the *Minneapolis Tribune,* was at the entire event that night at the auditorium and captured more than thirty pictures of the police assault on the dancers. He was subpoenaed to present photographic evidence in court that the dancers were associated only with an easy and ironic square dance, not a violent protest that denied the rights of anyone and certainly not the presidential candidate of racial segregation.

"Americans of every viewpoint must be deeply concerned over the intolerance which prevented candidate George Wallace from speaking in Minneapolis last night," announced President Lyndon Johnson. "Freedom to speak, freedom to listen, the full and open right to communicate and reason together are essential to our system of government and our fulfillments as individuals."

"The tricky politics of civil rights protected the police riot and a presidential candidate who demonstrated that he was antisemitic and a segregationist, but hardly the allemandes and good cheer of a square dance," said Basile.

"Heart stories are reversed in politics," said Big Rant.

"Mayor of hearsay missed the dance," said Where Now.

"The descendants of slavery are once again denied the right to dance for liberty, to dance with courage and humor in the very hollows of political separatism and sanctimony," said Master Jean.

Birchy seldom considered the sentiments of others, and she was convinced that bold gestures, audacity, and Bull Durham tobacco were evidence of a confident woman, and yellow fingers and the scent of cigarette smoke were noticed by the quiet, crusty, severe sectarian, and rigid conservative candidate for governor of North Dakota.

Leo Landsberger was an independent candidate for the gubernatorial election in North Dakota at about the same time that Birchy and Bat Tremain became cheery sycophants of the John Birch Society. They never forgot the music and the moment of a cigarette destiny at the contentious rally of George Wallace and drove that autumn to North Dakota.

Landsberger declared that as the elected governor he would terminate socialism, eliminate the position of the state governor, decrease state services, end trade with communist countries, and withdraw from the United Nations. Hardly credible, and no surprise that he supported the presidential candidacy of George Wallace, the segregationist, populist, and antisemitic governor of Alabama.

"Leo Landsberger was so extreme as a conservative that he was shunned by the John Birch Society," said Basile. "Maybe he was the first person who was ever banished for austere notions about segregation and communists."

"John Birch Society of blunt dimwits," said By Now.

"The menace of fear and folly," said Master Jean.

Birchy and Bat Tremain agreed to meet with Landsberger at the railroad hotel in downtown Bismarck. The two ecstatic soulmates, toadies, and poseurs were noticed by a political candidate, a significant moment of recognition, and easily convinced that they had landed in a conservative paradise on the prairie.

The reactionary notions of political destiny were enhanced even more by the various images in huge mirrors on the walls of every booth in the restaurant, a constant perception of motion and fusions of reflections. Leo Landsberger, the most extreme conservative candidate, bounced in four separate mirrors, and his calculated maneuvers, gestures, and wary gaze were escalated as the images of a hand puppet. The soulmates were enchanted by his many representations in the mirrors and equally elated when the candidate leaned into the booth and handed them cigarettes from a new pack of Camels.

Gerald Vizenor reported in the *Minneapolis Tribune* that the cozy residential basement office of Leo Landsberger was lined with the bound volumes of conservative publications of every investigation of conspiracies by the government. He acquired over many years an inconceivable private library of elaborate and fantastic conspiracies, a monument of reactionary obsessions about the collective plots and cabals that would terminate free markets, monotheism, democracy, and liberty. The necessary consideration of corruption by elected officials, corporate greed, tax evasion, bigotry, antisemitism, and the abuses of labor and civil rights were not likely listed in notations or indexes of the published investigations of conspiracies.

There were four black telephones mounted on a metal desk, one private national line, one private state line, one residential line, and the last private telephone connection was with his wife upstairs in the living room, and no one called that late afternoon while the journalist was present. The silence of the telephones for several hours was an ironic notice that the candidate for governor had been utterly banished by the John Birch Society.

Basile read a section from *The Blue Book of the John Birch Society* that the purpose was to "promote less government, more responsibility, and a better world ... So far, with many thousands of members, and two years of experience, we have dropped less than a dozen," and we "refused to accept just one chapter since the Society was founded, and this was because of the extreme racist views of some of its prospective members." No one was named at the dedicatory presentation of the John Birch Society, but racial segregation was not acceptable, and that alone would exclude Leo Landsberger and George Wallace.

Robert Welch, the founder of the John Birch Society in 1958, was a social conservative and promoted the preposterous hearsay of communist conspiracies about the government and contended that President Dwight Eisenhower was a communist agent. The United States and "Soviet governments are controlled by the same furtive conspiratorial cabal of internationalists, greedy bankers, and corrupt politicians," wrote Welch in *The Blue Book of the John Birch Society.*

Landsberger was a chain smoker, and as he lighted another cigarette the journalist mocked the gestures of smoking and noted with irony, "Leo, you smoke too much." Leo closely examined the cigarette and then casually responded, "For all I know, this is communist tobacco."

Communists were everywhere, in local, state, and national agencies of the government, he told the journalist, and when "Joe McCarthy passed away there was nothing to stop a communist takeover. We are living in one vast insane asylum. The John Birch Society is a fighting power, but what good will the members be behind barbed wire."

William Lewis Guy, the popular incumbent and member of the Democratic Nonpartisan League, easily won reelection as the governor of North Dakota on November 5, 1968. Guy received more than fifty percent of the vote, the Republican candidate won about forty-three percent of the votes, and Leo Landsberger, the independent candidate received almost one and a half percent of the votes to terminate the elected governor, end communism, and cut short the United Nations.

Birchy Iron Moccasin and Bat Tremain were despondent and melancholy over the results of the election, and the small number of votes for the conservative convinced them to return to the existential colony and leave the sway of reactionary conspiracies in the John Birch Society.

The Bureau of Indian Affairs personnel manager delivered more bad news and distress when they returned from North Dakota. The Indian intern positions had been deleted from the annual budget, and the soulmates would be terminated at the end of the month. Bat was always ready to leave in silence, and he was immediately accepted as a native trainee in a new security systems training program.

Birchy was antagonistic, as usual, and shouted at the silent manager and cursed the agency as "organized crime on federal reservations." Her customary petulant manner came with a turnabout that was easily compared to the avowals as a casualty of culture and victimry, and later a celebration, of course, of native pluck and endurance. She was furious over the change of policy that natives who were once only served on or near federal reservations were now supported on the existential colony, and predictably she demanded every assistance course and program that was available at the Bureau of Indian Affairs.

19

MONGRELS OF MERIT

Zenibaa cocked an ear and listened to the hard swish of snow on the dry leaves that autumn morning and moved the great wooden chair from the front porch to the living room near the bay window of the Oshki Theatre of Chance.

The Norwindian boys waved on the way to church, and at the same time two bushy gray squirrels paused upside down on the trunk of a giant elm tree and reigned over the entire scene and sudden turn of seasons. The squirrels danced in the snow and then strutted across the porch of chance near the bay window, a calculated tease of the mongrels and Big Foot.

Big Foot, the stowaway black cat, posed, blinked, and then chattered at the bold squirrels, and the mongrels rushed closer to the bay window with muffled barks. Trophy Bay raised his nose, puffed his hairy jowls, and softly growled. Dingleberry slowly danced on her tiny feet down the wide cold bay window, and the other mongrels circled the couch, crouched, and pretended they were ready to chase the squirrels.

Zenibaa, the stowaways, and the mongrels would never have envisioned that cold autumn morning that the spotted black and white spirited terrier with a wild yodel and quirky dance moves would suddenly quiver, faintly sough, stagger back from the window closer to the other mongrels, and then tumble over dead.

Tallulah, the bold beagle mongrel, raised her head and mourned in a haunting contralto bay, and the other mongrels circled the tiny spotted body of the great dancer and created harmonic moans of favor and solace. The mongrels nosed the tiny body of the dancer one last time with a sense of reverence and remembrance.

Zenibaa was teary and warmed the cold paws of the dead dancer to stay, and the silence of sorrow and anguish continued as the other mongrels leaned closer to the mute puppeteer on the couch. Dingleberry was brushed and shrouded in a red flannel shirt, the burial honors for a loyal mongrel.

122   GERALD VIZENOR

The stowaways were doubly downcast because they could not participate in the burial of the devoted dancer in a grave house near Spirit Lake on the White Earth Reservation. They were employed, obligated to services, and could not easily leave for a mongrel funeral two hundred miles away, and they would never consider a burial in the existential colony.

Later that night the stowaways related heart stories about the great dancer, the tender moment when the tiny loyal mongrel nudged each of the five runaways, the crucial cue of the mongrels to stay as stowaways at the Theatre of Chance. The mongrels cocked their heads and created harmonic moans and bays of tribute and sorrow that merged with the generous stories of the stowaways and memories of nudges, mercy, and heartfelt gestures at the Oshki Theatre of Chance.

Dingleberry, the fancy dancer, rightly earned an ironic nickname and would be buried with that distinctive name in a grave house near the other loyal mongrels who once lived with the mute puppeteer. Poesy May created a dream song to honor the dancer that night and slowly whispered the lines out loud near the shrouded body of Dingleberry.

> *dingleberry dancer*
> *loyal mongrel of chance*
> *nudged the five stowaways*
> *celebrities to stay*
> *yodels of native liberty*
> *tiny feet and perfect harmony*
> *puppets honor your name*
> *dream song in the clouds*
> *teases of memory*

Jacques Dazhim La Roque escorted the mute puppeteer in silence early the next morning to the front seat of the old station wagon, and the shrouded body of the great dancer was secured in a cardboard banker box and carried to the back seat. Tallulah and Trophy Bay sat next to the box and cocked their heads as a tribute to the dinky dancer on the way to a signature grave house near Spirit Lake. Zenibaa left a note for the stowaways. "The loyal dinky dancer honored my silence, mocked the arias of the divas, and now she hears the bays and stories at the grave houses of the other loyal mongrels, Fidèle, Papa Pius, Queena, Makwa, Miinan, and Snatch."

THEATRE OF CHANCE

Harmony Baswewe prepared a room in her cabin near Bad Boy Lake for Zenibaa and Dazhim La Roque. The Dingleberry grave house was constructed overnight from gray weathered boards and placed over a shallow pit near the other mongrel grave houses at Spirit Lake.

Dazhim chanted three times the dream song created by Poesy May. Zenibaa circled the mongrel grave house, raised her hands, and gestured in silence, brava, brava, brava, several times to honor, tease, and celebrate the heart stories and memory of Dingleberry.

Postcard Mary created and presented a clever puppet parley of mongrel hearsay that night of fond reminiscence for the dinky dancer and other mongrels from the theatre of silence, chances, tricks, ironies, and the grave houses of rapture, mockery, and mongrel memories of liberty.

Harmony rescued two pairs of wooly and mottled mittens and fashioned caricatures of mongrel hand puppets and started the parley with the distinctive falsetto voices of three grave house mongrels and a pedigree outlier, a small, smart, cosseted terrier, for the strategic hearsay parley. Queena, the rangy basset hound and golden retriever mongrel, a great diva with heavy ears, a steady slaver, and melodic chirrs, moans and bays, was named in honor of the celebrated coloratura soprano of the Metropolitan Opera. Fala, an evocative nickname for Murray the Outlaw of Falahill, the Scottish Terrier and devoted companion of President Franklin Delano Roosevelt. Fidèle, the loyal mongrel of the coureurs des bois with a distinctive baritone accent of barks and bays, was deserted at the end of the greedy fur trade near French Portage Narrows. Dingleberry, the mongrel yodeler and dancer, was buried in a grave house near Queena and Fidèle with a view of Spirit Lake.

> FIDÈLE: Mongrels bay about chance and presence.
> DINGLEBERRY: Barks are the real tease of memory.
> FALA: Finally, scent over the words and stories.
> DINGLEBERRY: Last bay of memory at the grave house.
> QUEENA: Mongrels carry on with great operas of memory.
> FALA: Mongrels of merit, but not presidential companions.
> FIDÈLE: Coureurs des bois abused mongrels in the fur trade.
> DINGLEBERRY: Danced to death over gray squirrels.
> QUEENA: Celebrities of nothing in a grave house.

FIDÈLE: The honesty of memory, *l'honnêteté de la mémoire.*

QUEENA: Remember the mongrel arias and heart stories.

DINGLEBERRY: Shared memories of dance stories.

QUEENA: Mongrels are divas in the opera of memory.

FALA: Mongrel remembrance with no royal bloodlines.

DINGLEBERRY: Mongrel shamans in the spirit of puppet parleys.

QUEENA: Creation stories in mongrel arias and bays.

FIDÈLE: Memories are the heart stories of the portage.

QUEENA: Mongrel moans with no personal pronouns.

FIDÈLE: Memories of the coureurs des bois.

FALA: The White House was a paradise of memory.

DINGLEBERRY: Mongrels dance in the operas of memory.

FALA: Mongrel poses of pedigree bloodlines.

QUEENA: Nothing more to chase in the operas of memory.

FIDÈLE: Portage operas of remembrance.

DINGLEBERRY: No favors, no grooms, no reason to hide bones.

QUEENA: Heart stories are the operas of remembrance.

FALA: Cats prance forever in mongrel stories.

DINGLEBERRY: Memories of the last chase of squirrels.

QUEENA: Mongrel operas at the grave houses.

Zenibaa, Dazhim La Roque, and two mongrels, Trophy Bay and Tallulah, returned to the existential colony a few days later, and the stowaways were eager to present the puppet parley created by Postcard Mary. Decorated paper bags served as the faces of the four dead mongrels, and Master Jean was the voice of Fala, Bad Boy was the accented voice of Fidèle, Poesy May was the great diva voice of Queena, and Big Rant was the voice and slight yodels of Dingleberry. Big Foot waited as usual on the room divider and stared, purred, and licked her paws several times during the hearsay parley of the mongrels.

The stowaways told ironic stories later that night about the characters and ironic situations of their work and study. Big Rant earned a native scholarship to study psychology at the university and could not resist talking about the ideas of liberty and fascism that were discussed in *Escape from Freedom* by Erich Fromm.

"Fromm is a psychoanalyst, philosopher, and escaped from the fever of antisemitism, the horrors of fascism in Nazi German, and moved to Columbia University to write about the destruction of communities and the sense of creative survivance," shouted Big Rant. "Fromm described my own perceptions of chance and liberty, as he raised questions about the actual burdens of freedom, and that was easy to understand as native resistance to the obvious burdens of separatism on reservations and how we learned as stowaways to counter with mockery and break away from predatory traditions and the deceit of federal agents."

Big Rant continued with a critical question by Erich Fromm. "Can freedom become a burden, too heavy for man to bear, something he tries to escape from? Why then is it that freedom is for many a cherished goal and for others a threat?"

The stowaways agreed late that night that some natives, the greedy fur traders and pork barrel bully boys were ready with derisive hearsay to give away native liberty to tradition fascists and poseurs only for a pathetic promise of recognition at a powwow, or the unintended mockery of native celebrations on the Fourth of July.

Big Rant continued reading from *Escape from Freedom*, is "there not also, perhaps, besides an innate desire for freedom, an instinctive wish for submission? If there is not, how can we account for the attraction which submission to a leader has for many today? Is submission always to an overt authority, or is there also submission to internalized authorities, such as duty or conscience, to inner compulsions or to anonymous authorities like public opinion? Is there a hidden satisfaction in submitting, and what is its essence?"

Zenibaa printed on a chalkboard that "puppet parleys are the spirit of native chance, hesitations, and natural motion and never hearsay, consent, or submission to tyrants, and heart stories and ironic puppet parleys are native gestures of liberty."

No one that night needed to be reminded that the loyal mongrels nudged five native runaways to stay as stowaways at the Theatre of Chance, favored to stay only because the five truants, or fugitives, were hesitant, related to irony, and trusted the spirit of chance and resistance over destiny and victimry. The stowaways had been abandoned and endured abuse on

126   GERALD VIZENOR

the reservation and were rightly insecure, and yet they intuitively countered
deception and predatory traditions. The mute puppeteer coaxed the five
stowaways to choose resistance as a vision of survivance and with clever
irony and mockery to overturn the enticement of the snow ghosts and the
tricky lures of suicide.

"The poseurs of traditions, menaces of party politics, and fascist federal
agents seldom outlast the resistance, irony, and creative counters of mockery in puppet parleys," shouted Hush.

"Celebrations of chance and native puppet parleys subvert the lures,
submissions, and catchy sway of priests and poseurs, and resistance is always necessary on treaty reservations and the existential colony," said Big
Rant.

"Reservation fascists banish the contraries," said Bad Boy.

"Some poseurs are fascists and armed, some camouflaged hunters are
devious and demonic, and federal agents are wicked, and mockery might
provoke some crazed natives to vengeance," warned Master Jean.

The Theatre of Chance was a coincidence of native liberty at the end
of the fur trade, the fortuitous outcome of the death of a lover in a forest
fire, the shamanic silence of a puppeteer, and the native convenience of
mercy, mockery, puppet parleys, and loyal mongrels. The stowaways were
once vulnerable to abuse, crude teases, and hearsay vengeance, but they
endured and learned from the mute puppeteer that heart stories, dream
songs, resistance, mockery of puppet parleys, and the tricky course of native liberty counter the constant lures of submission to the poseurs, priests,
and predators of tradition.

Poesy May was employed four or five hours a day as a clerk at the bookstore in Coffman Memorial Union at the University of Minnesota. The
books were new, pristine and tightly bound, and most of the student readers were bright and new, and most of the literature on the shelves was new,
or the translations were new. The Modern Library published hundreds of
hardbound books that were similar in design, style, and octavo dimensions.
The new books were the same color, and the most obvious variations on
the shelves were the width of the books.

She could not easily relate to only new and similar volumes and browsed
for used books with a history of readers on the untidy and uneven shelves
at McCosh's Book Store, located behind Bridgeman's Ice Cream in Din-

kytown. Melvin McCosh, the perceptive, ironic, bony, and bearded owner, slouched in a heavy chair near the entrance and hardly noticed the customers that entered the narrow store.

"Maybe some of the authors were ready to be discovered by a native stowaway, and the books were not neatly shelved for display, so *Zorba the Greek* by Nikos Kazantzakis, *The True Believer* by Eric Hoffer, and *Haiku: Eastern Culture* by Reginald Horace Blyth were the first books that reached out from the shelves and found a place in my memory," said Poesy May.

She read several pages of *Zorba the Greek* standing near the narrow stairway in the basement of the bookstore and later recited a short selection of the novel. "A cool, damp wind was blowing, the kind that follows rainfall. Some fluffy clouds were passing quickly overhead, sweetening the earth with haze; other clouds were climbing excitedly up the sky, covering and uncovering the sun so that the earth's features were brightened and then darkened like those of a living face shrouded by heavy fog."

"Clouds in natural motion with the sweet haze of shadows on the earth are native dream songs," said Poesy May. "Zorba must be a distant native stowaway ready for the tease of readers, the nudge of mongrels, and sweet mockery at the Theatre of Chance."

Eric Hoffer, an immigrant, wanderer, migrant worker at times, and later a longshoreman in San Francisco, read books at public libraries and created a memorable assessment of mass movements. The used copy of *The True Believer* was badly worn and that made the book an even more fortunate discovery that afternoon for Poesy May.

She read a section from *The True Believer* to the stowaways and the mute puppeteer that night after dinner. "Those who see their lives as spoiled and wasted crave equality and fraternity more than they do freedom. If they clamor for freedom, it is but freedom to establish equality and uniformity. The passion for equality is partly a passion for anonymity: to be one thread of the many which make up a tunic, one thread not distinguishable from the others. No one can then point us out, measure us against others and expose our inferiority."

Big Rant shouted, "The bully boys on segregated federal reservations create malicious hearsay about the mute puppeteer and native irony and rage against puppet parleys and creative stowaways only to crave authority and waste the heart stories of liberty."

128   GERALD VIZENOR

Poesy May paged through the four used volumes of *Haiku* shelved with poetry. The first volume was *Eastern Culture,* and there were three more volumes for the seasons, *Spring, Summer Autumn,* and *Autumn Winter.* Basile had read about the nuclear ruins of Hiroshima and the surrender and military occupation of Japan and related some information about the author, who was born in England, moved as a young man to Japan, and created a literary perception of haiku poetry as a professor of English at Gakushuin University in Tokyo. The four volumes of *Haiku* were published between five and seven years after the surrender of the Empire of Japan.

"Blyth was detained as an enemy alien during the war and later initiated occupation strategies with Lieutenant Colonel Harold Gould Henderson and other senior officers who served General Douglas MacArthur, the Supreme Commander for the Allied Powers, the strategies of the transition from war to peace in Japan," related Basile. "Blyth and Henderson first met in Japan before the war, and, more than a decade earlier, Henderson had published *The Bamboo Broom: An Introduction to Japanese Haiku.*"

Blyth published *A History of Haiku* in two volumes, more than a decade after the publication of the four volumes of *Haiku.* Poesy May, at the time, could only afford to purchase the first volume of *Haiku: Eastern Culture, The True Believer,* and *Zorba the Greek.*

Poesy May was alone in the basement of the bookstore and whispered out loud a short paragraph and a poem from the first volume of *Haiku,* and later with the stowaways she read the same paragraph and easily compared haiku imagistic poetry to native dream songs. "Haiku is the result of the wish, the effort, not to speak, not to write poetry, not to obscure further the truth and suchness of a thing with words, with thoughts and feelings."

"Haiku is the silence of a shaman," shouted Big Rant.

Poesy May continued to read selections from *Haiku.* "A haiku is not a poem, it is not literature; it is a hand beckoning, a door half-opened, a mirror wiped clean. It is a way of returning to nature, to our moon nature, our cherry blossom nature, our falling leaf nature, in short, to our Buddha nature. It is a way in which the cold winter rain, the swallows of evening, even the very day in its hotness, and the length of the night becomes truly alive, share in our humanity, speak their own silent and expressive language."

"Blyth as a mirror wiped clean," said Big Rant.

"Blyth could have recounted native dream songs, the poetic gestures, natural motion, and presence of nature in the imagistic sensation of summer in the spring and visionary words carried away in the clouds," said Poesy May.

"Matsuo Bashō, the haiku poet, was born in the seventeenth century, created visionary scenes with pithy images, *the old pond, or ancient pond, a frog jumps or leaps in, the sound of water*, and similar scenes of natural motion were envisioned in native dream songs, *walking in the sky, a large bird, a companion*, and now dream songs of natural motion are created every day by the stowaways and mute puppeteer."

Tallulah, Trophy Bay, Hail Mary, George Eliot, Daniel, the late Dingleberry, and other loyal mongrels in named grave houses were never slighted, sidelined, or considered an absence in native heart stories and dream songs. The gestures, dances, baritone moans, harmonic bays, and howls of liberty were heard, teased, and envisioned in every spirited scene of puppet parleys at the Theatre of Chance.

Master Jean was teased as a master of the mongrels, and he used that mockery of the stowaways to convince a dental surgeon that he was more than capable of caring for seven mongrels caged for a surgical research project at the University of Minnesota. He learned later that the first research assistant had resigned when the surgeon cut the vocal folds of the strays, and nothing more was heard in the cages than the rush of hoarse mongrels. The barks were hushed only to favor the moods and distemper of a surgeon.

The stowaways were angry about the cruel use of mongrels in scientific research, and to honor the sentiments of the strays, hushed their voices and only gestured with hoarse whispers that night over dinner. The loyal mongrels were moody and uneasy with the raspy tones, a strange mockery, and circled the table and moaned in need of some reassurance.

The dental surgeon administered an anesthetic, broke the jaws of the mongrels, and then used three distinct surgical procedures to mend the fractures. The purpose of the research was to provide dental surgeons with scientific evidence and procedures to treat fractured human jaw bones.

"The mongrels were eager to pose on a stainless steel table for a dose of narcotics, they raised a paw, leaned closer for the assistant to shave the hair from a vein on the front leg, and then waited to receive the injection of peace and silence," said Master Jean.

"Surgical savagery," shouted Big Rant.

"Barbaric research at the university," said Poesy May.

"Celebrate the fugitive mongrels," said La Chance.

"Yes, but now the mongrels are loyal to me, they can sense my presence in the building and bounce in the cages with hoarse barks," said Master Jean. "I prepare the best food, twice a day, and sometimes the mongrels are so excited to be near me they can hardly eat, and, of course, they must wonder if this is the time for another narcotic dose of serenity and liberty."

"Serenity and savagery," shouted Big Rant.

"The mongrels sense your anguish," said Poesy May.

"Gruesome, heinous, but the research is almost done, the broken jaws are healed, and nothing more than X-ray images as evidence, and that ends the narcotics," said Master Jean.

The stowaways continued the hoarse mockery for another day, and then considered a puppet parley to ridicule the dental surgeon as a creature of savagism, a cruel and greedy coureur de bois of the ancient fur trade who concealed his hatred of animals as a dental surgeon. The mute puppeteer raised her hands and shouted in silence, brava, brava, brava, and printed on a hand chalkboard, "Master Jean protects the jawbone mongrels from the deadly scientists that continue the cruelty of the fur trade."

Master Jean could not contain his rage a few nights later when he related the horror of the dental surgeon who executed one of the mongrels and sawed out sections of the healed jaw bone for preservation and scientific evidence.

"Later that night, when the research laboratory was closed, and the lights in the building were turned out, a disguised native mongrel of the slave trade quietly rescued six mongrels from certain execution and lead the pack of jawbone survivors to the wooded banks of liberty near the Mississippi River," said Master Jean. "I smiled and laughed, and then with a great sense of glory shouted out hallelujah and turned back to cover any traces of my presence, and in the darkness two jawbone mongrels nudged the back of my legs, and that was the moment that the stowaways must reverse the nudges for the two jawbone mongrels to stay at the Oshki Theatre of Chance."

The mute puppeteer raised both hands and shouted three rounds of brava, brava, brava in silence, as a gesture of native mercy and favors to stay, and the other loyal mongrels circled and nudged the two newcomers to the count of native heart stories. The faint hoarse moans of the jawbone mongrels lasted that first night and then turned to hoarse barks of liberty. The mute puppeteer named the two fugitive mongrels Jawbone and Throaty.

||||| 20 |||||

SHAME OF LIBERTY

Master Jean set the military bugle aside and bought a used brass trumpet and practiced major scales, overtones, and flutters at the back of the cold bus parked out of sight behind the Oshki Theatre of Chance. Several weeks after the fraught outcome of the presidential election he was ready to present the customary military sounds and celebrated "Fanfare for the Common Man," composed by Aaron Copland, at various events, soldierly and cultural, and at puppet parleys in the existential colony.

Richard Nixon won the election as president by less than one percent of the vote and declared that he would return the country to "law and order" for the "silent majority," and with no sense of irony, the sweaty face, shifty eyes, and moody manner of the president elect became one more political shame of liberty.

The Democratic National Convention in August 1968 was a political misadventure that served the "silent majority," not the protesters against the Vietnam War. Senator Eugene McCarthy, the persuasive and philosophical antiwar candidate with strong support from young democrats, almost defeated President Lyndon Johnson in the New Hampshire primary, and the outcome was not to pursue another term as president. Vice President Hubert Humphrey and Senator Robert Kennedy decided to enter the risky chase of the primaries.

Meanwhile, thousands of young demonstrators gathered in the renowned Lincoln Park the Sunday night before the Chicago Convention. Thousands of police officers and National Guard soldiers pushed, pummeled, and sprayed tear gas at the protesters that night, and many news reporters were hesitant to report any support of the protest or critical comments of the police violence. Television networks were cautious not to turn away commercial sponsors and the "silent majority" of television viewers, but there were several exceptional journalists at the convention.

"This is the most disgraceful night in the history of American political conventions," reported Eric Sevareid, one of the most trusted television journalists. Basile, Aloysius, By Now, and the stowaways had admired and respected the journalist for more than thirty years. Sevareid graduated from the University of Minnesota and was hired as a journalist at the *Minneapolis Star*. He wrote an accurate story about deadly police violence against union strikers during the Truckers' Strike in 1934. "Nearly all the injured strikers had wounds in the backs of their heads, arms, legs, and shoulders: they had been shot while trying to run out of the ambush." Not many journalists had the courage to report the savagery of the police at the Truckers' Strike or the police violence that night at the Democratic National Convention.

Master Jean honored the silent veterans of two world wars and the reserved, reluctant, and resistant soldiers of the wars in Korea and Vietnam but never the concocted and sullen silent majority. He played the "Fanfare for the Common Man" on the front porch a few days later in time for Sunday services at the Den Norske Lutherske Mindekirke. The gray squirrels were always curious about the stance of the mongrels and stowaways and paused to listen on the trunk of an elm tree in the front yard, and the parishioners waited at the entrance to the church for an account of the character and trumpet music that early morning.

"Trumpet music for the common man but not a ceremonial for the electoral college voters or the silent majority," shouted Big Rant. "Master Jean favors native fanfares for the survivance of soldiers and native liberty."

The Norwindian boys saluted the trumpeter, and the church elders waved at the stowaways on the way into the church. "The creative fanfares of consent and civil liberties were out of tune and sidetracked with the electoral college election of a bruised diplomat and paranoid president who was favored by the ironic silence of fascists and greedy war mongers," said Basile.

Zenibaa, Dazhim La Roque, By Now, Prometheus, Basile, and Aloysius considered the strange tangles of political parties, the outcome of the presidential election, and ordered several cases of moonshine from native bootleggers near Lake of the Woods. Doctor Wilde, Archie Goldman, Hush, Tedious, Where Now, Atomic 16, Noah Bear, and many others were invited to an ironic celebration of the shame of liberty and to participate in a puppet parley and mockery of a rogue reservation agent and President Elect Richard Nixon at the Oshki Theatre of Chance.

The make ready stories and creative hearsay of treaty teases and deceptive agents on separatist reservations started that cold and wild night after a dinner of baked chicken, roasted potatoes, and kidney beans. Basile presented several tributes with a raised glass of moonshine to honor the natives who had served in the wars of liberty and then mocked the tricky political chants and propriety of President Elect Richard Nixon.

"Nixon is the most mockable politician," shouted Hush.

"The candidate of political shame," said Where Now.

"Nixon counts tricks, kicks, and kinks," said Master Jean.

Aloysius painted two abstract caricatures on white paper bags, the feral, chary grimace of Richard Nixon and the twisted and wicked face of a federal reservation agent. Hush Browne was the voice of the agent and shouted out the hearsay blabber of annuities and treaty politics. Tedious Van Pelt was the voice of the president elect, and his gestures were nervous, hesitant, sly, and sweaty. The slight ironic notions of a reservation agent were created for the parley, and the words of President Elect Richard Nixon were actual quotations selected from a press conference when he lost the election for governor of California on November 7, 1962, and other quotations were from the recorded nomination acceptance speech at the Republican National Convention in Miami, Florida, on August 8, 1968. The puppet parley was first presented as a rehearsal that late afternoon near the public telephone booth in front of the Band Box Diner to an Elliot Park casual audience with burgers in hand and then later that night with a taste of native moonshine in the living room of the Oshki Theatre of Chance.

NIXON: We see cities enveloped in smoke and flame.

AGENT: The ruins of loggers on segregated reservations.

NIXON: We see Americans dying on distant battlefields abroad.

AGENT: The battles continue on treaty reservations.

NIXON: We see Americans hating each other.

AGENT: Nothing but hatred of federal agents.

NIXON: Decline in respect for public authority.

AGENT: The federal treaties were never respected.

NIXON: Millions of Americans cry out in anguish.

AGENT: Most natives probably cry out for the past.

NIXON: We've had enough of big promises and little action.

AGENT: Treaty reservations were deceptive promises.

NIXON: We need a policy to prevent more Vietnams.

AGENT: Policies to prevent the Ghost Dance Religion.

NIXON: We live in an age of revolution in America.

AGENT: Natives declare revolutions on every reservation.

NIXON: Crime is not going to be the wave of the future.

AGENT: Peace is not going to be the wave on reservations.

NIXON: To put it bluntly, we are on the wrong road.

AGENT: Segregated reservations are on the right road.

NIXON: The long dark night for America is about to end.

AGENT: The long dark nights of civilization.

NIXON: Far from being a great society.

AGENT: Run with natives on a sacred mountain.

NIXON: Ours is becoming a lawless society.

AGENT: Navajo witchcraft can solve that problem.

NIXON: Teachers, preachers, and politicians have gone too far.

AGENT: Nothing is perfect at the Bureau of Indian Affairs.

NIXON: There can be no right to revolt in this society.

AGENT: Agents respect the law on every reservation.

NIXON: No right to demonstrate outside the law.

AGENT: No right to demonstrate for native civil rights.

NIXON: This is my last press conference.

AGENT: There is always an agent to kick around.

Poesy May told more personal stories from the bookstore that night about a former medical student who stole one or two books at least once a week, a needy, speedy reader or a clinical kleptomaniac.

She was never certain at first about his thievery, but then noticed two empty spaces on the designer book shelves of the Modern Library, and politely whispered to the book thief to return or purchase the books that were hidden under a white medical gown. He flashed a toothy smile, returned the books, and that encounter became an invitation to meet a few days later near the campus at the Catholic Newman Center.

Lamy Crayone, the book thief, was playing classical music on a grand piano when she arrived with obvious hesitations and worries. The center was secure, and she was distracted when he declared, "Watch my fingers on the keys. My small hands cannot reach the entire chords, so it was necessary to score the music for a short fingered pianist, as you can plainly see in this piano concerto by Johann Sebastian Bach."

Poesy May was invited later to visit a pathology laboratory at the university medical school. Lamy entered a gown room with confidence and insisted that she wear a gown and mask to observe an actual appendectomy by surgery interns. He revealed later that he had quit medical school two years earlier.

"Why the music and surgery show?" asked Poesy May.

"More exciting as a spectator," said Lamy.

"Real surgery is not for spectators," said Poesy May.

"Spectators are observers and witnesses, and that makes more sense than the scrutiny of examiners in the great irony of music and medicine," said Lamy.

He smiled, of course, and assumed everything he said was understood and then waved an arm to follow, and he drove to a tidy suburban house for another surprise, not as a spectator but to meet his lively wife and two children. The stolen books were shelved in the living room, a monument of kleptomania, more than a hundred books published by Modern Library.

"Yes, stolen from the campus bookstore, one or two at a time over the past two years since my time as a student in the medical school," said Lamy.

Lamy was the principal orderly responsible for the custody and care of confined psychiatric patients at the Paraday Mental Hospital in North Minneapolis, a private hospital that carried out a lucrative schedule of electroshock treatments, drug therapy, and gender custody. His fast comments that afternoon were more evasive than critical of the electroshock of women, mostly married women with children, and at the same time casually revealed that he assisted a psychiatrist with the electric torture as treatment.

"We need an orderly, do you want the job?" asked Lamy.

"No, torture is not my idea of therapy," said Poesy May.

"The duties of an orderly are much more interesting, direct, and urgent and more necessary than operating a cash register or waiting to catch me stealing another book," said Lamy. He was generous and persuasive at first and then moved from one story to another to sidestep any hesitations or controversy.

Lamy explained that his given name was related to the city in New Mexico that his mother proclaimed as the place of his conception. When the mute puppeteer and the stowaways heard the stories about the book thief and electroshock orderly, they created several ironic nicknames in a few days, and the one that lasted was Guglielmo Libri, the nineteenth century inspector of libraries in France. Lamy became Count Libri in stories about the bookstore and mental hospital.

Basile was bemused when he first read the stories about the famous mathematician who was born in Italy and named a count. "Guglielmo Libri was a professor at the Collège de France, and later at the Sorbonne, and then designated the chief inspector of libraries in France in 1841, the perfect appointment to become a thief of rare manuscripts and books from libraries," said Basile. "Libri feared arrest seven years later and escaped to London with eighteen trunks of stolen manuscripts and books."

"Count Libri became the perfect nickname for Lamy, the hospital orderly and book thief in the strange world of medical school drop outs," said Big Rant. "Count Libri probably would have stolen the great books that we discovered in the ashes of the Nibwaakaa Library."

Bad Boy was eager to pursue the position as an orderly, and a few days later Poesy May introduced him to Count Libri, the book thief and principal orderly, and the native stowaway of classical literature was hired straightaway as a late shift mental hospital orderly. Bad Boy was given a uniform, white shirt and pants, and reported for mental hospital duty.

21

Salutary Nicknames

Bad Boy Aristotle was hired to care for five male patients, and carried out other orderly concerns and customs, in a single wing of the Paraday Mental Hospital. "My hospital duties were never ordinary, of course, and rather easy and cordial at first, even comfortable at times, but casual notions of care and custody changed on the third night when a patient simulated a heart attack, and nurses and orderlies with medical experience were absent, and that was the mentality of the hospital."

Harmony Baswewe, the reservation librarian, presented a copy of *The Divided Self* by Roland David Laing a few years ago along with several other books for the stowaways to read on the *Theatre of Chance*, a converted school bus, during a road trip to the Seattle World's Fair. Since then, that book has touched in some way every stowaway in a heart story of natural motion. Laing revealed the trouble and anxiety of human existence, the mental torments, resistance to separation, and cultural distance, and the overtime count of psychiatry.

Bad Boy was curious about the actual treatment of mental disorders and became more perceptive about his own memories of an abusive uncle on a reservation and resolved not to confirm that his ironic names were entered on a certificate of birth at the White Earth Hospital. He declared that federal documents alone were not a source of existential presence because he had earned recognition and confidence as a stowaway at the Theatre of Chance.

Bad Boy read selected paragraphs of *The Divided Self* several times, pondered over the critical concepts along with the classical thoughts about comic and tragic literature, and then compared the psychiatric notions of the schizoid or the divided self to situations of natives on segregated reservations and the ironic sensations of chance, presence, and liberty.

"Treaty separatism as a *santé mentale*," said Master Jean.

"Heart stories of an ironic presence," said Poesy May.

"Existential stays and a literary presence," said Bad Boy.

Laing reached out to perceive and appreciate the elusive nature of derangement, schizoid character, the obscure course of survivance, and wordbook depictions of psychiatric patients, and wrote, "As a psychiatrist, I run into a major difficulty at the onset: how can I go straight to the patients if the psychiatric words at my disposal keep the patient at a distance from me? How can one demonstrate the general human relevance and significance of the patient's condition if the words one has to use are specifically designed to isolate and circumscribe the meaning of the patient's life to a particular clinical entity?"

Bad Boy was motivated by that critical query and accepted with no hesitation the position as orderly at the Paraday Mental Hospital. Poesy May encountered an affable book thief and that directly related to the invitation to become an orderly, a chance connection in a bookstore provided the necessary experience to consider the critical theories about psychiatry in *The Divided Self* by R. D. Laing.

Bad Boy created one or more depictive nicknames for the patients, names that envisioned a singular character, and some patients, maybe most, would never want to hear a birth name separated by psychiatry and shouted out at a clinical distance in the cold custody of a mental hospital.

By Now, a registered nurse, experienced the trauma of war as a comrade in *La Résistance* and was critical of the practices in mental hospitals, and in casual talks and at conventions she condemned the dreadful diagnoses of individuals as distant and diminished and raged against the electroconvulsive treatments or measured electrocutions by psychiatrists.

"Most mental patients were deserted and then declared wards by court orders and expensive psychiatrists, an archaic medical, legal, and familial collusion based on the unbearable misconceptions of altered perceptions that became a course of custody," said By Now. "Some of those in custody were outliers, outcasts, solitaries, and strays, as many natives were outcasts and strays on the borders of commerce and corporate greed, vague natives caught in the absence of a future on a federal reservation, the remnants of cultural deception, disruptive at times over the contradictions of war, peace, and the church, and mostly as an inconvenience, but many strays carried on with the necessary resistance to the temptations of suicide, and for that entangled sense of a troubled presence the common psychiatric treatment tours are remedial drugs and electroconvulsive therapy."

"Electroshock for women of resistance," shouted Big Rant.

"Reservation shock for native resistance," said Bad Boy.

"Thorazine for veterans and moody men," said La Chance.

"Drugs to hush the shouts for liberty," shouted Hush.

"Shout out native dream songs," said Poesy May.

"Salutary nicknames as native cures," said Bad Boy.

"Powwow predators of tradition," said La Chance.

"Laing created a language of resistance," said Tedious.

"Shun psychiatry in an existential colony," shouted Hush.

"Nicknames of presence," said Master Jean.

"Nicknames of ironic recognition," said Bad Boy.

"The mute puppeteer and shaman of silence practiced the native cures of natural motion and teases of recognition, ironic stories of mercy, mockery, creative puppet parleys, and the shouts of shame, vengeance, and salvation were directed to the meadows of panic holes, and the stowaways resisted deceit and predatory traditions with irony and mockery and learned to celebrate their presence as celebrities of nothing," said Master Jean.

Nicknames at the Paraday Mental Hospital were depictive and ironic, and some patients might have believed the hospital was an outpost of transience and the torments of tricky treatment were tours of existence, but not likely as the existential sensations of an actual presence even with descriptive and ironic nicknames of recognition.

The hearsay and heart stories of native nicknames on treaty reservations were customary, necessary, sometimes salutary, and at the same time nicknames were mutable, the necessary, quirky encounters of cause, cultural maneuvers, associations, and the tease of chance and presence.

Predatory traditions and the nasty hearsay of the pork barrel bully boys were easily countered with mockery and bold puppet parleys. Native relations created nicknames as recognition and with care and irony, and nicknames were created by envious friends and with ridicule by enemies, competitors, arbiters, and blood rivals, but never as psychiatric theories or for the separation of patients in a mental hospital.

"Nicknames are ironic remedies," said Big Rant.

"Nicknames shed shame and pity," said Master Jean.

"Master Jean of double ironies," said Posey May.

"Nicknames of treaty separatism," said Big Rant.

"Mutable nicknames of recognition," said Tedious.

"Count my nickname an ironic story," shouted Hush.

Heartthrob, a toady with a slight hunchback and crepey skin, wore white slippers and a hospital gown tied at the back and occupied a room directly across the hallway from The Director, a short and wiry patient. Ordure, a precise nickname, was cared for in a corner room directly across the hallway from Hacksaw, a huge patient with the robotic hand gestures of sawing as he slowly walked in a haze of therapeutic drug ventures from one end of the hallway to the other. Quilty, or Forepaws, the fifth patient on the wing of the hospital, was short and stout with huge hands and a generous smile, and several times a day he soughed and swayed from side to side in random doorways of women patients.

"Heartthrob was the tricky start of my duties that third night at the hospital as he started to moan and shout loudly in agony," said Bad Boy. "I rushed to the central station to alert the principal nurse, but she was not there, and the entire corps of practical nurses and orderlies on the second floor of the hospital were absent.

"Heartthrob shouted louder that he was having a heart attack, and his breath seemed short and hollow, so, with no practical experience of heart attacks, I leaned over the patient, pounded on his chest to stimulate a heartbeat, but my urgent strategy was scary, and he turned from side to side in a panic and then started to pound on my arms and chest, and his shouts of agony became shouts of stop, stop, stop beating me," said Bad Boy.

The Director inspected the hallway every day at first light, and he wore a starched white shirt, black tie, tailored business suit and vest, gold watch chain, and polished shoes, ready to deliver operational orders to the nurses and orderlies.

The Director was once the actual director of a mental hospital in North Dakota. He lost the capacity to perceive the patients from the nurses and orderlies, a rather natural outcome over more than twenty years of mental hospital experiences, or to discern the necessary professional duties as hospital director, and then distant relatives obtained a court order to sentence him with no sense of irony as a patient to the Paraday Mental Hospital.

The Director roamed down the hallways of the hospital in the early morning and later in the evening and ordered nurses to provide care for certain patients, and several times every evening he directed the orderlies to carry out precise assignments, meals, and medications and to select appropriate television stations for the patients, the duties, of course, that had been carried out earlier by Count Libri and Bad Boy Aristotle.

"The directors of mental hospitals are always directors and after twenty years might stray as patients, a hospital distinction that is lost with psychiatric drug treatments and other dreads of custody," shouted Hush.

Ordure was a stout wanderer with hairy bow legs, and at times a delighted patient in a fancy shirt over the standard white gown, and on the other side of monthly cycles he groped women patients during television sessions, shouted out the window that he was a political prisoner, and then decorated the plaster walls of his room with feces. The last orderly resigned when he was ordered to clean the abstract feces smears from the walls.

"Count Libri never mentioned the odious duty to clean the walls of an abstract excrement artist," said Bad Boy. "Yes, to be an orderly, that was chance and necessary at the time, but not sure what my decision might have been with the ordure notice, yet the feces art show is carried out only once a month."

Hacksaw, the robust patient and former manager of a car dealership, slowly shuffled down the long hallway and moved his huge hands forward and backward, the slow motions of sawing, and paused at the end of the hallway. He sawed at the thick drapes, and then, gently turned around by an orderly, nurse, or patient, he sawed in the opposite direction.

Hacksaw sawed most of the day and delivered a few phrases in the presence of other patients. "Where you go now, Watch out by morning light, Maybe next week, Nobody comes back, Dance day and gone, gone, gone, My name, you know my face, Pontiac, my dog stays," were seven of the most common comments that he repeated daily. Thorazine, the drug for disorders of manner and mood, converted memory and motion and had other strange consequences, dose after dose, and turned a court reported menace into an eternal patient that simulated the motion of a hacksaw.

Quilty could have been an orderly. He was casual, wore blue jeans, and greeted everyone with smiles and hand gestures as he moved with the ease of a dancer down the hallways and, without an obvious reason, he paused in doorways of women patients and swayed from side to side, a strange motion of hesitation and separation. He smiled with a gentle touch on the shoulder and returned to the private and secure room that was decorated with patchwork pattern quilts and several magnificent star quilts.

Quilty was only secure at night under a star quilt, the same quilt he made for his mother as she slowly died at home of cancer, and that was the start of his separation from a familiar time and place. He swayed from side to side in public doorways, at the market, library, drug store, and post office. A distant relative visited the hospital and explained that he was a celebrated quilter, an international historian of quilts, and had lived his entire life only with his mother.

Marion Daunger, the handsome, muscular, principal nurse, and the others were at dinner and deliberately staged their absence as a prank and initiation to tolerate and treat the faker of heart attacks. Heartthrob simulated heart attacks once a day, and his sensitive feigns were more intense with every new nurse and orderly.

"Heartthrob complained to me that you pounded on his chest, a good strategy to scare him out of fakery, but he has never abandoned the absolute attention and personal recognition he receives with fake heart attacks," said Count Libri.

Marion never answered telephones, no matter the urgency or constant pitch of the ring. "This was obvious when she asked me to deliver a large envelope to her husband at their nearby residence," said Bad Boy. "The telephone rang and rang as she handed me the envelope, and then she turned away, and walked down the hallway in silence."

Count Libri smiled and with a familiar voice of guidance revealed that Marion, "a prescient principal nurse, never answered telephones, and the strange aversion to telephones was not a common experience but was more easily understood in a mental hospital."

Marion, or Fire Eater, an ironic nickname, had an absolute fear of fire in telephone receivers. "Marion fears that flames would come out of a telephone if she raised the receiver, and she never takes the risk to answer," said Count Libri. "Visitors sometimes gesture with the receiver, and Fire Eater rushes to another wing of the hospital and returns only when the flames are under control."

Bad Boy rang the doorbell as directed and then waited to hand over the envelope. The man opened the door and quickly stepped backward and seemed to resist the delivery. Bad Boy was instructed to throw the envelop into the hallway, not an actual handover, and the man slammed the door shut. A few days later, the strange behavior was revealed in a conversation with Count Libri. "Marion rescued a former Catholic priest from the hospital in this very ward a few years ago and now they live together. The priest was tormented by open doors and panics near thresholds, and for more than three years he has never crossed a threshold for fear that he would be struck dead," said Count Libri.

"Blasphemy at a homey threshold," said Bad Boy.

"Yes, the devil waits in doorways," said Count Libri.

"Demonic thresholds and telephone firestorms, and what else is considered normal at the hospital," said Bad Boy. "Out of body nurses, and orderlies with olfactory damage ready to wipe away the excremental art of a political prisoner?"

"Watch me, listen for the telephones, consider a simulated fire extinguisher, carry a heart attack detector, and sometimes the patients are much easier to understand than the nurses and psychiatrists," said Count Libri.

"Yes, everyone lives with fears and faints, flights and firestorms, nicknames of separatism, the mockery of winter ghosts on reservations, and sometimes sidelines the shaman poseurs of tradition," said Bad Boy.

"My kind of reservation," said Count Libri.

Bad Boy told emotive and incredible stories about nurses, orderlies, and patients almost every morning after breakfast and over coffee, and the stowaways and mute puppeteer sometimes insisted on more stories late at night. Some stories compared the nurses and patients with ironic and salutary nicknames that later became a puppet parley.

BAREFOOT PSYCHIATRIST

By Now, Bad Boy, and Master Jean created a puppet parley with the salutary nicknames of patients, nurses, orderlies, a chorus, and a psychiatrist at the Paraday Mental Hospital. Barefoot was R. D. Laing, and Fire Eater was the principal nurse. The Director, Heartthrob, Hacksaw, Quilty, Ordure, and Scheisse Curator were the patients. Bad Boy and Count Libri, the book thief and deputy to electroconvulsive therapy, were orderlies in the parley.

Big Rant fashioned the nine hand puppet characters with torn sections of a discarded sheet, and the huge puppet heads were stuffed with wads of paper. Aloysius painted caricatures of the hospital ensemble and printed nicknames on the foreheads of each white cloth puppet. The puppets were caped with slits at the sides for two fingers to simulate the motion of puppet arms. The ghostly puppets were bright, distinctive, and represented the patients, nurses, and orderlies with every bounce and gesture of the puppet chorus and salutary nickname parley.

Aloysius painted a miniature star quilt on the front of the puppet Quilty. The Director wore a tiny gold watch chain and simulated black fedora, and an abstract tie and vest were painted on his chest. Ordure was decorated with brown blotches. Hacksaw was decorated with a simulation of an automobile steering wheel on his white chest. Heartthrob wore only the cape painted with red stripes. Fire Eater was enhanced with flames on the front of the cape. Count Libri the puppet wore an image of an uneven row of books on his chest. Bad Boy, or Scheisse Curator, the chorus puppet, wore a sheet with words from *Poetics* by Aristotle, *instinct of imitation* and *imitation of action*, painted by Aloysius.

Laing, or Barefoot, a descriptive nickname for the existential psychiatrist who reconsidered the schizoid as a solitary chase of presence in cultures of deception and nostalgia, wore the same white cape as the patients with the Scottish word, *radge*, angry, furious, crazy, painted on the front, an ironic gesture of native favor.

"Doctor Laing changed the notions of mental illness, and he countered the entire wordbook of psychiatric diagnoses," said By Now. "He considered psychoses the strange poetry that conveys the agony, uncertainties, and visionary estrangements and the memory of unbearable experiences."

"The barefoot radge of schizoid liberty," shouted Hush.

"Laing was born in Scotland, studied psychiatric medicine at the University of Glasgow, served in the military, and a few years ago created with others the Philadelphia Association to advance new theories of treatment at Kingsley Hall, a community house of original psychiatric care in London," said Basile.

"Barefoot existentialist at Kingsley Hall," said By Now.

"The patients and psychiatrists actually lived together, an unusual course of treatment, and that curious notice comes from a British journalist who visited last year to write a feature story about the new fauvist art of Aloysius," said Basile. Barefoot, the psychiatrist, was quoted directly from his recent book, except for the first comment of the puppet parley, and the forthright and ironic comments of the other hand puppets with salutary nicknames were created by Master Jean, Big Rant, and By Now.

Master Jean was the voice of Barefoot, Bad Boy was the voice of Ordure, Dazhim La Roque was the voice of The Director, Poesy May was the puppet voice of Quilty, La Chance was the voice of the patient Hacksaw, and the voice of Heartthrob was Tedious in the puppet parley of salutary nicknames.

The lyrics of the chorus were created by the stowaways for the parley, and a few lines were selected from *The Divided Self*. Big Rant was the soprano voice of Fire Eater, Atomic 16 was the baritone voice of Count Libri, and Noah Bear was the tenor voice of Scheisse Curator, the three nicknames of the puppet chorus.

The stowaways and ensemble of hand puppets waited for a warm sunny day to present the parley of salutary nicknames on the lower steps in front of Northrup Memorial Auditorium at the University of Minnesota. The mongrels of chance circled the puppeteers as they raised the nine puppets, nodded together with huge caricature heads, and the fingers of the puppeteers wagged as arms.

Master Jean played "Fanfare for the Common Man" by Aaron Copland, and the mongrels circled the puppets and moaned and bayed in perfect harmony with the trumpet. The two new loyal mongrels returned to the university for the first time since they had been rescued from the dental executioner. Jawbone and Throaty raised their heads and delivered raspy bays as a memory of harmony.

Where Now Downwind chanted that autumn afternoon to the audience, mostly students, who were curious about the nine hand puppets, and the theories were selected and edited from the first chapter of *The Divided Self* by R. D. Laing.

"The clinical focus is narrowed down to cover only some of the ways there are of being schizoid or going schizophrenic. The account of the issues lived by the individuals studied in this book is intended to demonstrate that these issues cannot be grasped through the methods of clinical psychiatry and psychopathology as they stand today, but, on the contrary, require the existential and phenomenological methods to demonstrate their true human relevance and significance," Where Now chanted on the steps of Northrup Auditorium. "The form of human tragedy we are faced with here has never been presented with sufficient clarity and distinctness. I felt, therefore, that the sheer descriptive task had to come before all other considerations."

BAREFOOT: Mental health ironies are presented here in this hand puppet parley of salutary nicknames, and that includes me as the new barefoot stance of existential psychiatry.

DIRECTOR: Paraday parley and a grand chorus.

CHORUS: Paraday puppets with salutary nicknames.

BAREFOOT: You are expected to be able to recognize me.

QUILTY: Existential psychiatrist favors a star quilt.

CHORUS: Human relevance and significance overnight.

BAREFOOT: Everyone is subject to a certain extent at one time or another to such moods of futility, meaninglessness, and purposelessness, but in schizoid individuals these moods are particularly insistent.

ORDURE: The words circle me in a schizoid circus.

CHORUS: Schizoid chase of presence and aesthetic feces.

BAREFOOT: I am accustomed to expect that the person you take me to be, and the identity that I reckon myself to have, will coincide by and large.

HEARTTHROB: My heart attacks coincide with the tides.

CHORUS: Strange poetry of the trickster of misery.

BAREFOOT: The individual in the ordinary circumstances of living may feel more unreal than real; in a literal sense, more dead than alive; precariously differentiated from the rest of the world, so that his identity and autonomy are always in question.

DIRECTOR: My declarations are real now but not in the past.

CHORUS: Human relevance and significance.

BAREFOOT: If the individual cannot take the realness, aliveness, autonomy, and identity of himself and others for granted, then he has to become absorbed in contriving ways of trying to be real, of keeping himself or others alive, of preserving his identity, in efforts, as he will openly put it, to prevent himself loving his self.

HACKSAW: Nobody comes back.

CHORUS: Schizoid chase of presence with nicknames.

BAREFOOT: Each has his own autonomous sense of identity and his own definition of who and what he is.

DIRECTOR: The Director is favored as a patient.

CHORUS: Evaluations are quite irrelevant at night.

BAREFOOT: The term schizoid refers to an individual, the totality of whose experience is split in two main ways: in the first place, there is a rent in his relation with his world and, in the second, there is a disruption of his relation with himself.

HACKSAW: Where you go now?

CHORUS: Schizoid chase of presence with no destination.

BAREFOOT: The schizophrenic has to be known without being destroyed. He will have to discover that this is possible.

HACKSAW: Dance day and gone, gone, gone.

CHORUS: Haunted by the persistent dread of memories.

BAREFOOT: His whole life has been torn between his desire to reveal himself and his desire to conceal himself.

HEARTTHROB: My heart is a prisoner in a mental hospital.

CHORUS: Nature of anxiety, nature of phantasy.

BAREFOOT: We suggest that it was on the basis of this exquisite vulnerability that the unreal man became so adept at self-concealment.

HACKSAW: Watch out by morning light.

CHORUS: Strange poetry of concealed misery.

BAREFOOT: Generally speaking, the schizoid individual is not erecting defenses against the loss of a part of his body. His whole effort is rather to preserve his *self*.

DIRECTOR: The duties as director start with the early light.

CHORUS: Schizoid chase of presence overcame an absence.

BAREFOOT: The schizoid individual fears a real live dialectical relationship with real live people. He can relate himself only to depersonalized persons, the phantoms of his own phantasies . . . perhaps to things, perhaps to animals.

HACKSAW: Pontiac, my dog stays.

CHORUS: Schizoid chase of presence with totemic animals.

BAREFOOT: It is well known that temporary states of dissociation of the self from the body occur in normal people. In general, one can say it is a response that appears to be available to most people who find themselves enclosed within a threatening experience from which there is no physical escape.

HEARTTHROB: My heart attacks are real, real, real, let me go.

CHORUS: Mighty sounds of a wild heart in custody.

BAREFOOT: Many schizoid writers and artists who are relatively isolated from the other succeed in establishing a creative relationship with things in the world, which are made to embody figures of their phantasy.

QUILTY: The most secure place is under a star quilt.

CHORUS: Strange poetry of misery under a pattern.

BAREFOOT: If there is anything the schizoid individual is likely to believe in, it is his own destructiveness. He is unable to believe that he can fill his own emptiness without reducing what is there to nothing. He regards his own love and that of others as being as destructive as hatred.

DIRECTOR: Count the nicknames in my hospital.

CHORUS: Only the hate of being hated being more hated.

BAREFOOT: No animal is without enemies. Being visible is therefore a basic biological risk; invisible is a basic biological defence. We all employ some form of camouflage.

ORDURE: Fecal art is my camouflage in custody.

CHORUS: Haunted by a persistent dread of custody.

BAREFOOT: One of the greatest barriers against getting to know a schizophrenic is his sheer incomprehensibility: the oddity, bizarreness, obscurity in all that we can perceive of him.

ORDURE: You always know me by my abstract fecal art.

CHORUS: Schizoid chase of presence in excremental art.

BAREFOOT: To the schizophrenic, liking someone equals *being like* that person: being like a person is equated with being the same as that person, hence with losing identity. Hating and being hated may therefore be felt to threaten loss of identity less than do loving and being loved.

HEARTTHROB: The nurses love me for my heart attacks.

CHORUS: Love the hatred and the menace of being loved.

BAREFOOT: The self-conscious person is caught in a dilemma. He may need to be seen and recognized, in order to maintain his sense of realness and identity. Yet, at the same time, the other represents a threat to his identity and reality.

DIRECTOR: Hate the patients and mock the chase of hatred.

CHORUS: Strange poetry of misery in the absence of identity.

The puppeteers bowed in silence at the end of the parley, and the audience of mostly students raised their arms and came forward to touch the hand puppets. One student shouted out the nicknames of Heartthrob, Ordure, and Barefoot the psychiatrist, and other students praised the serious parley about patients in mental hospitals. No one mentioned natives, the mute puppeteer, reservations, or loyal mongrels, and most students were hesitant and listened to others comment on the selection of quotations from *The Divided Self* by R. D. Laing.

The mongrels roamed through the crowd of students and faculty, raised their noses, and teased with gentle bays. Trophy Bay sneezed twice near an older, bearded, lean, heavy smoker that Poesy May identified later as the poet John Berryman who taught at the University of Minnesota. The jumpy poet moved with clouds of cigarette smoke through the crowd and smiled over the caricatures of the hand puppets.

Tallulah nudged the legs of a young woman in a plaid skirt, and finally she raised a hand to be recognized and with serious hesitations related a family heart story. "My great aunt was sent to a mental hospital, and she only wanted to be an aviator, to fly an airplane around the world, or somewhere, and nothing more, but she was shocked out of flying at a mental hospital."

"Crashed in electro convulsions," said Master Jean.

The audience was silenced by the story of the psychiatric capture and electroshock crash of flight and liberty. A faculty member waited for the perfect moment of silence to encourage students to raise doubts and queries about the authenticity of native hand puppets and caricatures as more comic and ironic than cultural, and with that moment of authority, he declared that mental health has never been advanced by mere mockery. The professor of cultural anthropology flaunted his tutorial guile and presence and became more puppet caricature than parley, a mere poseur and bully boy of cultural hearsay.

"Native puppets shun the poseurs," shouted Big Rant.

"More apology than native heart stories," said Poesy May.

"Celebrate native mockery, a double shock of culture ploys, and praise anyone who would shock anthropologists out of their pretentious and magisterial theories of native cultures, and that would be a grand evolution of consciousness," said Master Jean.

The students stared at the haughty anthropologist, counted in a tweed sport coat, composed and separate on the higher steps to the auditorium, and then the students saluted and cheered the puppeteers, and the mongrels bayed in harmony. That moment of mockery was secure in native heart stories.

"Last year, an archeologist directed a seminar of graduate students to unearth native remains," shouted an older student. "Yes, and with each secure scoop and brush of a native bone, the archeologist turned and twitched, and the involuntary motions of his body became wild, and then he vanished one summer night with no explanation or notice."

"Shamans captured his bones," shouted Big Rant.

"The grave scene was abandoned by the students when the bones vanished one by one," said the student. "A few weeks later the archeologist was rescued in a canoe adrift on Lac la Croix in Canada and was treated with electroshock therapy to stimulate his memory of native bones."

"Double shock of shaman bones," said Master Jean.

An older graduate student who studied philosophy and literature pointed at the puppet Ordure and inquired about the actual situation of the patient with that nickname. The mongrels nosed the student as Bad Boy related a concise version of the patient who decorated his room with excrement at the Paraday Mental Hospital.

The student was a military veteran, and the creative situation of excrement that he recounted that afternoon on the steps of the auditorium could not have been a better conclusion to the puppet parley. He moved closer to the puppets and then turned slightly to the audience to express some regret for the use of direct language about a memorable experience ten years earlier as a soldier at the basic training camp at Fort Knox, Kentucky.

"There was a rush every morning after breakfast to visit the latrine and to defecate," said the graduate student. "No privacy at the latrine, of course, and more than a dozen soldiers were seated on a row of toilets, and the second rush was a quick bowel movement to avoid the stench in the latrine.

"One soldier in the barracks was assigned to clean the sinks and toilets for the morning inspection by the camp officers, the duty of every recruit at least once every other week, and the week of this story, a clever soldier rushed to clean the latrine and scrubbed one particular toilet several times, and then he fashioned two thick lumps of peanut butter into simulated turds and dropped them in the clean bowl and waited on the toilet. The officers arrived to inspect the latrine, but instead of standing at attention the clever soldier leaned over the toilet, raised a turd from the water, and started to eat as he turned and smiled at the officers.

"That soldier was secured as a mental patient that morning, and in less than two weeks the post psychiatrist recommended a medical discharge, and he returned home with no shock or shame," said the graduate student. "Mostly, the other soldiers in the barracks respected authority and carried out the orders and duties of military service, completed basic combat training, and they were directly ordered to serve in the Korean War."

"Lost and found memories," shouted Big Rant.

"Peanut butter discharge," shouted Hush.

"Maybe latrine lemonade," said Master Jean.

The mute puppeteer shouted brava, brava, brava in silence and then reached out to touch the graduate student and veteran with the hand puppet. They linked arms with the others, puppet to puppet, as Master Jean raised the trumpet and played retreat. The loyal mongrels, including the two raspy fugitives, circled the puppeteers and moaned and bayed with perfect harmony.

ⅠⅠⅠⅠⅠ 23 ⅠⅠⅠⅠⅠ

PARADAY CUSTODY

Count Libri was the principal orderly and assistant to the psychiatrists that executed the electroconvulsive treatments two or three times a week at the Paraday Mental Hospital. Bad Boy was directed one afternoon to prepare a young married woman for shock treatment.

Mary was described in the obscure notes by the psychiatrist as "vague," and "she resisted the duties of a wife and was not responsive to sexual attention," according to the testimony of the husband, and based on that vague and dubious concoction of wifely demeanors, the court decided in favor of custody, care, and electroconvulsive therapy at the Paraday Mental Hospital.

Ugo Cerletti, or Ugoletti, was a nickname created by the nurses and orderlies for the psychiatrists that presided over the primitive electric shock treatments, or the severe punishment for resistance and dissociation. Cerletti was an Italian neurologist who studied the effects on animals shocked with electricity and later named the practice that shocked, stunned, and numbed actual humans electroconvulsive therapy.

"Shock and leave psychiatry," shouted Hush.

"Native shamans tease the motion of the night and catch for a moment the distant whispers of the spirits, the strange sounds that bury the snow ghosts and heal memory," said Master Jean. "Psychiatrists dumb down the shamans and spirits and catch the money with a shock button."

"Ugo Cerletti became a prominent doctor that used electric shocks on humans partly because the other methods of severe chemical treatments for dissociation and schizophrenia were dangerous and deadly," said By Now. "The chemical therapies were poisons, and some patients died in convulsions, but shocks to the brain were not considered as dangerous, and yet the practice of short jolts of electricity have never been confirmed as an effective treatment, and the outcome has never been more than wild body jerks, broken bones, and erasure of memories."

"More shocks for the money," shouted Hush.

"Cerletti died a few years ago," said By Now.

"Lost dream songs and broken bones," said Poesy May.

"Ugoletti would never shock his wife," said La Chance.

"Wait, wait, wait, for the ironic shock psychiatrists are convinced that electric jolts to the brain cure bad memories and dissociation in a culture of deceptions, medical deceit, and the mendacity of peace and liberty," shouted Hush. "Plainly mistaken, and they should be escorted to custody and shocked several times out of their psychiatric delusions."

Count Libri secured the young woman on a medical counter in the treatment suite and attached the bilateral electrical contact pads to the sides of her temples, set the torture machine, and then waited for the psychiatrist to execute the gruesome shock and convulsions that deleted the bother, tease, and tributes of melancholy and memory and terminated an elusive sense of irony, or the chance of meditation and shamanic silence.

Bad Boy was somber and worried later that night as he related to the stowaways the entire shock treatment scene, the absence of decency, human reach, or contact with the patient. No common traces of compassion or motion of mercy were demonstrated by the psychiatrist.

"Ugoletti entered the treatment suite, slowly removed his tailored suit coat, washed his hands in silence, looked away to avoid eye contact, checked the blood pressure of the patient, examined the bilateral shock pads, and then ordered me to hold the ankles of the patient as he pressed the button that released a bolt of electricity through the brain of the woman, the first of ten shock treatments scheduled over several weeks.

"Mary was struck by lightning, breathless in a storm of convulsions, taut muscles, thrusts and seizures, brutal strains of menace, rapid heartbeats, bones bounced on the padded counter, and then she was overcome with a strange motion, ankles jerked in my hands, a barbaric electrical torture that chased away fright, terminated the memories of chance, closed the visions of shamans and the rights of hesitations, resistance, and shared stories over mistaken contrition," related Bad Boy.

Bad Boy was mortified by the crude shock and convulsions of the patient, haunted by the memory of the treatment that could not be abated with irony or mockery, and pleaded to be forgiven by the stowaways because he should have removed the contact pads and liberated the young woman from the brutal course of psychiatry and torture of electroconvulsive therapy.

"Master Jean rescued the mongrels from execution by a dental surgeon in the strange opera of hoarse barks, and no one can forget that patients in custody at a mental hospital convey a cultural distance, and at the same time natives wait for the chance to counter and mock the trust and shock of psychiatry," said By Now. "The stowaways are celebrities of nothing and favor heart stories, mockery, and shamanic silence and are ready to shock psychiatry other remedies of resistance on reservations and in the existential colony."

"Shock of absence on reservations," shouted Big Rant.

"Shock of segregation on reservations," said Tedious.

"Shock of promises and starvation," said Master Jean.

"Shock of soldiers at Wounded Knee," said Bad Boy.

"Shock of psychiatry and suicide," shouted Hush.

"Shock of rich psychiatrists," said Poesy May.

"Shock of great thunderstorms," said La Chance.

"Shock of lightning and hesitations," shouted Big Rant.

The mute puppeteer listened to the heart stories and tacks of conscience about mongrels and patients that night and printed a dream song on the chalkboard to counter the shock treatment of a woman in custody and the regrets of Bad Boy.

hoarse mongrels
grand opera of liberty
overnight bravas
forlorn women of psychiatry
chance of lightning

Thousands of natives on hundreds of treaty reservations were once downcast over cultural partitions and outlasted the greedy timber barons and miners by chance, resistance, and mockery and surely would have sidetracked the conceit of psychiatry and electroconvulsive treatment with the menace of snow ghost stories. The shock of native spirits, the shamanic presence of silence in heart stories, and the hesitations of thunder in the natural motion of lightning storms might have erased or recast the wordbooks of psychiatry.

Bad Boy prepared a resignation letter critical of the brutal shock therapy but was convinced by the stowaways and mute puppeteer to counter with

THEATRE OF CHANCE

mockery rather than the shame of a passive departure, and he discovered once again that native derision is a creative art. He mocked the tailored suits and detachment of psychiatrists and never again participated in electroconvulsive treatments.

"Mockery parties for psychiatry," shouted Hush.

"Laing would honor the mockery," said Bad Boy.

"Reservation psychiatrists would have diagnosed native hearsay and nicknames, captured the play but not the irony of hand puppet parleys, and weighed at a distance the mongrel nudge of stowaways to stay at the Theatre of Chance," said Master Jean.

"The stowaways learned how to counter hearsay with irony and mockery from the mute puppeteer, and we became the first native celebrities of nothing on the reservation, and now creative mockery is even more essential in the existential colony," said La Chance.

"Existential celebrities of hesitations," shouted Hush.

Bad Boy easily countered the nasty hearsay and the churchy course of shame and pity on the reservation, but as an orderly he was distracted by the brutality of shock therapy and lost a sense of resistance and heart stories of survivance. He was back in the sway of a stowaway in a few days and mocked the psychiatrists, nurses, and orderlies, and created salutary nicknames for patients at the mental hospital, and countered with hearsay and derision the punitive shock treatment of patients in custody.

"Existential celebrities of custody," shouted Hush.

Bad Boy mocked the secure manner of psychiatrists, the deliberate gestures, meticulous hand washes, fussy maneuvers with rubber gloves, slight hesitations over the shock button for the money. The mockery was noticed by some of the patients.

Ordure was curious, hesitant, and rather pleased that his excremental art was compared to the abstract expressionist and cubist painters, and at the same time, and with no grasp of the irony, he pretended to understand the mockery of the "strange scent and sensations of excremental cubism" for a few days every month.

Bad Boy created other salutary nicknames for some of the patients. Ordure became Caca Picasso. Heartthrob pretended to resist his new nickname, Blood Count. Hacksaw, the robot, became Corvette Stingray, a nickname that teased his experience with automobiles, and he practiced a few more phrases of contact with ghosts in the hallway, Outside dares, Chase the streetcars, Count over today. The Director deserved at least two nicknames, Big Warden, and, as a military veteran, Parade Rest. The benign star quilter smiled, swayed, and then frowned when he heard a new nickname, Jiibay Anang, the words for a ghost star in the language of the Anishinaabe.

Count Libri continued to serve the psychiatrist that executed electroconvulsive treatments and teased the one time assistant of shock therapy as an effete native with a fear of lightning, a perfect derision that resolved critical hearsay at the hospital. The artless nurses refused to hear serious comments about shock therapy and were hesitant to endorse new nicknames for the patients. They were the celebrities of equivocation and overly concerned about the ethics of care and custody and any changes in the routine of the Paraday Mental Hospital.

Bad Boy created nicknames with the least sense of irony for the nurses, Godly Smirk, Back Time, Clever Charm, Heart Tuner, and continued with new salutary nicknames but heightened the ironic depictions to counter the distance of patients in a mental hospital. The patients related to every new nickname, a spirited encounter with a recast of presence, irony, recognition, and diversions, and with no shocks, absence, shame, or drugs. Thorazine, though, was the steady dose of exclusions, the setback of memory, and a muted futurity.

Bad Boy created another round of nicknames a few months later to enliven the spirits, perception, and ironic recognition of the patients. The Director, or Parade Rest, became Sergeant at Arms, Caca Picasso became the Superintendent of Sanitation, Corvette Stingray became the Secretary of Transportations, Blood Count was delighted as the Sheriff of Paraday, and the quilter Jiibay Anang was distracted, as usual, with another nickname, Mother Cover, the tease of star quilts and his mother. Some of the patients started to tease each other over the ironic nicknames, and the most enthusiastic players were the Sergeant at Arms and the Sheriff of Paraday. These two patients teased each other in the hallway several times a day.

The Sergeant at Arms was on duty early in the morning, and later he became The Director and warden of the entire hospital. The Sheriff of Paraday raised a hand one night in the hallway and announced a new grand nickname for The Director and Sergeant at Arms, who checked the time on his pocket watch at least every hour and for that reason earned the nickname Great Northern Conductor. That surprise became the start of salutary nicknames created by the patients, minimal and tentative at first, and with an obvious pleasure and ironic notice of mutable nicknames in the Paraday Mental Hospital.

The patients became more observant of gestures, generous teases, and manners and created salutary nicknames with no hesitation and with no expectation of approval from the nurses or orderlies. Paraday nicknames were created with a perception of mood, manner, and gestures and not based on the overstated shape, weight, or contours of body parts.

The Great Northern Conductor created a new nickname, Curator of Art, for Caca Picasso, and the Sheriff of Paraday, the simulator of heart attacks, boldly created the nickname Blaze Nightingale for the principal nurse, Marion Daunger.

The patients became pluckier and more confident and soon created perceptive nicknames for the nurses, orderlies, and other patients. Count Libri was given the nickname Sly Shocker, and Bad Boy, the actual creator of salutary nicknames at the hospital, earned the nickname Tricky Liberty.

Bad Boy told the stowaways about the detestable monthly chore of excrement removal from the walls of the patient, Ordure, and at least once a week a patient learned to mock the duties and pleasures of the orderlies, and that was a comparable course of ironic hearsay and perception.

By Now and Master Jean created the ironic nickname Scheisse Curator for one of three chorus puppets in a parley at the University of Minnesota. The Paraday patients were not aware of the excremental and curatorial nickname for the puppet parley.

"Doctor Samuel Wilde assured me that it was not unusual for patients to imitate nurses and orderlies at a mental hospital and to pretend to change the course of care and custody," said Bad Boy. "So, that was the obvious and necessary reason to create salutary nicknames and encourage the patients to do the same, but the pleasant surprise was how perceptive and creative the patients became about ironic nicknames."

Later that summer the patients created another round of creative nicknames for nurses, orderlies, and patients, and with great pleasure the Sheriff of Paraday, once known as Heartthrob and later Blood Count, and the recent Great Northern Conductor, once named The Director, The Warden, and Sergeant at Arms, created for a favored orderly the ironic nickname Name Jumper. Bad Boy never convinced the patients that his given names were documented on a reservation public health birth certificate and not mutable, but the patients were certain that Bad Boy Aristotle was an orderly nickname.

The patients shouted out new nicknames in the hallway that night with a creative confidence. Caca Picasso laughed out loud when he heard the double shouts of his ironic nickname, Maybe Matisse, and a nurse with gray curly hair was given the nickname Hungry Head. The shout outs of creative nicknames were perceptive and ironic and continued for several days, and then five patients gathered in the hallway after dinner and celebrated the play of nicknames and became the overnight celebrities of sobriquets. Most of the nurses were troubled by the nickname mirth of the patients, not the usual burdens of custody, and since the creation of patient nicknames, a mentality of liberty emerged and changed the character of custody at the Paraday Mental Hospital.

The patients were more perceptive about ironic nicknames than the nurses were about treatment, and one night during a communal television session, five patients, Sheriff of Paraday, the Great Northern Conductor, Corvette Stingray, and the inimitable excremental fauvist artist, Maybe Matisse, were engaged in a lively conversation about birthrights, care, and custody at the Paraday Mental Hospital.

The Great Northern Conductor wore a signature dark suit and vest and slowly fingered a gold watch chain as he listened closely to the patients talk about care and custody, the medical treatment and television, the weather and deserts, the recognition of nicknames and a sense of presence, and that night the quick stories, slight teases, and gestures of irony were perceptive, and the buoyancy of the patients in the hallway was more memorable than the tiresome nursey diversions, social evasions, shifty undertow of caste, and pastime chitchat of the nurses on late duty.

Bad Boy listened to the conversations of the patients for several nights and could easily favor the character and substance of the patients compared to the nurses. The patients had become spirited celebrities of sobriquets in every conversation, and the nurses caviled and equivocated the promises of politics and the economy, but the patients were more generous and had learned the pleasure of irony and liberty in a nickname, and the nurses skirted around any mention of chance, mental hospital ethos, ironic prognoses of care and custody, or the Vietnam War.

Bad Boy related to the stowaways some of the nickname stories of the patients, the generous irony of creative names and the discovery and tease of presence in a mental hospital. Every salutary nickname created by the patients was compared to the tedious notations of the nurses over time, care, and custody. Bad Boy Aristotle made his decision to resign at the end of the month as an orderly at the Paraday Mental Hospital.

\\\\\ 24 /////

SUE FOR MOCKERY

Basile, Aloysius, and By Now were not surprised that the ironic sway of hand puppet parleys had gone astray, after more than twenty years, and the clever portrayals and gestures of puppets on the reservation were misconceived in the existential colony. The mute puppeteer and stowaways celebrated the stories at the recent parley at the university, and at the same time they were distracted by the reluctance and cultural distance of the student audience.

"Bouncy comeback at the Waite House," said Big Rant.

"Spirited at the Oshki Theatre of Chance," said Bad Boy.

"Mother Jones was favored by the audience in the parley with Andrew Carnegie," said By Now. "The Cristóbal Colón and Erik the Red parley was lively, the skinwalker witchery masks scared most of the students, and the caricatures of puppet patients at the Paraday Mental Hospital no doubt touched the dark fears and insecurities of the students."

"Native hearsay and puppetry are not the same in the existential colony," said Basile. "Mockery, ironic nicknames, and puppet parleys on the reservation are hardly comparable to the speculations and daily chitchat in the existential colony."

"No bully boys here," said Bad Boy.

"Clever parleys, but sometimes scary," said Big Rant.

"Chitchat and ironic Paraday stories," said Poesy May.

"Paraday parleys close to home," shouted Hush.

"The students might feel more comfortable with the stories of book thieves," said Poesy May. "Most of the students thought at least once about stealing a book, the secret, risky adventure of stolen knowledge."

"Stolen but never read," shouted Hush.

"Dreamy, easy, and mundane," said La Chance.

"Except, of course, for kleptomaniacs," said Bad Boy.

"Scary masks and hand puppet caricatures are strangers in the existential colony," said By Now. "The parleys and mockery of survivance are not ordinary experiences, so we must recast the manner of native puppetry."

THEATRE OF CHANCE

"More existential colony trickery," shouted Big Rant.

"Bunraku puppet theatre," said Poesy May.

"Bossy chants of bigger puppets," said La Chance.

"The Bunraku Doll Theatre of Japan was presented at the Seattle World's Fair at the same time that we attended the play *Waiting for Godot* by Samuel Beckett," said Poesy May.

"The mute puppeteer once carved the heads of puppets from chunks of fallen birch, and the characters were spectacular," said Master Jean. "She enhanced the intricate wrinkles on the face of Samuel Beckett."

"Beckett as a Bunraku puppet," said La Chance.

"Chant the eternal wait for Godot," said Bad Boy.

"Bunraku is a theatre of memorable chanted scenes, and the gestures of puppet figures are carried out by two or three creative operators," said Poesy May. "Forget the operators and movable eyes, the heads carved by the mute puppeteer can easily simulate misery, enchantment, and shame."

"Bunraku chant with native puppets," said Big Rant. "The celebrities of nothing could wear carved masks and chant the outcome of creative trickster dives and the creation of earth with no reservations," said Big Rant.

Poesy May, a few days later, searched the basement shelves at McCosh's Book Store and found a copy of *Bunraku: The Art of Japanese Puppet Theatre* by Donald Keene. The illustrated book was published three years earlier, and the author pointed out in the introduction that Bunraku "occupies a most important place in Japanese literature and theatrical history alike, and by no means belongs to the frivolous class of entertainments associated with puppets and marionettes in other parts of the world."

"Native puppets are not frivolous," shouted Big Rant.

"Keene was not keen about native hand puppets," said By Now. "Maybe he was right about the waggish marionettes but not about the mute puppeteer, not about natural motion, native nicknames, and mockery in a parley."

"Donald Keene deserves a nickname," said Bad Boy.

"Keen Cant for a just start," said La Chance.

"Bun Boy in the existential colony," shouted Hush.

"Bun is literary, raku is delight, and our native hand puppet parleys are the chance of literary mockery," said Poesy May.

"No native word for delight," said Bad Boy.

"Only *onzaamenimo*, elated or excited," said Poesy May.

Poesy May continued to read out loud the introduction of *Bunraku* by Keene. The great "tragic dramatist, Chikamatsu Monzaemon, wrote not for actors but for the Bunraku puppets, and the audience today as in the past is there to enjoy a true dramatic performance rather than an amusing display of the dexterity of the operators."

"Native puppet parleys are more than amusing displays of dexterity," said By Now. "Keene has never attended a parley on the reservation, and with that experience he would have included native hand puppets and parleys as ironic and literary."

Poesy May was prepared a few nights later to present more relevant selections of the book to the stowaways, and the outcome was to create hand puppets that were inspired by the Bunraku of Japan.

"The simple movements of a stick puppet operated by a medium intoning ancient legends are, of course, a far cry from the sophisticated art of Bunraku, but even in its most primitive form we can detect one peculiar feature of the Japanese puppet theatre: the medium makes no attempt to conceal the fact that she is manipulating the puppets," wrote Keene.

"The sculpted puppet faces are deliberately fashioned so that the expression can be markedly altered by moving the eyes, eyebrows or mouth, but these movements are employed relatively seldom, so as not to weaken their effect in the climactic scenes. Changes of expression normally come from the successive poses of the puppet's body.

"Part of our pleasure in watching Bunraku today comes from an awareness, however imprecise, that every gesture by the puppet, every shift in inflection of the chanter's voice, every intensification of accent in the shamisen accompaniment is the product of conscious efforts over many years to achieve a perfect balance between realism and non-realism. It is said to take a chanter eight years to master the art of weeping," wrote Keene in *Bunraku*.

"Japanese Bunraku survived the war. The chanters, puppet operators, and shamisen players endured the great hunger at the end of the war, and loyal audiences for puppet theater survived the fire bombs and nuclear destruction of two cities," declared Basile. "Native puppeteers, dream songs and heart stories, the great mask carvers, shaman chanters, and the elation of puppet parley mockery survived the fur trade, colonial wars, and treaty separatism on reservations and outwitted churchy shame, pity, and destiny."

"Bunraku chance, not destiny," shouted Big Rant.

THEATRE OF CHANCE

"Bunraku without the shamisen," said Bad Boy.

"Bunraku with my trumpet," said Master Jean.

"Bunraku and creative native chants of heartbreak, parleys of creation and chance, trickster conversions, cultural duties and duress, and the uneasy string tones of the shamisen could easily become the clear, brassy, and melancholy timber of the trumpet," said By Now.

By Now, Dazhim La Roque, Atomic 16, Where Now, Hush, Tedious, the stowaways, and the mute puppeteer decided that night to create a memorable parley for the last presentation of native puppets in the existential colony.

Big Rant, Poesy May, and Bad Boy were inspired by the description of Bunraku puppetry and were ready to create distinctive native puppets for a sensational parley. First they considered totemic puppets, the sandhill crane, golden eagle, beaver, marten, otter, bear, and others that survived the colonial fur trade, chemical pollution, nuclear downwind poisons, and avarice, and later they were convinced that the great puppets must be enhanced caricatures with a creative sense of presence to counter the churchy stance of salvation.

The stowaways never expected the mute puppeteer to carve six distinctive heads from blocks of birch bark in time for a parley that late autumn, and the wooden heads would be too heavy for easy gestures. Tedious proposed puppet heads formed with plastic, but the facial details, wrinkles, brows, and frowns, were too complicated to fashion.

Basile read out loud that morning a front page story in the *Minneapolis Tribune*, "Three Are Removed From Mass After Attempting Dialogue," November 18, 1968, by Gerald Vizenor. The stowaways mocked the priest over the expulsion of dissident parishioners and prepared to present a new paddle puppet parley at a Catholic church.

Three young protesters were "physically removed" from Our Lady of Victory Catholic Church in North Minneapolis as they appealed for a serious discussion of the war, poverty, and racialism, and they were critical of the priest because he omitted the sermon. More severe than the deletion of a homily was a brutish father who "followed his daughter to the church and slapped her in public for associating with the dissident Catholics he accused of being 'Communists' and 'outlaws.'"

"James McDonnel, a former priest and member of the dissident group, was the first to speak out. He asked the priest why the sermon had been omitted, but his questions went unheeded when the congregation sang the offertory hymn," wrote the journalist.

Our Lady of Victory was the "fourth attempt of the group to create a 'meaningful dialogue' in conservative Minneapolis parishes," but the priest anticipated the disruption and "omitted the sermon and conducted the entire mass in Latin."

Father Joseph Musch warned Gerald Vizenor, a staff writer for the *Minneapolis Tribune*, that "no newspapermen are allowed" at the mass in Latin. "It is my option who attends the mass," said the priest. "I might have to sue you."

"Sue for peace, not shame," shouted Hush.

"*Dona nobis pacem*," chanted Master Jean.

Father Musch might sue the stowaways and hand puppet caricatures for mockery and create sensational hearsay about the conservative revisions of the Mass and Holy Communion at Our Lady of Victory. The stowaways might sue the churchy dictator for existential threats and because he sidestepped the homily or reverent dialogue about crucial issues in the nation and the world, poverty, slavery, and the war in Vietnam.

"Sue for peace and mercy," shouted Hush.

"Sue for peace and mockery," said Bad Boy.

"Our Lady of Victory is the Blessed Virgin Mary, and that commemoration of victory is about an ancient war," said Basile. "That ironic tribute of victory should be reason enough to discuss poverty, racialism, and war."

"Sue the priest for hearsay," shouted Big Rant.

"Sue the priest for promises of salvation," said La Chance.

"Sue the priest for exclusions," shouted Hush.

Tedious arrived at the Oshki Theatre of Chance a few days later with six rusted and badly worn handheld school crossing signs. He smiled, raised and slowly turned a paddle sign, and the stowaways envisioned the six puppet caricatures, Samuel Beckett, George Lincoln Rockwell, Rachel Carson, J. Robert Oppenheimer, Gertrude Stein, and Father Joseph Musch, painted on each side of the octagonal paddle signs, with two distinctive expressions.

Aloysius cleaned and painted the signs with several coats of glossy white paint, printed the puppet names on the paddle, and then created enormous black and white caricatures on each side of the paddle, a side view with broad features, and on the other side a direct stare with a raised eyebrow, an expression of doubt, hesitation, or exotic temper. The puppet caricatures were created from published photographs.

Samuel Beckett, the novelist and playwright, was depicted with bright blue eyes, wire rim spectacles, swirls of wrinkles on one side of the paddle, and with one curved eyebrow on the other side.

George Lincoln Rockwell, the former Navy commander, reconnaissance pilot in the Second World War and the Korean War, and fascist founder of the American Nazi Party, was pictured on one side of the paddle with a dark stare, puffy cheeks, and a chevron moustache and on the other side as a caricature with curled lips and a wide open mouth of fascist rage.

Rachel Carson, the author of *Silent Spring,* was depicted with neat short hair and a slight, mannered smile and on the other side with a grimace and one finger raised as a cautionary notice about the chemical and radiation poison and death of the natural world.

J. Robert Oppenheimer, theoretical physicist and director of the Manhattan Project, was pictured with pale pensive eyes. He held a tobacco pipe on one side of the paddle and on the other side wore a rumpled fedora with a wide brim.

Gertrude Stein, the ironic and esoteric author, was depicted with a broad forehead and very short hair on one side of the paddle, and on the other side a caricature with a slight smirk and puffy cheeks.

Father Joseph Musch was born in Poland, graduated at Cretin High School and Saint Paul Seminary, served as a captain in the United States Army Air Corps during the Second World War, and, with no permanent parish, the young priest celebrated Holy Communion in the Camden Theater and several years later established Our Lady of Victory. The caricature of the priest was stern, a haunted stare on one side and enhanced jawbones on the other, and wore a confessional stole.

The facial gestures of the caricatures were reversible, and the stowaways decorated the octagonal paddles with bright ribbons fastened to the handle, and the ribbons waved with every turn of the puppet caricatures. Father Joseph Musch, the most austere puppet caricature, was not decorated with ribbons.

Dazhim, Where Now, Hush, Atomic 16, Big Rant, and Poesy May selected the citations from published sources for the parley of the paddle puppets, and the stowaways were ready to chant the citations for the caricatures. The trumpet tones, chants of the stowaways, and the slow ecstatic motion of the sandhill crane created a totemic theatre of chance.

Poesy May earned the ironic nickname Rapture Totem for the stately sandhill crane, an enormous puppet fashioned with chicken wire, plastic tubes, and canvas painted the colors of the totemic crane.

The elegant sandhill crane was about eight feet high, more than twice the proportions of the demure puppeteer, and was mounted on four plastic tubes. Two tubes were glued to a fitted shoulder harness, and the other two were connected to the thick canvas wings of the sandhill crane. The puppeteer slowly leaned in the natural motion of the totemic crane and raised the wings in marvelous flight.

Master Jean saluted the spectacular sandhill crane puppet with melodious trumpet tones, a great moment of creative motion and totemic presence. The mellow sound of the trumpet was a native substitute for the twang of the stringed shamisen, an expressive celebration of the Bunraku Theatre of Japan and the creative puppeteers at the Oshki Theatre of Chance.

The paddle puppets, caricature parley, and totemic sandhill crane were presented for the first time on the grand stone steps of the Cathedral of Saint Paul at Selby and Summit Avenue in Saint Paul on Sunday, December 1, 1968. The crew of paddle puppeteers and the mongrels arrived early that morning and parked the bus nearby on Summit Avenue. The stowaways decided at the last minute to leave the loyal mongrels in the bus to avoid any resistance or fear that the parishioners might have about nosy mongrels on the steps of the Cathedral of Saint Paul.

The mute puppeteer fashioned loose black shirts for each of the paddle puppeteers, a modest costume to create a sense of invisibility similar to the traditional operators of the puppets in the Bunraku Theatre. The paddle puppet masters were ready to chant the actual quotations of the caricatures that were selected from publications. Where Now Downwind chanted citations from *The Unnamable* by Samuel Beckett, Atomic 16 was the voice of J. Robert Oppenheimer, Big Rant Beaulieu was the voice of Rachel Carson, Bad Boy Aristotle was the fascist chant of George Lincoln Rockwell, Hush Browne chanted the eccentric proverbs written by Gertrude Stein,

THEATRE OF CHANCE 169

and Truman La Chance chanted only two epigrams in natural motion, "sue for peace," and "sue for mockery," as the caricature of the stern Father Joseph Musch.

The totemic sandhill crane and six paddle puppets waited on the wide stone steps that cold morning for the early service at the Cathedral of Saint Paul. The puppeteers advanced from step to step, never close to each other, and chanted the citations of the puppets with slight pauses as the paddles turned, and the wings of the enormous sandhill crane moved slowly through the parishioners as they mounted the steps of the Cathedral of Saint Paul.

BECKETT: I'm all these words, all these strangers, this dust of words, with no ground for their settling, no sky for their dispersing.

ROCKWELL: Being prepared to die is one of the great secrets of living. Perhaps I will go to hell for doing what must be done.

CARSON: Everywhere was the shadow of death.

OPPENHEIMER: There are no secrets about the world of nature. There are secrets about the thoughts and intentions of men.

GERTRUDE: Romance is everything. Suppose no one asked a question, what would be the answer.

FATHER MUSCH: Sue for peace.

BECKETT: The voice that speaks, knowing that it lies.

ROCKWELL: Nazism says that women are absolutely equal to men. But they're different. And thank god for the difference.

GERTRUDE: Remarks are not literature.

FATHER MUSCH: Sue for mockery.

CARSON: Radiation has changed the nature of the world.

OPPENHEIMER: We knew the world would not be the same. A few people laughed, a few people cried, and most people were silent. I remembered the line from the Hindu scripture, the Bhagavad Gita. Now I am become Death, the destroyer of worlds.

FATHER MUSCH: Sue for peace.

BECKETT: I shall not be alone, in the beginning. I am of course alone. Alone. That is soon said. Things have to be soon said. And how can one be sure, in such darkness?

FATHER MUSCH: Sue for mockery.

ROCKWELL: The color of your skin is your uniform in this ultimate battle for the survival of the West.

FATHER MUSCH: Sue for peace.

CARSON: Spring without voices.

OPPENHEIMER: There is no place for dogma in science. The scientist is free, and must be free to ask any question, to doubt any assertion, to seek for any evidence, to correct any errors. Science is not everything, but science is very beautiful.

GERTRUDE: Argument for me is the air I breathe.

FATHER MUSCH: Sue for mockery.

BECKETT: These are futile teasers. Let them put into my mouth at last the words that will save me, damn me, and no more talk about it, no more talk about anything.

ROCKWELL: I am a political soldier. I mean to win. I do not hesitate to admit that I would do anything, absolutely anything, to ensure the survival and happiness of our White, Western People.

FATHER MUSCH: Sue for mockery.

CARSON: Dangerous chemicals from birth to death.

OPPENHEIMER: In some sort of crude sense which no vulgarity, no humor, no overstatement can quite extinguish, the physicists have known sin; and this is a knowledge which they cannot lose.

GERTRUDE: Everybody knows if you are too careful you are so occupied in being careful that you are sure to stumble over something.

FATHER MUSCH: Sue for mockery.

BECKETT: I can feel it, they're going to abandon me, it will be the silence, for a moment, a good few moments, or it will be mine, the lasting one, that didn't last, that still lasts, it will be I, you must go on, I can't go on, you must go on, I'll go on.

ROCKWELL: I don't believe in democracy.

FATHER MUSCH: Sue for peace.

CARSON: Pollution has rapidly become almost universal.

OPPENHEIMER: If atomic bombs are to be added as new weapons to the arsenals of a warring world, or to the arsenals of the nations preparing for war, then the time will come when mankind will curse the names of Los Alamos and Hiroshima.

FATHER MUSCH: Sue for peace.

GERTRUDE: Explanations are clear but since no one to whom a thing is explained can connect the explanations with what is really clear, therefore clear explanations are not clear.

FATHER MUSCH: Sue for mockery.

BECKETT: You must say words, as long as there are any, until they find me, until they say me, strange pain, strange sin, you must go on, perhaps it's done already, perhaps they have said me already.

FATHER MUSCH: Sue for mockery.

ROCKWELL: I realized that National Socialism, the iconoclastic worldview of Adolf Hitler, was the doctrine of scientific, racial idealism, actually, a new religion for our times. I saw that I was living in the age of a new worldview.

FATHER MUSCH: Sue for peace.

OPPENHEIMER: Our own political life is predicated on openness. We do not believe any group of men adequate enough or wise enough to operate without scrutiny or without criticism.

CARSON: Writing is a lonely occupation at best.

FATHER MUSCH: Sue for mockery.

BECKETT: Perhaps they have carried me to the threshold of my story, before the door that opens on my story, that would surprise me, if it opens, it will be I, it will be the silence, where I am, I don't know, I'll never know, in the silence you don't know, you must go on, I can't go on, I'll go on.

FATHER MUSCH: Sue for mockery.

The children were entranced by the motion of the sandhill crane, and probably would have stayed with the magic of the totem and paddle puppets rather than with the parents or the priest or the monumental cathedral. The chants of the puppets wavered in the cold air with a solemn sense of presence, and most of the parishioners paused on various levels of the great stone steps to listen, as they were prepared to hear the gospel or a priestly homely. The clear resonance of the trumpet, the magical motion of the great sandhill crane, and the melodic chants of the puppet caricatures that cold morning were lasting heart stories in the existential colony and the Cathedral of Saint Paul.

||||| 25 |||||

Jour Éternel

John Ka Ka Geesick, the venerable shaman and storier, died yesterday, December 6, 1968, in Warroad, Minnesota. The native *midewi*, a healer in the observance of the *mediwiwin*, was born in 1844, a hundred and twenty four years ago, at Buffalo Point, Lake of the Woods, Prince Rupert's Land, the colonial territory of British North America, and later he moved to a weathered cabin located on treaty land near Muskeg Bay in Minnesota Territory.

The Anishinaabe healer heard trickster stories of creation and the hearsay of native trade routes, the natural motion of continental liberty, catchy mockery of cultural conversions, and with a visionary name, Gaagige, forever, and Giizhig, day, heaven, or sky. Later, the coureurs des bois and colonial newcomers to Lake of the Woods, or *Lac des Bois*, rushed to reign and roughly transcribed the distinctive sounds of the two native words and then translated and archived the name as John Ka Ka Geesick, or Everlasting Sky.

John Tyler was president when the shaman was born in the spring, and at once he was overlooked by the colonial count of native obscurity, and fifteen years later he was enticed by the greedy course of the fur trade. Gaagige Giizhig was seventeen years old when Abraham Lincoln was elected as the antislavery president of a nation that was entirely divided by barbaric slavery in 1861.

Gaagige Giizhig was more enlightened as native healer and storier of the inner bark of willow and natural motion of totemic animals than the chase of political promises and outlived twenty five presidents of the United States of America. The equable shaman of survivance was eighty years old when natives on federal treaty reservations were recognized for the first time as citizens of the nation with the enactment of the Indian Citizenship Act of 1924.

By Now arrived for dinner with the news of his death and related the early stories about Gaagige Giizhig and an eighteen year old native woman with a silk cloche hat who was born at French Portage Narrows, an elusive station and watery scene between two islands, Skeet and Coste, in Lake of the Woods.

The bright young woman of the narrows earned at least three expressive nicknames, or portage names: La Taquine, the clever teaser of the coureurs des bois, Mazina, a contraction of *mazinaigan*, a book or document, because she was a sovereign native reader at the wane of the fur trade and was never in the custody of mission schools, and Zenibaa, the portage nickname contraction of *zenibaawegin*, the native word for silk.

Zenibaa sat near the bay window and watched the snow shimmer under the corner street light as she waited for her lover Dazhim to return from Banks, the warehouse of goods salvaged from fires and other disasters and the regular source of dinner surprises of canned vegetables with burned labels at the Oshki Theatre of Chance. The mongrels nosed the rims of ice on the window, and the mute puppeteer waved with both hands as the two Norwindian boys and parishioners marched to an evening event at Den Norske Lutherske Mindekirke.

The mute puppeteer might have countered ironic portage names of chance and situations of presence as she listened in silence to the stories of early adventures, and there were many versions of the silk escapades related at the post office, and later she was demeaned by the pork barrel bully boys on the White Earth Reservation.

The heart stories, scenes of chance, and ironic pleasures of hearsay and mockery recounted at the post office were enhanced and elaborated as grand gestures of esteem and recognition of the mute puppeteer by Postcard Mary.

"The portage teaser wore that silk cloche hat for several years as a tribute to the silkworms and the turn of fabric fashions in Europe that saved the beaver and totemic animals, and silkworms slowly brought about the denouement of the continental fur trade, and the memories and melancholy manner of the coureurs des bois on Lake of the Woods," related By Now.

"Zenibaa was eighteen years old at the wane of the fur trade and smartly paddled a scraped, dented, patched, and leaky birch bark canoe with Fidèle, the loyal mongrel abandoned by the coureurs des bois, at the bow from French Portage Narrows to Muskeg Bay and Warroad, Minnesota.

"The teaser in the silk hat raised a canoe paddle and waved to an old man near the shoreline, and then she shouted out *boozhoo* and *bonjour*

174   GERALD VIZENOR

several times, an enthusiastic gesture of ironic recognition, the native version of the greeting in French," related By Now.

"Gaagige Giizhig raised a hand and waved back, smiled in silence, reached out to drag the canoe ashore, and then counter teased the young native woman with an ironic story about a trickster who wore a classy round silk hat and taunted the lake spirits with the pose of elegance, *apiitendan*, pride, and the savoir faire of elusive natives from the French Portage Narrows.

"Fidèle cocked his head and with a mongrel smile delivered a memorable countertenor bay and then bumped the old shaman several times on the legs, and that great bay and gesture of salutation delighted the storier.

"Gaagige Giizhig lived alone that summer, his wife and daughter were with relatives across the border at Buffalo Point in Manitoba, Canada," related By Now.

"Fidèle was the first loyal mongrel," said Poesy May.

"First countertenor mongrel," said Master Jean.

"Other mongrels teased his bay," said Big Rant.

"French fur trade bay accent," said Poesy May.

"Zenibaa teased the healer for several days, and at first she worried about the mighty sway of conscience and spirits of the *midewiwin*, the catch and tease of heart stories, mockery of native nicknames, and spirit of a trickster, but the more she teased the more she trusted the gestures and heartfelt character of the old shaman.

"She continued on the journey of chance, a creative chase of totemic presence, and the necessary escape from the remorse of the coureurs des bois," related By Now. "Zenibaa told the shaman to change his name from the translation of Everlasting Sky to a more stately, elusive, and visionary translation, Jour Éternel, or Forever Day."

The mute puppeteer was amused by that version of heart stories, the tease of company, and turned away from the cold bay window. She shouted in silence, brava, brava, brava, and then wobbled across the living room to embrace By Now.

"Jour Éternel, heart stories of chance," said Poesy May.

"Jour Éternel, heart stories of irony," shouted Big Rant.

Zenibaa and Fidèle wandered through great forests for more than a month that summer, and at last they were invited to stay at Bakegamaa

Lake, a lively native community near Pine City, about a two day walk south of Hinckley, Minnesota. Most of the post office hearsay and spirited heart stories about the great fire and the death of her lover Nookaa, a perceptive and tenderhearted lumberjack, were benign, reverent, and ironic, but reliable.

Bakegamaa Lake, Mission Creek, Sandstone, and several other communities, more than three hundred square miles of forest, and hundreds of natives and other citizens were burned to mounds of gray ashes in the Great Hinckley Fire of 1894. Zenibaa and Fidèle escaped by chance, the sudden shift of the wind, and the firestorm moved in another direction.

Many years later the mute puppeteer created a dream song about the great rush of animals, predators, wolves, bobcats, bears, and the woodland prey, deer, squirrels, mice, moles, and racoons that escaped the firestorm with each other in the natural motion of survivance and feral unity.

autumn firestorm
tributes of silence and ashes
natives at bakegamaa lake
predators and prey
natural motion of unity

Zenibaa and Fidèle survived the Great Hinckley Fire, and since then and for more than seventy years she has gestured the tributes of chance, survivance, and natural motion, and created clever puppet parleys about feral unions, and abided in silence the death of a lover with the spirited manner of a shaman. The stowaways created the obvious nicknames of the shaman of silence as the mute puppeteer.

26

FUNERARY MOCKERY

Zenibaa, Dazhim, By Now, and the stowaways, mongrels, and native troupe decided to gather at the public funeral services for Everlasting Sky and Jour Éternel on Tuesday, December 10, 1968, at the high school auditorium and the burial ceremony at the Indian Burial Grounds in Warroad, Minnesota.

La Chance and Bad Boy painted over the old watchwords, *Célébrité de Rien*, Celebrity of Nothing, on the sides of the bus later that cold night under a street light. The catchy words were once creative mockery six years ago when the mute puppeteer, eager stowaways, mongrels, and the entire native troupe traveled to the Century 21 Exposition, or Seattle World's Fair.

The sides of the bus were frosted overnight, the paint froze on the metal, and traces of the watchwords were more noticeable, a double irony after the hurried attempt to erase the weary words.

"Last journey as celebrities of nothing," said Master Jean.

Harmony Baswewe, the retired librarian, moved from the White Earth Reservation to Bemidji, Minnesota, and invited the stowaways and the entire troupe to camp on the floor of her tiny bungalow near Lake Bemidji.

"The Oshki Library of Nibwaakaa," said Big Rant.

"Harmony a dream song library," said Big Boy.

Postcard Mary and Harmony announced they would ride along with the mute puppeteer, stowaways, mongrels, and others as two more celebrities of nothing in the converted school bus rightly named the *Theatre of Chance*. Master Jean, the troupe of mourners, and the mongrels in the front seats were on the road for three hours that early morning to Warroad.

"Hundreds of citizens walked past the *Theatre of Chance* on the way to the funeral services, and only the students waved at the solemn mongrels in the front row seats," said Big Rant.

Jour Éternel was stowed in a metal casket and dressed in a baggy blue suit, white shirt, and striped necktie for the showy funeral service that morning in the auditorium of the Warroad High School.

THEATRE OF CHANCE 177

The mortician was dressed in a black tailored suit, and he was nervous about the natives that encircled the casket mounted on a trolley and sternly warned not to touch the body or move the casket. The natives were surprised and stared in silence at the strange spectacle. The mortuary cosmetologist had puttied the great wrinkles on the face of the shaman and neatly tucked the body away in the ornate crepe interior of a brushed steel casket.

The funerary camouflage and unintended irony of the shaman in a blue suit was a moment of incredulity and was easy to recount later in trickster stories with ironic tributes to the mortician and cosmetician of demises.

"Cosmetic disguise of a shaman," shouted Big Rant.

"Funeral parlor puppet parley," whispered Poesy May.

"Puttied face of absolute silence," said Bad Boy.

"Poseurs of masks and mercy," said Poesy May.

The Everlasting Sky was praised to high heaven by the good citizens of Warroad, and as the outliers of a native presence they waited with caution and reserve outside of the auditorium. The curious students peeped as cultural spies through the narrow space between the double doors, a bright row of blue and brown eyes that blinked and waited for a glance of native ghosts or the spirits of the dead and to hear the risky waver of native singers.

"The outliers might have counted on the timeworn traces of the coureurs des bois and the ironic tease of the fur trade, and any regrets over the dead native trader in a cheap blue casket suit were overcome with the great romance of colonial portage songs and churchy favors of salvation," said By Now.

The slight trace of an expressive wheeze, faint whisper, hesitant cough, mature crack of bones, heavy tread, and haunting squeak of rubber trolly wheels echoed in the auditorium. The natives slowly turned the casket around several times, a tribute to natural motion and the secret spirits of the dead shaman and to tease the dour mortician, who had abandoned wit and irony in the distant past and diverted the tease of spirits with the menace of his black suit and wide necktie.

Zenibaa printed on a chalkboard, "Jour Éternel would wear a blue suit only to tease the wary newcomers, and native spirits stay to mock the mortuary clothes." The citizens remembered or heard stories that the old native wore moccasins, a buckskin jacket, and in winter a muskrat hat, not a blue suit on the streets of Warroad.

Daniel Raincloud, the native *midewi* healer of a *midewiwin* observance, or the Grand Medicine Society, from the nearby Red Lake Reservation, slowly raised both arms, turned slightly to the side, reached over the casket, and started the steady beats of a small rattle, an echo of heartbeats, and with a tremulous voice he honored in song the spirits that stay with the last stories of natural motion and recounted memories and the chase of reveries and regrets at death.

Raincloud and two *midewi* singers created a transcendent sense of sacred motion with songs of honor and steady beats of the rattle in a native theatre of silent spirits and native liberty, and with the favor of that ceremonial moment, the natives around the casket imagined the wild wrinkles and the body of the shaman bound in wide swathes of birch bark for the eternal stories of a spiritual journey.

Zenibaa, Basile, By Now, Master Jean, Postcard Mary, Poesy May, Raincloud, Big Rant, Bad Boy, and Gerald Vizenor, a native citizen of the White Earth Reservation and staff writer with the *Minneapolis Tribune*, encircled the casket and slowly waved their hands over the body of the shaman, the natural motion of silence, reverence, and the tease of eternity for the last flight of spirits in the heart of Jour Éternel.

Raincloud placed in the casket a small bundle of food for the journey, a pack of cigarettes, and a pair of red cotton gloves that hasten the journey of spirits from the body. The mortician reached out to remove the native benefaction, and the stowaways pushed him away from the casket.

Zenibaa unfurled the red and blue silk scarf, once a special present from the stowaways, over the gaudy suit in the casket as a favor and ironic bounty of cast and tease of the shaman who mocked the silk cloche hat when she first paddled ashore that summer more than seventy years ago at Muskeg Bay on Lake of the Woods.

"Zenibaa wore silk as the bounty," said By Now.

"Zenibaa favors shamans with silk," said Poesy May.

"Zenibaa shouted bravas in silence," said Big Rant.

"Zenibaa almost covered the blue suit," said Bad Boy.

"Zenibaa leaned closer to the casket and sang in silence to honor the spirits of the shaman, and then with easy gestures mocked the haughty manner of the stony mortician," said Poesy May.

"Maybe the spirits rush away with the last silent breath of the shaman, and maybe there are native stories that are more poetic and memorable than excessive secrets of the *midewiwin* observance," said By Now. "The trickster stories of creation are necessary, and chancy stories are more curative as mockery and diversions than the rush of adoration with rattles, murmurs, and songs, and the mortuary betrayal of the shaman and storier in a blue suit, and maybe the spirits are celebrities of nothing and hang around for nothing more than death and liberty."

"Celebrity spirits of nothing," shouted Big Rant

"Mockery of shamanic stories," said La Chance.

"Bounty of chance and liberty," said Master Jean.

"Rattles chase the heartbeats," shouted Big Rant.

"Maybe every native spirit has a spirit," said Poesy May.

"Spirits are not predators or prey," said Bad Boy.

"Native spirits are in words, dream songs, and stories, and in the tease and temper of a last breath," said Poesy May. "The spirits wait in every scene of a story, and we heard the spirits of words in the ashes of burned books at the Nibwaakaa Library."

More than three hundred citizens chattered and mumbled as they roamed down the wide aisles of the auditorium, a customary course at most public school events. Once the casket was moved to the front, the audience united in solicitude and mercy.

The Reverend Leonard Lindholm of the Evangelical Covenant Church convened the funeral service and then reached out to summon a common recitation of the Lord's Prayer, Our Father in heaven, hallowed be your name, your kingdom come, your will be done, on earth as in heaven.

"Jour Éternel craved ironic recitations," said Bad Boy.

"Jour Éternel mocked paradise," said Poesy May.

"Jour Éternel teased godly reigns," shouted Big Rant.

Gaagige Giizhig, the shaman and storier, was buried forever as a celebrity of nothing in a blue suit with a red and blue silk scarf, red cotton gloves, cigarettes, and magnanimous analogies of churchy humility and salvation at a cold gravesite near the grave of his brother Na Ma Puk at the Indian Burial Ground. The names, Ka Ka Geesick, Everlasting Sky, were sandblasted on a granite gravestone.

The loyal mongrels bounded, bounced, and pawed every grave stone in the snowy native cemetery and then paused in reverence and circled the grave of Jour Éternel. George Eliot raised her head and delivered a magical sough and soprano moan, and Tallulah, the bold beagle, balanced the melancholy pitch with a contralto bay, and the other mongrels created the bays of an honorable chorus. Jawbone and Throaty, the mongrels liberated from a death sentence at the dental school, softened their raspy barks and created a background sound with a distinct rhythm of condolence.

The Christian services and sentiments to honor a treasured native resident who lived on treaty land never prevailed in the pose of godly harmony and never over the cosmetic conversion of a wrinkled shaman in a bulky blue suit, tucked evermore in a decorated casket.

Cozy memories of the old native were carried out with the churchy poses of reverence, and sentiments of romantic novels of the fur trade and beaver wars, but a sense of native presence, chance, survivance, and ironic stories of creation and native liberty were diverted by the homey perceptions of salvation.

"Clichés count more than natives," shouted Big Rant.

"Mockery counters cozy memories," said La Chance.

"The ironic war paint and putty and bright blue suit scared away the spirits that had teased the old shaman for more than a hundred years," said By Now.

"Jour Éternel favored irony not mercy," said Basile.

"Jour Éternel was a celebrity of nothing," said Bad Boy.

Master Jean slowly maneuvered the *Theatre of Chance* out of the parking area of the high school auditorium. The mongrels were solemn in the front seats, noses at the frosted windows, and after the ceremonies more students than parents and preachers waved to the mongrels.

Big Rant related what the mute puppeteer had printed on two chalkboards as the *Theatre of Chance* cruised through Baudette late that afternoon on the road back to Bemidji. She moved to the front of the bus near the mongrels and shouted out the scenes over the noise of the engine.

"Fidèle and the loyal mongrels of the Theatre of Chance were buried with nicknames in native grave houses near Spirit Lake, but the tricky spirits of my loyal friend Gaagige Giizhig, an ironic shaman and celebrity of nothing, were buried in a metal casket and hushed forever by the hearsay of newcomers under a granite marker, a churchy death sentence with no chance to tease the spirits that created his native name."

The stowaways, mongrels, and entire troupe on the bus honored the silence and perception of the mute puppeteer, the silent bravas of native presence, the timely mockery of the mortician, and the churchy death sentence of a shaman, and every native on that grave journey of spirits would salute chance and the eternal irony of grave houses for the loyal mongrels and a blue suit burial with a translated name on a granite marker.

Harmony and Postcard Mary prepared a feast of walleye as a gesture of respect and recognition for the mute puppeteer and stowaways, and the stories that night were constant, a creative mockery of every grimace, grave gesture, and solemn frown at the funeral services for Jour Éternel.

Harmony presented five new books to the stowaways that night, a gesture that has continued every year since an arsonist destroyed the Nibwaakaa Library. *House Made of Dawn* by N. Scott Momaday, *Summer in the Spring: Lyric Poems of the Ojibway* by Gerald Vizenor, *Armies of the Night* by Norman Mailer, *The Population Bomb* by Paul Ehrlich, *The Teachings of Don Juan: A Yaqui Way of Knowledge* by Carlos Castanada, *The Joke* by Milan Kundera, *The Painted Bird* by Jerzy Koziński, and *Vietnam: Inside Story of the Guerilla War* by Wilfred Burchett.

Basile read selected paragraphs out loud from "Ojibway, Christian Funeral Rites Conducted for State Indian" by Gerald Vizenor in the *Minneapolis Tribune* the next morning, December 11, 1968, as the *Theatre of Chance* roared south past the city of Saint Cloud and the long mighty gray granite walls of the Minnesota State Reformatory on the highway back to the existential colony and the Oshki Theatre of Chance.

"Daniel Raincloud, the Midewiwin medicine man from the nearby Red Lake Reservation, conducted the Ojibway service in the auditorium while the minister and those attending the Christian service waited outside.

"Raincloud sang two Ojibway honoring songs over a small bundle of food and a package of cigarettes. He accompanied himself with a small rattle. Raincloud then placed a pair of red cotton gloves in the coffin to accompany Ka Ka Geesick to the grave.

"The uncertainty of Ka Ka Geesick's birth was resolved in 1964 when the Warroad village council passed a resolution establishing his date of birth as May 16, 1844. On the same day the council decreed that the name of Muskeg Bay should be changed to Ka Ka Geesick Bay two years after the death of the Indian medicine man.

"Tom Lightning, now 94 and recognized as the oldest Indian in Warroad, said of Ka Ka Geesick that 'he was an old man when I was a little boy in the village.'

"Ka Ka Geesick was dressed in a blue suit, white shirt, and blue striped tie. But he was remembered by residents of Warroad as always wearing moccasins, a buckskin jacket and in the winter, a muskrat hat," wrote Gerald Vizenor.

Zenibaa, Dazhim, By Now, Basile, and Aloysius convened Doctor Samuel Wilde, Archie Goldman, Noah Bear, Harmony Baswewe, Postcard Mary, Corporal Samuel Hutson, Tedious Van Pelt, Hush Browne, Gunner Sandberg and Anders Bolstad, the Norwindian boys, and the stowaways, the entire troupe, on Sunday, December 15, 1968, to observe the formal decree of the Oshki Theatre of Chance, Existential Colony, Minneapolis, that the historical names of Muskeg Bay and Warroad, Minnesota, had been changed that day and forever to Jour Éternel Bay, Lake of the Woods, and Jour Éternel, Minnesota.

Doctor Wilde observed the native decree, shouted hallelujah several times, and later blessed and lighted the first candle on the Hanukkah menorah that the mute puppeteer had acquired earlier from an antique dealer as a present and celebration at the start of the Jewish festival that Sunday.

The good doctor provided music for the Jewish festival, "Ma'oz Tzur, Rock of Ages," and chanted the first lines of the liturgical poem. "The rock is my salvation, rock of ages, let our song praise thy saving power, you amidst the raging foes were our sheltering tower."

Zenibaa handed Doctor Wilde a note that she wrote for the celebration of the name change and the first day of Hanukkah. Big Rant read out loud the tribute to the good doctor. Big Foot licked a paw and turned toward the bay window. The mongrels circled the mute puppeteer in the wooden chair. Hail Mary was restless, George Eliot cocked an ear and moaned, and the two raspy mongrels leaned against Master Jean.

"The eight candles of the menorah might be a native puppet parley of eight trickster stories about the tease of a natural union of predators and prey and the chance of survivance on the risky course of nicknames, hearsay, promises, silence, and perception of irony by a cardiologist who smiled when he listened to the shamanic beat of my heart. The native trickster of creation and contradictions somehow caught the daily light of eight candles of the menorah, and that has become the celebration of natives and Jews at the Oshki Theatre of Chance in the Existential Colony."

27

Rainbow Herbicides

By Now Rose Beaulieu and her lover Prometheus Postma reminisced about covert operations of *La Résistance* during the Nazi Occupation of Paris. Prometheus was a mime with white gloves and gathered information about the location of enemy soldiers. By Now was a nurse and treated downed aviators, fugitives, and agents in the chancy colonies of resistance. The betrayal of the traitors and fascist collaborators was deadly in the honorable course of liberty in France.

Basile Hudon Beaulieu wrote fifty descriptive letters to the heirs of the fur trade between October 1932 and January 1945, or from the decline of the French Third Republic to the end of the Second World War in Paris. The fifty letters were printed and circulated on the White Earth Reservation.

By Now read out loud short selections from two letters from almost thirty years ago, "Secular Barricades," Saturday, 2 March 1940, and "Rocky Unions," Friday, 13 December 1940, that winter night of wistful remembrance at the Oshki Theatre of Chance.

"This letter to the heirs of the fur trade celebrates the first wood violets, primroses, lilies of the valley, daffodils, tulips, and bright cherry blossoms, only two days after emergency surgery in the American Hospital of Paris. My appendix was removed on a leap year day with no medical complications.

"Docteur Thierry de Martel, the surgeon, examined the sutured gridiron incision yesterday and told me that the pouch at the end of my intestine was swollen but had not burst. He assured me, as he looked out the window, that the hospital stay should not be more than a week, and complete recovery in a month or two.

"The American Hospital of Paris was turned over to the military about five months ago with the official declaration of the war, and at the same time the directors changed the name to *L'Hôpital Américain Bénévole de Guerre*, the Volunteer American Hospital of War.

"Companies of enemy soldiers invaded the solitude of the Jardin des Tuileries, and we longed to hear the piano music of Erik Satie. The royal pigeons march around the benches as usual, the liberty trees have already flaunted their bright leaves to honor the memory of the revolution, and now the silent rows of bare branches stand as solemn reminders of the weary season of the Nazi Occupation."

Basile was disconcerted by the stories of the hospital stay because he was there for an appendectomy, not as a wounded soldier. By Now continued to read the scene about the puppet parley at the American Hospital of Paris. "The doctor and nurses were surprised as Aloysius raised two hand puppets from a shoulder pouch. Docteur Appendice on the right hand, a royal gesture, and on the other hand, Adolf Hitler, a comic caricature with a toothbrush moustache and three arms. Docteur Martel frowned and then turned away, obviously not pleased with the ironic subject of the puppets."

Aloysius said he raised the hand puppets, face to face, and then imitated the steady voice of Docteur Appendice. Coyote Standing Bear, an honorable native poseur, one of many native poseurs in Paris, simulated the whiney pitch and vain drone of the fascist chancellor of Germany, Adolf Hitler.

> ADOLF: *Mein Kampf* is my truth and glory.
> DOCTEUR: Grammar struggle for dopey readers.
> ADOLF: Third Reich is my vision of liberty.
> DOCTEUR: Nothing more than savagery.
> ADOLF: My vision has changed the world.
> DOCTEUR: Putsch and prison boasts are not a vision.
> ADOLF: Third Reich hospitals in Paris.
> DOCTEUR: Not with three arm salutes.
> ADOLF: Surgeons serve the Third Reich.
> DOCTEUR: Delusions of a fascist painter.
> ADOLF: Swastikas will wave on the Eiffel Tower.

Hush Browne, Tedious Van Pelt, and the stowaways were attentive, of course, but the memories and melancholy about the puppet parleys of *La Résistance* were not relevant or related to the conversions and resistance of conscription to the savagery of the Vietnam War.

"Resistance to war against the shadows of communism is more conscionable than covert. A creative sense of ethos and native mockery is more decisive at the moment than espionage and sabotage of the enemy," said

186 GERALD VIZENOR

Master Jean. "More precise mockery of politicians and military commanders than exposure and stealthy destruction of defoliant companies," said
Master Jean.

By Now recognized the mood of the stowaways and read one last sentence from the letter by Basile. "Docteur Thierry de Martel, the surgeon
who removed my appendix earlier this year injected a suicide dose of strych-
nine on a bright sunny day, 14 June 1940, and died as Nazi soldiers com-
mandeered the Hôtel de Crillon, raised huge swastika banners, marched to
the Arc de Triomphe, and occupied Paris."

Hush, Where Now Downwind, Tedious, and the stowaways were courageous comrades of a new native resistance. "Stand by for the sway of conscientious mockery of the war maestros, wild ridicule of the state cabals,
and tease of military poseurs ready to cut short communism with napalm
and herbicides that defoliate and poison the natives, seasons, forests, and
harvests in Vietnam," shouted Hush.

"Poisoned in a shower of herbicides," said Bad Boy.

"Children stained by Agent Orange," said Poesy May.

"Families napalmed as communists," said Master Jean.

"Mist of poisons at sunrise," shouted Hush.

Basile and Aloysius slowly trudged through almost a foot of snow that
first week of December to deliver groceries and a block of frozen walleye
from the Red Lake Reservation. The sides of the bay window were iced,
and the mongrels circled the kitchen table and nudged the stowaways after
a late breakfast. Dazhim and the mute puppeteer were on the couch with
two mongrels, Hail Mary and George Eliot, at their side. Big Foot, the
black cat, was poised at the bay window and moved her ears with the slow
tumble of snow from the trees.

"The peace of overnight snow, and at the same time curious children
watch the enemy aircraft overhead and are poisoned by rainbow herbicides,
the combat pilots were ordered to terminate the communists in the trees, in
the great curves of rice fields, and in the bright eyes of children," shouted
Hush.

Basile gathered everyone together in the living room to hear a grave report, "My Lai: An American Tragedy," the cover story in *Time*, the news
magazine, on December 5, 1969. Aloysius teased the mongrels Jawbone

and Throaty and then in a low voice said the news report would change the course of the stowaways and the Oshki Theatre of Chance.

Seymour Hersh, the investigative journalist, published the first reports about the military savagery a few weeks earlier in several newspapers. The most common responses to news of the massacre were shame, rage, repugnance, and doubt, and later many citizens were convinced the reports were political and concocted only to encourage resistance to the war against communism.

The My Lai massacre and the Tet Offensive a year earlier actually weakened public support for veterans and for the war, and at the same time three of the most popular books that year were *The Godfather* by Mario Puzo, *Portnoy's Complaint* by Philip Roth, and *The Selling of the President 1968* by Joe McGinniss. Vito Corleone of the New York Mafia, Alexander Portnoy, the evocative lecher, and the stagy political campaign of Richard Nixon evidently engaged more serious comments than the savagery of the Vietnam War.

"I pledged in my campaign for the Presidency to end the war in a way that we could win the peace," declared Richard Nixon in his address to the nation on November 3, 1969. "Let us be united for peace. Let us also be united against defeat," and then he delivered the most reasonable sentiment. "North Vietnam cannot defeat or humiliate the United States. Only Americans can do that."

Zenibaa listened to the president on radio, and on a hand chalkboard mocked his elusive promises. "End the crazy war and secure peace at the same time, otherwise lose the war with double talk." She has mocked every president, every cut and run politician, every reservation agent, and everyone who pretended to represent others in the maneuvers of party politics and churchy salvation.

President John F. Kennedy was a character of favor in heart stories of the mute puppeteer, the only president she has saluted and in silence shouted, bravo, bravo, bravo. Ulysses S. Grant was president the year she was born at French Portage Narrows, Lake of the Woods, Canada, in 1876. The mute puppeteer mocked three early presidents, Grover Cleveland, Theodore Roosevelt, and Woodrow Wilson, and almost saluted Harry Truman and Dwight Eisenhower, or Whitey Dwighty. The manner and cozy drawl of

Lyndon Johnson, the absence of natives in the Civil Rights Act of 1964, and Richard Nixon, the moody double talker about war, peace, and liberty, were mocked in bold print on chalkboards.

"In a terrible way that he did not mean or likely imagine, those words of Richard Nixon's came true last week as the nation grappled with the enormity of the massacre of My Lai," reported *Time*. "A young Army lieutenant, William Laws Calley, Jr., stood accused of slaying at least 109 Vietnamese civilians in the rural village in South Viet Nam and at least 25 of his comrades in arms on that day in March 1968 are also being investigated.

"Only a shadow of a doubt now remains that the massacre at My Lai was an atrocity, barbaric in execution. Yet almost as chilling to the American mind is the character of the alleged perpetrators. The deed was not performed by patently demented men. Instead, according to the ample testimony of their friends and relatives, the men of C Company who swept through My Lai were for the most part almost depressingly normal.

"The massacre may be only one betrayal of American ideals; but is it possible that there have been other betrayals? My Lai is a token of the violence that trembles beneath the surface of American life; where else, and in what ways, will it explode? How much injustice and corruption distort the reality of democracy that the U. S. offers to the world? The answers are debatable, the questions are not," reported *Time*.

"The mass murder of civilians at My Lai, a search and destroy mission in Vietnam, must be compared to the cavalry massacres of natives at Marias River, Sand Creek, and Wounded Knee," shouted Hush.

Where Now reported that the American Association for the Advancement of Science resolved that the use of Agent Orange and other herbicides as a weapon should be investigated, and thousands of scientists from around the world petitioned to end herbicide warfare in Vietnam.

"Operation Ranch Hand is the name of the military use of herbicides that started about seven years ago," said Where Now. "Some reports estimate that thousands of civilians and millions of acres of land were poisoned with the military spray of several herbicides."

"War with rainbow herbicides," said Poesy May.

"Rachel Carson warned about pesticides," said La Chance.

"Pesticides now, herbicides forever," shouted Big Rant.

"Chemical warfare everywhere," said Bad Boy.

"The last breath of dream songs," said Poesy May.

"The use of herbicides is the calculated horror of chemical warfare in a savage campaign against nature and the concocted and wacko wrath about communism," shouted Hush.

"Colonial warfare of defoliants," said La Chance.

"Spray the gardens of the generals," said Bad Boy.

"Children catch a breath of poison," said Poesy May.

"Silent spring of herbicides," said Master Jean.

"Strategies of death by defoliants," shouted Big Rant.

"Cavalry caste of search and destroy," shouted Hush.

"War is darkness, peace is light" were the watchwords of a protest in Dinkytown last year against the Vietnam War, and later that month Martin Luther King Jr. visited the University of Minnesota in Saint Paul and ardently demanded a new phase of the struggle, a coalition of conscience about racism, poverty, and war and the actuality of justice for everyone.

"Pathetic slogan, darkness and light," said Master Jean.

"War is sheer savagery, and the righteous temper lasts more than a generation, maybe centuries as an elusive silence of fatal maneuvers to oust communism in the world," shouted Hush.

Reverend King pronounced a more direct denunciation of the Vietnam War in "Beyond Vietnam: A Time to Break Silence," a measured recitation at the Riverside Church in New York City two years ago on April 4, 1967. He was assassinated on the same day last year at the Lorraine Hotel in Memphis, Tennessee. Basile read several critical paragraphs from the antiwar speech out loud later that week at the Oshki Theatre of Chance.

"I come to this platform tonight to make a passionate plea to my beloved nation," chanted Reverend King. "This speech is not addressed to Hanoi or to the National Liberation Front. It is not addressed to China or Russia. Nor is it an attempt to overlook the ambiguity of the total situation and the need for a collective solution to the tragedy of Vietnam." Tonight, "I wish not to speak with Hanoi and the National Liberation Front, but rather to my fellow Americans.

"There is at the outset a very obvious and almost facile connection between the war in Vietnam and the struggle I, and others, have been waging in America. A few years ago there was a shining moment in that struggle. It seemed as if there was a real promise of hope for the poor, both black and white, through the poverty program. There were experiments, hopes, new beginnings. Then came the buildup in Vietnam, and I watched this program broken and eviscerated, as if it were some idle political plaything of a society gone mad on war, and I knew that America would never invest the necessary funds or energies in rehabilitation of its poor so long as adventures like Vietnam continued to draw men and skills and money like some demonic destructive suction tube."

"Tubes of chemical corporations," said Big Rant.

"Politicians and war marketeers," said Tedious.

Basile paused, and then shouted out the last sentences, the devastation of "hopes of the poor at home," and recited more from the published speech. Military commanders send "their sons and their brothers and their husbands to fight and to die in extraordinarily high proportions relative to the rest of the population. For the sake of those boys, for the sake of this government, for the sake of the hundreds of thousands trembling under our violence, I cannot be silent."

"Natives were not counted," said La Chance.

"Reservations of silence, not a nation," said Bad Boy.

"Resistance breaks the silence," shouted Big Rant.

"Save mockery, disarm the cavalry," shouted Hush.

"Resistance of native heart stories," said Master Jean.

"Dream songs dead with the draft," said Poesy May.

"Natives are the heirs of a continental liberty, and natives served with honor in every war and then waited in silence for six years after the end of the First World War to be named citizens by hesitant politicians who never served in the military," said By Now.

"Legislators lost touch with chance and the natural world, the creative stories of native sovereignty, justice, and liberty, and removed natives to reservations, and now politicians chase the communists around the world in deadly military games with the catchwords of enlightenment," shouted Hush.

Master Jean, Bad Boy, and La Chance were worried about the military draft lottery for service in the Vietnam War. The three stowaways created a conscientious resistance with blunt mockery of politicians who were tormented by communism and gestures of democratic socialism and now provide deferments for college students and poseurs with the necessary medical documents.

Master Jean and La Chance were casual house painters, and Bad Boy was employed as a page at the university library and attended selected advanced seminars in literature and philosophy but never applied for admission to the university.

Basile and Aloysius served in combat in the First World War, and later By Now and Prometheus were close comrades in *La Résistance* during the Nazi Occupation of Paris. Historians and politicians continue to salute those who countered fascism in the world wars.

"Recognition of dissent today is the outright evasion of conscription and service in the savage war against communism, and native resistance is a heart story of peace and liberty," said Where Now.

Several hundred thousand young men evaded conscription or burned draft cards as a protest, and only a few thousand were convicted and sent to prison. Those with money, political favors, and other connections could easily obtain medical deferments for various health conditions, asthma, weak eyes, anal cysts, crooked spines, bent trigger fingers, bone spurs, and other timely delusions of disability.

Natives were outsiders with no political connections, no historical traces of exceptions or easy deferments to conscription, and most natives were expected to continue the sentiments of courage and honor of military service in combat that had been demonstrated in previous generations of native warriors.

"The nostalgia of heroic poseurs," shouted Hush.

"Contradictions of service and deferments," said Big Rant.

"My resistance is native mockery," said Master Jean.

"Mockery is the conscience of resistance," said Bad Boy.

"Dream songs of native resistance," said Poesy May.

"Native tributes in dream songs," said Big Rant.

"Native justice is in the clouds," said Bad Boy.

Basile reminded the stowaways of the native relations who served in the First World War. "Private John Clement Beaulieu served as a combat engineer. Private Ignatius Vizenor was killed in action at Montbréhain, France, near the Hindenburg Line on October 8, 1918, and about a hundred miles away on that same misty morning his brother, Corporal Lawrence Vizenor, engaged the enemy in face to face combat at Bois-de-Fays in the Argonne Forest and was awarded the Distinguished Service Cross."

Zenibaa, the mute puppeteer, created dream songs and heart stories for natives who served in the First World War, the Second World War, the Korean War, the persistent wars with reservation agents, and now for the new native resistance to the war against distant communist natives in Vietnam.

> *flame trees at sunrise*
> *shimmer in the mist*
> *rainbow herbicides of shame*
> *catch children in a game*
> *last breath of liberty*

Basile and Aloysius contacted Norton Stillman, a regional book distributor and bookstore owner to publish and distribute the native dream songs of the mute puppeteer. The Nodin Press had published other native imagistic poetry, and the native dream songs would include original abstract art by Aloysius.

28

NATIVE WATCHWORDS

Master Jean painted two lines of declaratory watchwords in bold letters on a wide canvas and fastened the esoteric banner to the posts on the porch of the Oshki Theatre of Chance.

Wounded Knee and My Lai
Lock and Load for More Massacres

Big Foot was sensitive to the slightest flits and dance of birds in the huge elm trees, the constant tease of shadows and sparrows on the porch, and reigned over the entire bay window during the migratory rush of birds in autumn and spring. She chattered that morning over the natural motion of Baltimore orioles, grosbeaks, robins, and warblers, and the mongrels respected the stalwart poses of the sovereign of the house and bay window.

Big Foot ruled over the bay view of the porch for more than the flit of birds on churchy days. She waited with a wet nose, whiskers and ears in natural motion, and faintly wheezed at the slightest sound of a distant clunk of a heavy car door, the prance of parishioners on the sidewalk, and chattered over the simulated catch of a grosbeak, or a child in churchy clothes, or the shadow of a common sparrow.

Big Rant counted the parishioners that paused to read the porch banners of native resistance and mockery. The congregants smiled politely, and some feigned curiosity over the banners of a native existential colony, and others winced, and a pack of sturdy men raised their fists and waved away the contentious messages on the way to services that Sunday morning at Den Norske Lutherske Mindekirke.

"Sunday salvation and massacres," said Master Jean.

"Churchy parodies of peace," said Poesy May.

"Ghost Dance remembrance," said Bad Boy.

"No churchy sermons of My Lai," shouted Big Rant.

"Massacres here, war crimes there," said La Chance.

"Nothing private about a massacre," shouted Hush.

"France received more than two billion dollars from the United States to rout the communists in the First Indochina War, and now the cost is more than a hundred billion, and the military and civilian casualties are enormous in the Second Indochina War," said Basile, who had written a critical essay on military massacres for peace and democracy. "French colonial soldiers were outmaneuvered, surrounded, and defeated by General Vo Nguyen Giap and the Viet Minh at the Battle of Dien Bien Phu and ended the First Indochina War in May 1954."

Sunday morning fifteen years later in the native existential colony and there were no churchy shouts or pouts that conveyed even the slightest outrage about another war over the elusive torments of the domino concoctions of communism. "One more round of salutes over colonial dominance and no one mocked the banner, Lock and Load, or shamed, or shouted, or condemned the soldiers of massacres and war crimes," said Master Jean. "There was almost a churchyard silence over the imminent defeat of the United States in the Second Indochina War."

"Presidents Dwight Eisenhower, John F. Kennedy, Lyndon Johnson, and Richard Nixon were benefactors of colonialism for thirty years in Indochina," said Basile. "The Japanese occupied the former colony, and at the end of the Second World War the French boldly recovered a colonial possession, and less than a decade later Ho Chi Minh and the communists almost changed the course of colonialism in Indochina.

"President Eisenhower avoided direct involvement in the colonial war but provided financial and material support to the French. President John F. Kennedy authorized the deployment of more than five hundred Special Forces to South Vietnam eight years ago, and a year later there were more than ten thousand military advisors, and then hundreds of thousands of combat soldiers were ordered once again to terminate the menace of communism in the ironic war strategy of dominos," said Basile.

"Politicians and cavalry soldiers were brutish benefactors of the removal of natives and carried out comparable massacres at Wounded Knee, Sand Creek, Bear River, and many others since the colonial fur trade" shouted Hush. "The Ghost Dance, a native observance of visionary ethos, probity, peace, and liberty, was demeaned by politicians and ravaged by the military as the dance of savages and war."

Thousands of students and untold citizens countered the gratuitous strategy and outright futility of ideological wars over economic and cultural theories and accused the military of war crimes for the massacre of children and civilians at My Lai and other villages in Vietnam.

Natives and young men born in poverty, and others, had never earned or assumed the contacts, relations, or academic favors to defer military conscription. Tens of thousands of young men resisted the draft, and many others in uniform turned to desertion, fugitives of the military, and that conscientious sway of ethos, resistance, and unease became a domino course of aversion to military service in the Second Indochina War.

Master Jean, Bad Boy, and La Chance were marked for the draft and combat service in the war games over communism and never regarded churchy convictions or the moral manner of conscientious objection to the Vietnam War. Their resistance was traced to native visions, heart stories of liberty, and mockery of communist shadows.

The stowaways declared a distinctive sense of presence as the heirs of native stories of resistance that were derived from relations and thousands of years of continental trade routes and liberty, from the cavalry war crimes at Wounded Knee, South Dakota, to, more immediately, the massacre of children and civilians at My Lai in Vietnam.

"Natives on reservations and in existential colonies are the successors of a conscientious resistance to a nation that decorated the soldiers that massacred natives," said Master Jean. "The stowaways rightly declared their resistance to conscription and military service in a nation that has carried out slavery and war crimes."

Big Rant read out loud selections from *Vietnam: Inside Story of the Guerilla War* by Wilfred Burchett. Nguyen Huu Tho of the National Liberation Front "made a prophetic remark: 'If the Americans continue to intervene in a small way, they face a small defeat; if they decide to intervene in a big way then they face a big defeat.'"

"Decisive maneuvers for a big defeat," shouted Hush.

"Big defeat at the Little Bighorn," said Master Jean.

"The only criteria seem to be to wipe out anything that lives or moves," wrote Burchett. To "destroy anything that shows signs of life or habitation and to provide mass slaughter by famine or flooding." American soldiers removed more than thirty thousand peasants from about seven hundred acres of land for a "super air base." That base was "used to bomb and spray toxic chemicals on liberated villages in Bien Hoa province."

Hush Browne, Master Jean, Where Now, and Atomic 16 selected quotations from *Vietnam: Inside Story of the Guerilla War* and actual news reports for a decisive puppet parley between Wilfred Burchett, the journalist who was in South Vietnam for eight months with the National Liberation Front, President Lyndon Johnson, Vice President Hubert Humphrey, Ronald Reagan, the defeated candidate for president, General William Westmoreland, the commander of the United States military for the past four years of the Vietnam War, and the acclaimed television news anchor, Walter Cronkite.

Aloysius painted six caricatures on each side of three large white paper bags, and the puppets were mounted on three canoe paddles and turned with the parley. The caricature parley was rehearsed several times and first staged at Peavey Park near the Waite Neighborhood House, and the second parley, with a lively audience, was held outside of McCosh's Book Store in Dinkytown near the University of Minnesota.

Atomic 16 practiced the Australian accent of the celebrated journalist Wilfred Burchett, who he encountered in the nuclear ruins about a month after Little Boy was detonated over the city of Hiroshima on August 6, 1945. Corporal Samuel Hutson served in ferocious combat in New Guinea, Leyte, and Luzon, and later he was exposed to radiation and earned the nickname for the strong odor of sulfur, the atomic element.

Atomic 16 related the story once again that he touched, ate, and inhaled radioactive dust along with other occupation soldiers and observed a journalist sitting alone on a chunk of radioactive concrete with a portable Hermes typewriter. Wilfred Burchett was thirty-four years old at the time and wrote for the London *Daily Express* and transmitted that first report by Morse code about the sulfurous pitch of a deadly radioactive landscape, the vapors that "drifted from fissures in the soil and . . . a dank, acrid, sulfurous smell."

Atomic 16 easily remembered the banner headline, "The Atomic Plague," and recited from memory the first paragraph of the report published in the *Daily Express* on September 5, 1945. "In Hiroshima, thirty days after the first atomic bomb destroyed the city and shook the world, people are still dying, mysteriously and horribly, people who were uninjured in the cataclysm, from an unknown something which I can only describe as the Atomic Plague."

Big Rant imitated the drawl of President Lyndon Johnson, La Chance was the cozy voice of Hubert Humphrey, Hush mocked the persuasive cinematic temper of Ronald Reagan, Master Jean was the mannered voice of General Westmoreland, and Tedious was the homey television broadcast voice of Walter Cronkite.

BURCHETT: The war is being escalated to a bestiality that blurs the exclusive image of what one used to think was the unmatchable and never-to-be-repeated bestiality of the Nazis.

PRESIDENT: I have asked the commanding general, General Westmoreland, what more he needs to meet this mounting aggression. We cannot be defeated by force of arms. We will stand in Vietnam.

BURCHETT: Another major question was how, when, and where the war in South Vietnam started, because this is a war which seemed to have no precise starting point in terms of time and place.

GENERAL: I am absolutely certain that, whereas in 1965 the enemy was winning, today he is certainly losing.

BURCHETT: All of a sudden it was there with half a million South Vietnamese and twenty thousand Americans engaged in a major war against what appeared to be jungle shadows.

HUMPHREY: There has been progress on every front in Vietnam. Military, substantial progress. Politically, very significant progress. There is no military stalemate. There is no pacification stalemate.

BURCHETT: But if the Americans wanted a face-saving way out, they had already staged two coups. Why not a third, with someone prepared to negotiate on the basis of peace, democracy, independence, and neutrality?

CRONKITE: We have been too often disappointed by the optimism of the American leaders, both in Vietnam and Washington, to have faith any longer in the silver linings they find in the darkest clouds. For it seems now more certain than ever that the bloody experience of Vietnam is to end in stalemate.

BURCHETT: Nguyen Huu Tho thought Washington would probably try out a few more personalities and have to suffer some more defeats before they would be willing to permit negotiations on any realistic basis.

REAGAN: We should declare war on North Vietnam. We could pave the whole country and put parking strips on it and still be home for Christmas.

BURCHETT: Short of using the hydrogen bomb and wiping out all Vietnamese and many of their neighbors, the Americans will never succeed in South Vietnam by trying to impose a military solution.

CRONKITE: To say that we are closer to victory today is to believe, in the face of the evidence, the optimists who have been wrong in the past. To suggest we are on the edge of defeat is to yield to unreasonable conclusions. To say that we are mired in stalemates seems the only realistic, yet unsatisfactory conclusion.

The stowaways mocked the political and military obsession to chase communism out of the country, out of memory, and then revise the scenes of massacres and war crimes to represent the deliverance of an elusive democracy over communism in Vietnam.

Military massacres, war crimes, torture, willful killing, and inhuman treatment that causes great suffering, the extensive, unnecessary, and catastrophic destruction of property, taking hostages, attacks against civilians, the use of chemical weapons, and more have been discovered and documented as grave violations of the United Nations Geneva Convention and provisions of the Hague Convention.

TRICKSTER OF HEARSAY

Jacques Dazhim La Roque was away that first week of May to visit his sister and friends at Naytahwaush on the White Earth Reservation. The mute puppeteer counted on his spirit and trust, yet she was never alone with the good cheer of the stowaways and the nudges of the loyal mongrels, and the memories of silent and intimate moments with the clever hearsay man easily diverted any sense of loneliness or melancholy. The generous mockery, native irony, and nickname teases were a constant sense of presence and never the memory scraps of absence in the silence of dream songs and heart stories.

Zenibaa dozed overnight with the mongrels on the lumpy overstuffed couch near the bay window. The street light on the corner cast slight shadows of an elm tree in motion on the porch, and later the black cat raised her head and cocked an ear, and that roused the loyal mongrels. Jawbone rushed to the window and was ready to deliver a raspy bark at the shadows.

Big Foot reigned over the mongrels and slowly marched across the back of the couch, stretched out on the belly of the mute puppeteer, and then purred with the steady motion of gentle wheezes. George Eliot, Trophy Bay, and Tallulah leaned on one side of the puppeteer, and Hail Mary and Daniel were on the other side. Jawbone and Throaty, the newcomers, warmed the swollen ankles of the puppeteer on the giant fake leather footstool.

"George Eliot is the most devoted," said Poesy May.

"Mushy bays and a heavy lean," said Bad Boy.

"Hail Mary courts the weary," said Big Rant.

"Daniel bays for me and liberty," said Master Jean.

"Trophy Bay is the bay baritone," said Poesy May.

Zenibaa walked several times a week in the morning with the mongrels to nearby Peavey Park. The mongrels would never forget the lively meanders through the woods to the reservation post office as they bounced, bayed, barked, and circled the favors of every tree at dawn. The mongrels nosed the air and pranced side by side in the existential colony, roamed around Mount Sinai Hospital, and then raced around every tree and the Den Norske Lutherske Mindekirke to the Oshki Theatre of Chance.

The mute puppeteer teased the mongrels on the porch that balmy morning with small chunks of pemmican, and with every round of bites she sat on the stone stairs and slowly chewed as the loyal mongrels wagged and waited for more. Jawbone, the buoyant fugitive, bumped the thighs of the puppeteer and then delivered a raspy bay of gratitude, and the other mongrels were united in bays and muffled barks of appreciation.

Zenibaa created a dream song on a chalkboard that spring morning and later read random pages, a practice she learned as a sovereign reader at French Portage Narrows, from three recent novels, *House Made of Dawn* by N. Scott Momaday, the celebrated native author, *The Joke* by Milan Kundera, the Czech novelist exiled in France, and *The Painted Bird* by Jerzy Koziński, the most controversial Polish and American novelist, and copied scenes and creative comments about the novels along with dream songs in a leather bound notebook.

loyal mongrels
park trees and pemmican
favors in an existential colony
celebrities of remembrance
french portage narrows

Zenibaa envisioned the "house made of dawn" as a dream song in the summer clouds over French Portage Narrows at Lake of the Woods. The house of dawn "was made of pollen and rain, and the land was very old and everlasting," wrote Momaday.

The "portages at dawn are everlasting in my heart stories," wrote the mute puppeteer in the leather notebook. "The fur trade portages, and the ice breaks are envisioned with migratory birds and coureurs des bois, an eternal house of pollen and rain at dawn." The mute puppeteer created portages at dawn and dusk from visionary memories, and from the native scenes related in the fourth person voice of a shamanic presence.

Momaday wrote, the "land was still and strong, it was beautiful all around," and the mute puppeteer created concise comments about the first poetic scenes of native trade routes, natural motion, and the celebrities of remembrance were "still and strong" and all around the portage.

"Milan Kundera is a trickster of hearsay," wrote the mute puppeteer in the leather notebook. "The trickster is a joker, a portage farceur, and can stand on one leg and at the same time create a new earth in a few days with hearsay and hunks of muck with the help of a diving duck, and that is a memorable trickster start of the earth and a book, native hearsay, creative heart stories, and hunks of showy muck."

Zenibaa quoted several scenes from *The Joke*, and the selections were read out loud after dinner by Big Rant. "Reciting poetry makes me feel as though I'm talking about my feelings and standing on one leg at the same time," wrote Kundera.

Kundera contracted history as a poetic shimmer, "no more than a thin thread of the remembered stretching over an ocean of the forgotten, but time moves on, and an epoch of millennia will come which the inextensible memory of the individual will be unable to encompass; whole centuries and millennia will therefore fall away, centuries of painting and music, centuries of discoveries, of battles, of books, and this will be dire, because man will lose the notion of his self, and his history."

Zenibaa was captivated by unearthly scenes of a painted raven in *The Painted Bird*. The section she copied was read out loud by Hush Browne, who remembered the ravens and torments described in the novel. He "trapped a large raven, whose wings he painted red, the breast was green, and the tail blue. When a flock of ravens appeared over our hut, Lekh freed the painted bird." A battle was underway, and the painted bird was "attacked from all sides. Black, red, green, blue feathers began to drop at our feet." And "suddenly the painted raven plummeted to the freshly plowed soil. It was still alive, opening its beak and vainly trying to move its wings. Its eyes had been plucked out, and fresh blood streamed over its painted feathers. It made yet another attempt to flutter up from the sticky earth, but its strength was gone."

The mute puppeteer envisioned the presence of painted birds in native dream songs and heart stories, "the tease of painted birds, a visionary presence in trickster creation stories, and shamans painted the first birds and tricksters created the raven stories, an abstract creation and mockery of the first migration ready to be told again, and again, and painted birds were cursed on reservations by the rogue count of native blood and the treachery of jealous fascists of tradition," she wrote in the leather notebook.

The concentration of the sovereign visionary reader was diverted from the scenes of novels to the urgent news reports restated that afternoon by Poesy May.

"The treachery of citizen soldiers was carried out that afternoon on earnest college students, the painted birds of peace, resistance, and liberty," said Poesy May.

National Guard Soldiers executed four college students and wounded thirteen at Kent State University in Ohio. The mute puppeteer was walking with the mongrels and never heard the radio news reports that day. She learned about the mass murder when the stowaways returned home for dinner, a somber meal of beans and rice. Master Jean and Bad Boy were reminded of the recent discussions about fascism, native conscription, the war, and the bold banner messages of Wounded Knee and My Lai.

"Lock and load for a brutal irony," said Master Jean.

"Massacres at My Lai and Kent State," shouted Big Rant.

"Shot the communists and students," said Poesy May.

"President Nixon caused this horror with his speech last week about the invasion of Cambodia," shouted Big Rant. "We listened to him double talk the withdrawal of soldiers and at the same time increase the horror of war, and thousands of students were ready to protest."

President Nixon addressed the nation about Cambodia and Vietnam last Thursday, April 30, 1970. "Tonight, American and South Vietnamese units will attack the headquarters for the entire Communist military operation in South Vietnam. This key control center has been occupied by the North Vietnamese and Vietcong for five years in blatant violation of Cambodia's neutrality," declared Nixon. "We take this action not for the purpose of expanding the war into Cambodia but for the purpose of ending the war in Vietnam and winning the just peace we all desire. We have made and we will continue to make every possible effort to end this war through negotiations at the conference table rather than through more fighting on the battlefield."

"Nixon triple talked the war," shouted Big Rant.

"Crazy peace prize double talk," said Bad Boy.

THEATRE OF CHANCE 203

"Lock and load for a just peace," said Master Jean.

"Nixon, no trickster of hearsay," shouted Big Rant.

"My fellow Americans, we live in an age of anarchy, both abroad and at home," proclaimed Nixon in his speech to the nation. "We see mindless attacks on all the great institutions which have been created by free civilization in the last five hundred years. Even here in the United States, great universities are being systematically destroyed. Small nations all over the world find themselves under attack from within and from without."

"My fellow natives and citizens of the existential colony, we have endured the deceptive and dopey sermons on the salvation of war with defoliants and the progress of massacres in the ruins of civilization," shouted Hush Browne.

"Nixon is the lame triple talker," said Poesy May.

"Blames students, anarchists, communists," said Bad Boy. "Where are the tricksters of hearsay," said La Chance.

Basile arrived at the Oshki Theatre of Chance in the late morning and slowly read out loud the solemn story, "Four Kent State Students Killed by Troops" on the front page of the *New York Times*, May 4, 1970.

"Four students at Kent State University, two of them women, were shot to death this afternoon by a volley of National Guard gunfire. At least 8 other students were wounded.

"The burst of gunfire came about 20 minutes after the guardsmen broke up a noon rally on the Commons, a grassy campus gathering spot, by lobbing tear gas at a crowd of about 1,000 young people.

"In Washington, President Nixon deplored the deaths of the four students in the following statement: 'This should remind us all once again that when dissent turns to violence it invites tragedy. It is my hope that this tragic and unfortunate incident will strengthen the determination of all the nation's campuses, administrators, faculty, and students alike to stand firmly for the right which exists in this country of peaceful dissent and just as strongly against the resort to violence as a means of such expression.'

"Frederick P. Wenger, the Assistant Adjutant General, said the troops had opened fire after they were shot at by a sniper. 'They were under standing orders to take cover and return any fire.'

"This reporter, who was with the group of students, did not see any indication of sniper fire, nor was the sound of any gunfire audible before the Guard volley. Students conceded that rocks had been thrown, heatedly denied that there was any sniper," wrote John Kifner for the *New York Times.*

"Robinson Memorial Hospital identified the dead students as Allison Krause, 19 years old, of Pittsburg; Sandra Lee Scheuer, 20, of Youngstown, Ohio, both coeds; Jeffrey Glenn Miller, 20, of 22 Diamond Drive, Plainview, L. I.; William K. Schroeder, 19, of Lorain, Ohio."

Big Rant shouted out the names of the students, Allison Krause, Sandra Lee Scheuer, Jeffrey Glen Miller, William Schroeder, three times that late morning to honor their spirits in a heart story at the Oshki Theatre of Chance.

Hush Browne listened to the protest anthem "Ohio" by Neil Young a few days after the record was released as a single and bought three copies, one for the mute puppeteer and the second copy for the stowaways.

Big Rant wound the phonograph and played the single record several times that evening, only a few days after the United States Senate repealed and reversed the Gulf of Tonkin Resolution on June 23, 1970. The resolution was first passed by the House of Representatives and Senate six years earlier, and that consent was the formal start of the War in Vietnam.

> *Tin Soldiers and Nixon Coming*
> *We're Finally On Our Own*
> *This Summer I hear the Drumming*
> *Four Dead in Ohio*

Neil Young composed and recorded the emotive song about two weeks after National Guard soldiers murdered four students at Kent State University, and the record was released the following month in June 1970. The *Portage Theatre of Chance* departed on July Fourth for French Portage Narrows at Lake of the Woods.

30

PORTAGE STAYAWAYS

Zenibaa moved the huge wooden chair closer to the bay window. The elm trees were in bloom last week, and the slight green leaves were the tease of summer in the existential colony, with a gentle wave of native memories and heart stories of mercy that morning. The mute puppeteer reached out to touch the loyal mongrels, one by one a touch of tribute and solace, and then she turned away in sorrow, an intense shadow of misery and obscure silence, a shamanic silence.

Master Jean painted a new massacre message in bold red letters, "Wounded Knee, My Lai, Kent State," and fastened the huge banner to the posts on the porch. Strangers paused on the street to consider the banner and shouted out both sorrow and derision of the college student massacre. Later that night the mongrels leaped from the couch, rushed to the bay window, and howled and barked at two men who slashed the banner and shredded the names of the massacres.

Zenibaa was awakened by the vigilant barks, waited with the loyal mongrels at the bay window, and swayed with the gusts of wind in the elm trees and the gentle pitch of shadows on the porch, a distant sense of native presence that somber night.

"Renata Tebaldi came to mind, the magnificent soprano in the great tremors of the season," the mute puppeteer wrote on a chalkboard later at the hospital. She wound the hand crank phonograph and played a record of two arias that converged with meditation and shamanic silence, "Si mi chiamano Mini" in the first act of the opera and "Quandro me'n vó" in the second act of *La Bohème* by Giacomo Puccini.

Big Foot was perched on the wide arm of the wooden chair and purred with the same favor and insistence as the soprano, the desire of an aria and cri de coeur visionary dream song to honor the four students murdered at Kent State University.

Later the black cat purred louder, leaned closer, nosed the cold wrinkled cheek of the mute puppeteer, and paused to listen for a breath. The mongrels raised their heads, sensed the grave silence, and moaned and bayed in harmony with the spirit of the opera. Jawbone and Throaty, the fugitive mongrels, were unsure and delivered hesitant raspy bays. George Eliot nudged a cold hand. Tallulah, Trophy Bay, Hail Mary, and the other reservation mongrels recognized the arias, and they leaned closer to the mute puppeteer.

Big Rant and Poesy May were awakened by the moans and raspy bays. They rushed down the stairs, and once again the mute puppeteer was in the chancy state of a shamanic silence. Master Jean called Basile and Aloysius and made the decision to move her to the emergency department at Mount Sinai Hospital. The stowaways carried the mute puppeteer on a kitchen chair about three blocks from the Oshki Theatre of Chance to Mount Sinai Hospital.

Doctor Samuel Wilde, the consultant cardiologist, reviewed the extensive emergency examination and blood tests early the next afternoon and compared the overnight medical reports to a similar emergency about seven years earlier, when the heartbeat and respiratory rates of the mute puppeteer were hardly noticeable after several days of continuous news reports and eyewitness accounts of the assassination of President John F. Kennedy on November 22, 1963.

Dummy Trout, an abusive nickname delivered by the pork barrel bully boys on the reservation at the time, was changed to Zenibaa when she was transported by ambulance from the public health hospital on the White Earth Reservation to Mount Sinai Hospital in Minneapolis.

Zenibaa, the shorter word for silk, *zenibaanh* or *zenibaawegin* in Anishinaabe, was a secure native nickname in the existential colony, a creative mute puppeteer who had lived with five native stowaways, three men and two women, and seven loyal mongrels in ramshackle cabins at the Theatre of Chance near Spirit Lake.

Doctor Wilde confirmed that Zenibaa was listening to the same arias of the opera *La Bohème* by Giacomo Puccini when she entered a "persistent temper of shamanic silence." He reviewed the combined medical records at first in the necessary formal and medical manner. "Your blood, heart, and cognitive functions are normal, and there is no evidence of any serious health conditions, and that is remarkable for a woman in her nineties." The doctor smiled and then declared, "Naturally, you are a great shaman of eternal silence that cannot be observed by the customary course of medical examinations."

"My silence is a native opera, and you are the cardiologist of my opera, and we come together in the meditation of shamanic silence," the mute puppeteer wrote on hospital stationery.

"President Richard Nixon, the triple talker of war, peace, and deadly defoliants, replaced Edward Teller, the double talker of thermonuclear bombs, and Joseph McCarthy, the senator who chased communist shadows, and seven years later there are new political demons and diseases, and then as now my shamanic silence is not a disease," she wrote to the doctor.

Doctor Wilde slowly read the two messages on hospital stationery and then paused and smiled as a student of opera entered the private hospital room with the stowaways, Basile, Aloysius, By Now, Prometheus, and Hush Browne. Several nurses were aware of the surprise and arrived later to hear an emotive aria for the mute puppeteer. Doctor Wilde invited a music student and soprano to sing an aria from the second act of *La Bohème* by Giacomo Puccini.

"Renata Tebaldi and the aria 'Quando me'n vó' has been your choice of opera music the last three times you withdrew from the torment of an absence and envisioned an absolute shamanic silence," said Doctor Wilde. "Your visionary silence, my medical curiosity, and our shared appreciation of opera came together because of the great arias in *La Bohème* by Giacomo Puccini."

"Heart doctor and shaman of silence," said By Now.

Madeleine Deere, a graduate student in music and opera at the University of Minnesota and a celebrated soprano, sang the aria "Quando me'n vó," or "Musetta's Waltz," from memory, and the translation of each line was a slight chant by Hush Browne. Madeleine and Hush were close friends at the university, and the ironic whispers by the native advocate of shouts enhanced the emotive sense of presence and timbre of the soprano.

MUSETTA'S WALTZ

Quando me'n vó soletta per la via
When walking alone through the streets
La gente sosta e mira
People stop and stare

E la bellezza mia tutta ricerca in me
And look at my beauty
Da capo a piè . . .
From head to foot
Ed assaporo allor la bramosia
And then I savor the subtle desire
Sottil, che da gli occhi traspira
Which transpires from their eyes
E dai palesi vezzi intender sa
And from the obvious charms they perceive
Alle occulte beltà
The hidden beauty
Così l'effluvio del desìo tutta m'aggira
So the scent of desire is all around me
Felice mi fa!
It makes me happy!
E tu che sai, che memori e ti struggi
And you, knowing, reminding and longing
Da me tanto rifuggi
You shrink from me.
So ben,
I know it well,
Le angoscie tue non la vuoi dir,
You don't want to express your anguish.
Ma ti senti morir!
But you feel like you're dying.

Everyone was moved by the voice of the soprano, and the mute puppeteer raised her hands and shouted in silence, brava, brava, brava, and wrote on the hand chalkboard, "You are a shaman of sopranos, and the sound continues in heart stories."

George Eliot danced in circles at the first sight of the shaman of silence in the hospital lobby and rushed inside behind a visitor and leaped into the arms of the mute puppeteer, and the nurses shouted, "No dogs allowed in the hospital!" The loyal mongrel nudged, leaned, licked the hands and cheeks of the puppeteer, and then raised her head to deliver a soprano bay of devotion, and with three perfect muffled barks, the mongrel gesture of brava, brava, brava.

Dazhim returned from the reservation that afternoon, and after the teases about shamanic visions, the mute puppeteer and the hearsay man snuggled together on the couch, and the loyal mongrels were treated with bites of pemmican. George Eliot and Big Foot were granted lean rights on the couch, and the other mongrels moaned and stretched out on the floor near the bay window.

Zenibaa listened to the stowaways talk every day for several weeks that summer about the war and resistance to conscription and military service. The stowaways were reservation natives in an existential colony with no political relevance or deferments. Bad Boy reminded the stowaways that he was once an orderly at the Paraday Mental Hospital and could easily coach the character contractions, deportments, and derangements of mental patients as a creative resistance to conscription.

"Crazy feigns are too obvious," shouted Hush.

"Run away, we know how to do that," said Bad Boy.

"Conscription runaways," said Master Jean.

"Stowaways become the stayaways," said Bad Boy.

Zenibaa printed five words on the hand chalkboard the next morning at breakfast, "French Portage Narrows stayaways tomorrow," and then waited for a response from the stowaways.

"The portage name was clear but not tomorrow," shouted Big Rant.

"Renounce the existential colony and conscription now for native liberty at the French Portage Narrows," Zenibaa wrote on the hand chalkboard. That was probably the first time in more than seventy years or since the first time she met Gaagige Giizhig at Muskeg Bay on Lake of the Woods and the Great Hinckley Fire that she mentioned the portage. The mongrels were alerted by the unusual gestures and serious tone of voices and waited for the outcome and directions.

Bad Boy carried out research in the library reference room at the University of Minnesota, along with other assignments, about draft evaders and deserters that escaped to Canada. "Evaders and deserters are considered immigrants, and natives are granted border rights to enter Canada," he told the stowaways that night over dinner. "The Jay Treaty of 1794 is about the rights of natives to cross the border for trade and travel because natives were

210   GERALD VIZENOR

not included in other treaties between the colony of Great Britain and the United States."

"Lock and load, pack and row," said Master Jean.

"Pack and move to the portage," said La Chance.

"Stayaways from the existential colony," said Bad Boy.

"Stayaways from conscription," said Master Jean.

"Stayaways never had much to pack, and native heart stories are in the clouds," said Poesy May. "Overnight, the stowaways are the stayaways on the course of an immigrant, a native refugee from the existential colony, and now we wonder how to survive at French Portage Narrows."

Bad Boy contacted the native manager of Panic Radio, the late night station of ironic dread and dismay that was broadcast without a license from a rickety camper van, for technical advice about how to operate a covert radio station from a boat on the French Portage Narrows.

The Panic Radio van parked near native colonies on the wooded shoreline of the Mississippi River near the University of Minnesota. The overnight station broadcast native news and featured live native shouters, poetic hollers, creative ironic roars, and great cheers of mockery to overcome native hesitations.

Hush Browne cured her hesitations, pauses, and doubts with shouts on Panic Radio. She shouted almost every night for several months about poseurs and shamers, the churchy curse of destiny, and creepy politicians and learned how to overcome hesitation with more strategic and precise shouts as an advocate and then serious student of political science at the University of Minnesota.

Bad Boy secured the basic radio transmission equipment and was eager to broadcast, but he could not find a large inexpensive boat to buy, rent, or borrow that summer on Lake of the Woods. Basile and By Now provided the money to buy a used houseboat large enough to ferry the mute puppeteer, the hearsay man, five stayaways, and seven loyal mongrels to French Portage Narrows.

The *Portage Theatre of Chance* was inaugurated first as a converted school bus to Muskeg Bay and then as a houseboat and radio station at French Portage Narrows. The bus was packed, and the stayaways and mongrels departed from the existential colony for Lake of the Woods early on the Fourth of July, 1970.

Big Foot, the territorial black cat, remained as the sovereign of the house, and that weekend By Now and Prometheus moved to the former Oshki Theatre of Chance. Gunnar Sandberg and Anders Bolstad, the Norwindian boys, were ready to board the bus and become native stayaways. The church elders held back the two boys and disguised their gestures of delight to see the last of the mongrels and stowaway banners on the porch of the Oshki Theatre of Chance.

"Stayaways for the season," shouted Hush.

"Stayaways to the end of the war," said Tedious.

Poesy May Fairbanks established a used bookstore and lending library on the portage, named the Sovereign Reader in honor of the mute puppeteer. Master Jean Bonga taught music to three portage students that summer, composed a native opera, and played the trumpet at dawn, dusk, and death. Big Rant Beaulieu and Truman La Chance created lively puppet parleys about native shouts of liberty and honored the early families of the portage, Boucha, McPherson, Cutler, and Beacham.

Bad Boy Aristotle launched Portage Radio on the houseboat and broadcast opera arias, puppet parleys with the names of coureurs des bois of the portage, a native literary evolution created from the burned margins of pages of *Poetics* by Aristotle, and *The Essays* by Michel de Montaigne.

Bad Boy hosted a daily course of portage hearsay and ironic heart stories, essential cues of native mockery, the just teases of snow ghosts in the ruins of the fur trade and civilization, and the ethos of dream songs and heart stories from the burned books in the arson fire of the Library of Nibwaakaa.

Mazina, the mute puppeteer, resumed the manner and mercy of her third and expressive nickname, an abbreviation of the word *mazinaigan*, a book or document. She rightly earned the nickname as a creative storier of the coureurs des bois and the fur trade and easily perceived native irony and the mockery of craves and fancy in trickster scenes, partly because the sovereign reader was never in the custody of mission schools.

She learned to read random pages out loud surrounded by the seasons of natural motion and sounds of bird migration and the coureurs des bois at French Portage Narrows. The fur traders delivered lost and abandoned books to the sovereign reader, and she shouted out the first random scenes from *Pride and Prejudice* by Jane Austen and overstated the curious characters and phrases from *A Christmas Carol* by Charles Dickens.

Mazina read *The Whale* by Herman Melville at age sixteen, the most sensational literary venture of the sovereign reader, first as random scenes and then the entire visionary venture of the novel, from "Call me Ishmael" to "Now small fowl flew screaming over the yet yawning gulf; a sullen white surf beat against its steep sides; then all collapsed, and the great shroud of the sea rolled on as it rolled five thousand years ago."

"Call me Mazina," shouted Big Rant.

"Call me Mazina," said Poesy May.

The coureurs des bois were charmed by the native visionary reader that shouted out scenes about whales as they paddled on the French Portage Narrows. Mazina shouted, "Death and be murdered, in order to light the gay bridals and other merry makings of men, and also to illuminate the solemn churches that preach unconditional inoffensiveness by all to all."

"By all to you," the coureurs des bois shouted back.

"By all to you with no beaver," shouted Mazina.

Two years later the three volume novel, published in London in 1851, was burned in the Great Hinckley Fire of 1894. Many years later she received, as an extraordinary gift, the three volumes of *The Whale* from John Clement Beaulieu, an admirer of the mute puppeteer, at the Leecy Hotel on the White Earth Reservation.

Mazina was a sovereign and visionary reader, nurtured by totemic animals and the migration of birds and, in the winter, the thunder of the ice. She read *The Whale* that winter, and by the time the ice melted in the spring, she had copied more than thirty quotations from the novel. The coureurs des bois expected the usual teases of bird sounds from the sovereign reader, but that last easy season on the portage she shouted out short selections from the novel, and then she compared the shame of the continental fur trade massacre to the slaughter of the whales, only for the flighty fashion of fur and oil for lamps.

The fur trade ended, but the coureurs des bois never forgot the spirit and resolve of the native sovereign reader and shouter of *The Whale* in their romantic and embellished stories about the fur trader and French Portage Narrows.

Bad Boy selected a quotation from *The Whale* to be read as a tribute on Portage Radio to the author, Herman Melville, on the hundred and fiftieth celebration of his birth, August 1, 1819, and to honor the sovereign reader

THEATRE OF CHANCE

213

who shouted out the same selection to the coureurs des bois more than seventy years ago at French Portage Narrows. The radio houseboat was anchored for the covert broadcast near Coste Island, Lake of the Woods.

Bad Boy never revealed the name of the broadcast reader who chanted the selection from *The Whale* in clear and steady whispers. "The more I consider this mighty tail, the more do I deplore my inability to express it. At times there are gestures in it, which, though they would well grace the hand of man, remain wholly inexplicable. In an extensive herd, so remarkable, occasionally, are these mystic gestures, that I have heard hunters who have declared them akin to Free-Mason signs and symbols; that the whale, indeed, by these methods intelligently conversed with the world."

Dazhim, the hearsay man, was moved by the radio reading and denied any knowledge about the name of the actual whisper chanter of the selection on Portage Radio. Big Rant and Bad Boy were almost convinced the whispery radio voice was the mute puppeteer, the first words she had spoken for more than seventy years. Master Jean was not convinced that the radio voice was the mute puppeteer.

"Shamanic whispers," said Poesy May.

"Secret whispers, mute no more," shouted Big Rant.

"Stories of the coureur des bois," said Bad Boy.

"Whispers are not a presence," said Master Jean.

"During the broadcast there was a faint bay, very faint and in the distance, and the tone of the bay was perfect, and could only be the spirited bay of the loyal mongrel George Eliot," said La Chance.

"Distance creates the sense of a perfect sound, a clear bay, and that would never be enough to declare with certainty the bay was delivered for radio broadcast by George Eliot," said Master Jean.

"Ishmael, a dream song in the clouds," said Poesy May.

The stayaways could not remember any other background sounds or other cues that might reveal the actual name of the whisper chanter of a selection from *The Whale*. The mongrels might have a keener sense to hear the hushed tone of the radio voice of the mute puppeteer, but the broadcasts were not recorded, and the chanter remains forever a mystery at French Portage Narrows.

About the Author

Gerald Vizenor is a prolific novelist, poet,
literary critic, and citizen of the White Earth Nation
of the Anishinaabeg in Minnesota. He received the
2022 Mark Twain Award for Distinguished Contributions
to Midwestern Literature. His novels *Shrouds of White
Earth* and *Griever: An American Monkey King in
China* won American Book Awards, and the latter
also earned a New York Fiction Collective Award.
https://geraldvizenor.site.wesleyan.edu/